USA Today bestselling author

LINDSAY McKENNA

brings you another action-packed,
emotion-filled story featuring the men and women

MORGAN'S MERCENARIES!

* * *

"What's happening?" Akiva asked unsteadily.

"Nothing that isn't good, gal," Joe whispered rawly, holding her hand up in his larger one. "You deserve some goodness in your life, Akiva. I'm sorry for what happened to you. I wish…well, if I'd been there…"

Warmth and happiness suffused her unexpectedly. Akiva pulled her hand free because she was suddenly frightened by how she was feeling. Wrestling with the happiness throbbing through her chest and warming her lower body, she folded her hands deep in her lap. The tender flame burning in Joe's gray eyes nearly unstrung her. There was nothing, absolutely nothing, to dislike about this man. And that scared her badly.

* * *

"Lindsay McKenna continues to leave her distinctive mark on the romance genre with… timeless tales about the healing powers of love."
—*Affaire de Coeur*

LINDSAY McKENNA

Destiny's Woman

Silhouette® Books

Published by Silhouette Books

America's Publisher of Contemporary Romance

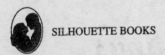

SILHOUETTE BOOKS

DESTINY'S WOMAN

ISBN 0-373-48460-7

Copyright © 2002 by Lindsay McKenna

This edition published by arrangement with Harlequin Books S.A.

® and TM are trademarks of Harlequin Books S.A., used under
license. Trademarks indicated with ® are registered in the United States
Patent and Trademark Office, the Canadian Trade Marks Office and in
other countries.

Visit Silhouette at www.eHarlequin.com

Printed in U.S.A.

To KaraHand's Home in Lower Hutt, New Zealand, and the heart-centered women who care for those in need: Helen Henderson, RN, homeopath, Deborah Mustard, RN, Reiki healer, and Cathy Garton, RN, homeopath. I salute the "Coyote Sisters," who work with the disabled, the mentally handicapped, the children who require twenty-four-hour-a-day attention. Thank you for being there to help so that the parents of these children can have a day off from their labors of love. You are truly pioneers in this area of help for such families. I honor your compassion toward those in need. Truly, the three of you are Jaguar Clan members in the finest tradition of healers for our world. Thank you for being who you are—great role models for the rest of us to follow.

Chapter 1

"Maya, you can't ask me to go on a mission of this type with a male copilot in the back seat of my Apache helicopter," Akiva said as she sat tensely in the chair before her commanding officer. Her words were low and tortured. Pleading. Without realizing it, Akiva curled her fingers into fists on her tense thighs. Anxiously, she searched her C.O.'s narrowed, emerald eyes for her reaction.

Sighing, Maya sat back in her creaky chair, which had seen better days. Ordinarily, at the Black Jaguar Squadron headquarters, hidden deep in the Peruvian jungle about fifty miles from Machu Picchu, everyone got along with everyone else. Because of the importance of their mission, the U.S. Army had upgraded their facility from a base to squadron status. The change was good for morale, as well. Rarely was there an outburst of dissension such as the one Chief Warrant Officer Akiva Redtail was giving her right now. Propping her fingertips together, Maya leaned back and gave Akiva time to settle down.

"Look," Maya finally murmured in her husky voice, "the Perseus psychologist, Jenny Wright, came down here earlier this month and interviewed everyone who wanted to volunteer for these upcoming missions. Of all the applicants, she chose you to lead this clandestine jungle mission in Mexico. Jenny lobbied hard for you, Akiva, despite the fact that she's more than a little aware of your prejudice against Anglo men."

Akiva's nostrils flared and her eyes flashed with anger. "I've made no bones about my prejudice toward white men, Maya. I *never* have."

"Which is what got you in so much hot water when we were being trained to fly the Apache gunships at the army helicopter facility back in Fort Rucker."

"Yes," she said through gritted teeth, "I'm guilty as charged."

As Maya studied Akiva, who was one of her best combat helicopter pilots, she withheld the bulk of her comments, knowing they would only hurt or inflame Akiva at this point. She knew Akiva well from years of working with the stalwart woman pilot. Akiva was half Chiricahua Apache and half Lakota Sioux, and a warrior of her people. The red headband Akiva wore indicated she had passed all the brutal physical and mental trials the Apache people had challenged her with in order to reach warrior status. Not only that, Akiva proudly wore what was known as the third braid of the warrior, as well. Her waist-length, lustrous black hair was down today, the small braid, which began at the center part, hung down among the thick locks streaming across her proud shoulder. Only an Apache who had fulfilled specific demanding tasks could wear such a braid.

Because Maya wanted Akiva to embrace who she was, as she did every woman pilot at Black Jaguar Squadron, she allowed her to proudly wear the signs of her warrior status. After all, the prejudice against them as women combat pilots had been horrendous enough. Though the army was struggling mightily against old prejudices against women, Maya knew it was a wound that would be long in healing for most of the women pilots. Akiva certainly hadn't taken to being treated like a second-class citizen at Fort Rucker, where she and Maya and many of the other female pilots on the squadron had trained.

Leaning forward, Maya placed her elbows on her cluttered desk and slowly clasped her hands together. Akiva's face was filled with anger, hurt and confusion. Not surprising, since she was the most aggressive gunship pilot at the base—she'd bagged a Russian Kamov to prove it. Akiva was Maya's best pilot. Maybe it was her Apache blood, Maya thought, that gave her that natural aggression that was so needed in air combat. But being a pilot was one thing; being asked to command a small, hidden operation in Mexico was another matter entirely.

Akiva was in her element here at the squadron. She'd thrived as a combat pilot and more than earned her keep. But now she was being asked to step into a command situation, and that was a whole other story. Not every officer had the capability, intelligence, sensitivity or desire to manage a base operation. If Akiva took the assignment, she'd be sorely challenged to develop new skills. Could she? Would she?

Worst of all, Akiva's prejudice against white men would be the test. Could Akiva lay her prejudice aside and treat everyone fairly, including her second-in-command, Joe Calhoun? Though Joe was half Comanche, Maya knew Akiva thought he was white. However, Maya decided not to bring this point up because Akiva had to learn to deal with not only white men, but men in general. Joe would be a real challenge to Akiva. Maya already knew that Joe realized Akiva would be a challenge to him. He already knew Akiva didn't like him, but he didn't understand why. It wasn't Maya's job to fix this. It was up to Akiva and Joe to hammer out a truce for the higher goal of the mission.

"Let's look at this possible assignment another way," Maya said, purposely keeping her voice low and soothing. Ordinarily, she left the door to her office wide-open; it was one of her policies here at Black Jaguar—an open door to the C.O. so that everyone knew they counted and could walk in and speak to Maya whenever they had a problem. That plan had worked well, but today, Maya had closed the door. She knew about the explosion to come, and did not want Akiva embarrassed by her knee-jerk reaction to what would be asked of her.

Opening her hands, Maya continued, "I'm asking more of you, Akiva, than I've ever asked before. This assignment is not about a guy named Joe Calhoun who has been chosen as your copilot and executive officer at this new base ops. It's really a question of whether or not you want to take on a commanding officer's role or not. You must rise above your personal prejudice. That is what a good C.O. does. Everyone should be treated equally and with respect."

Nostrils flaring again, Akiva felt an internal trembling from her gut up to her throat. She was breathing chaotically because she was upset. Her fists tightened on the fabric of her black, body-hugging Nomex flight suit. "I would go to hell and back for you, Maya. Anything you've ever asked of me, I've tried to do to the best of my ability." Her voice broke. "If you gave me a woman copilot and X.O., I'd say without hesitation that yes, I'd try my best to be a leader. But you're throwing this white guy into the equation. Isn't it enough that it's going to be damn dangerous, with a lot of stress on the three-person ground crew and two pilots involved? Why throw in white bread?''

Mouth quirking, Maya said, ''We don't always get everything we want in life, Akiva. You know that better than most.''

''No kidding.'' Her voice grated as she exclaimed, ''I *want* this assignment, Maya. I *know* I can do it. I just don't what an anglo along for the ride and in my rear seat.''

''Joe Calhoun is our best night operations pilot. He taught night ops back at Fort Rucker for the last two years. He's here now, teaching all our pilots on the Apache Longbow upgrade. You even took training from him. You know how good he is at what he does. This little experiment in a bottle that the Pentagon wants us to undertake in Mexico in order to disrupt drug shipments across the Gulf to U.S. soil, is very important. The government is modeling this mission based on the success we've had down here in Peru, stopping cocaine shipments to Bolivia with our Apache gunships. Mexico is home to one of the big drug cartels. The Feds want to set up this base in the jungle—a place near what was once used by drug dealers as a touch-and-go ops to land and take on a lot of drugs. It's the perfect locale for us to hide.

''I want this black ops experiment to be successful, Akiva. I need you to rise above your own prejudice toward white men and look at the larger picture. Through our work here, we've halted fifty percent of the drugs flowing to Bolivia for shipment across the world. That's fifty percent less on the world market. The Pentagon is finally interested in the plan that I initiated here years ago. At long last they're willing to invest time, money and coordinated effort to see if they can apply what we've learned here elsewhere.''

Maya got up and jabbed her finger at her colleague. ''And you're the best pilot for this, Akiva. I need your aggression, your nose for combat, your fearlessness because we don't know what you're up against once we get that Apache helo, that three-woman ground crew and your copilot set up in the jungle. I don't want to see our years of hard work screwed up because you can't get a handle on your prejudice.''

Lips flattening, Akiva looked up at her C.O., who stood six feet tall in her black flight uniform. Maya's ebony hair shone with reddish highlights beneath the fluorescent lights. Maya wore no insignias on her uniform—standard operating procedure for a black ops covert operation, so as not to reveal any hint of who they were or where they came from. Still, Maya was a powerful woman, and Akiva's respect for her transcended her own anger and frustration.

''Listen,'' Akiva growled, ''I don't want to screw up your plans. I agree with them. I want to see what we've carved out here in the jungle put to use elsewhere, too. My gun sights are on the druggies. It does my heart good to turn them back or down 'em. Please…I don't mean to be a pain in the butt about this. I know I am.''

''Yes,'' Maya said mildly, ''you are definitely being a pain in the butt, Akiva.'' She came around her desk and sat on the edge of it, facing the pilot. Placing her hands beside her, Maya let the tension in the room build along with the silence. Akiva's jaw was set, her full mouth a slash as she struggled to suppress her emotions. One of the many things Maya appreciated about Akiva was that she was always a straight shooter and honest about her thoughts and feelings. That was okay as a pilot. But as a commanding officer, Akiva couldn't afford to use bald, undiplomatic words with the people on her team; it would cause immediate problems for everyone.

"You know, there's a big difference between being a gunship pilot and being an officer in command of a base."

"I know that." Her mouth puckered, her arched brows knitted, Akiva flashed her a frown as Maya regarded her thoughtfully. "And I feel I can do it."

Maya had her doubts. Pilots were a fraternity; and although they faced many stresses, not to mention outright danger, Maya knew from her own experience that it was easy to be a pilot than a manager of people.

"You know, when I hatched the plan for the Black Jaguar Base ops at Fort Rucker, I was mad as hell at the army establishment, at the prejudicial way they were treating our company of women training for Apache gunship flight."

"You took your anger and did something proactive with it," Akiva agreed in a low voice. She tried to relax. Sitting back, she folded her arms against her chest and crossed her legs. "And every one of us women were with you all the way on your concept for this base."

"Yes, that made it easy for me to get on with my plans." Maya saw the defensiveness in Akiva's body. The intent expression on her oval face and the predatory look in her flashing, gold-brown eyes told Maya that Akiva wasn't really listening to her; she was still wrestling with the fact that Chief Warrant Officer Joe Calhoun was to be her second-in-command.

"If you think that putting this ops into place was easy,

Akiva, you'd be wrong. It wasn't. I had never thought of myself as a C.O. All I wanted was to be allowed to fly combat and do what I loved most. I never entertained the idea of being here in this capacity, believe me.''

Akiva looked up at Maya, her eyes flat with confusion. ''Who else did you think would do it? You created this place, this idea, out of nothing. Sure, we all helped, but you were the guide. You're the one who had the vision.''

''Vision…hmm… Yes, that's the right word to use here, Akiva.'' Maya smiled slightly. ''Among your people, the Apache, do you have vision quests? A ceremony where you don't eat or drink for three to four days, and you pray to your spirits for guidance and help to reveal the future?''

''Yes, we do.''

''And you've gone on such vision quests?''

''Growing up on the res, I did. Why?'' Akiva was becoming uncomfortable. She saw that glint in Maya's emerald eyes and sensed she was up to something. That got Akiva's attention, for her superior was a woman of immense mystical powers. Oh, everyone in the BJS— Black Jaguar Squadron—talked about Maya's secretive background. It was whispered that she was one of the elite Black Jaguar Clan, a group of mysterious and powerful spiritual warriors who kept a very low profile, yet were out there on the leading edge, fighting the darkness. Akiva believed those stories about Maya, because among her own people, the jaguar was a living spirit. At one time, in the Southwestern U.S., jaguars had roamed freely—until miners had killed them all off and made coats out of their beautiful black-and-gold skins. Often Akiva had wanted to ask Maya about her background, for the rumors about her and her healer sister, Inca, were well known at the base.

"When was the last time you were on a quest?"

Shrugging, Akiva muttered, "Five years ago, I suppose. Why?"

"Aren't vision quests about deprivation? You don't drink water. You don't eat. You starve your physical body in order to make it a receptacle so that spirit can come to you and give you a dream...a vision that will help you grow and become an even better warrior than you are now, right?"

"Yes..." Akiva eyed Maya with growing distrust. She felt her C.O. heading toward some unknown goal with this unexpected maneuver in their conversation. She knew Maya's mystical training had taken place among her people in Brazil, where she was born. Oh, Maya never talked about it, mysticism was not a common topic of conversation on the Black Jaguar Base. Daily combat missions and the interdiction of drug shipments was what their lives revolved around. So it was a big surprise that threw Akiva off balance when Maya started talking to her in an intimate, knowing tone about her own background and belief system. Native Americans had vision quests; it was one of the sacred rites they chose to undertake, sometimes on a yearly basis.

It was a time of cleansing, a time to pray for healing of any bleeding wounds within them. And it was a brutal physical test, draining participants on the physical dimension in order to leave them open for spirit to speak to them—if they were fortunate enough to have that happen. An individual could go on a vision quest for four days and receive no vision, nothing. That was about the worst thing Akiva could imagine happening.

"Where are you going with this little analogy?" she demanded huskily, watching her superior like a hawk. Akiva could feel the energy shift, change and become

very solid around Maya. Akiva was not clairvoyant, but
she had a kind of all-terrain radar that she called "blind
faith knowing." It had saved her butt many times out on
gunship missions when deadly Black Shark Kamov helicopters, flown by Russian mercenary pilots paid by drug
lords, had hunted her. She could sense the Kamovs before
she ever saw them. Apache helicopters couldn't pick up
the radar signature on the Kamov, so all the pilots in the
Black Jaguar Squadron had to more or less rely on their
well-honed intuition to be able to feel the enemy out
before the drug runners shot them out of the sky.

Raising one eyebrow, Maya said quietly, "I want you
to consider this new mission like a vision quest, Akiva.
You will go in knowing there's likely to be physical deprivation and emotional demands placed upon you that
you aren't sure you can deal with adequately or appro-
priately. In the process, there's going to be surrender to
a higher power, just like on a quest. You have a hatred
of white men. You're going into this vision quest with
the opportunity to transcend your wounds by trying to
rise above them." Maya's eyes glittered knowingly.
"You're going to have to put your people and the mission before your own personal pain. In a vision quest,
you are asked to put all your personal feelings aside and
concentrate on praying to the Great Spirit for guidance,
support and help. This black ops mission is well beyond
you in some ways, and we both know it. I'm putting my
money on you—that you'll transcend the fires, become
better than you are presently, and grow into the job re-
quirements. I'm not asking you to do anything more than
you would in a vision quest, where the demands are just
as brutal."

Akiva stared at Maya as her huskily spoken words
went straight to her hurting heart. The truth behind them

reverberated through her like an earthquake, and Akiva
sensed the greater stage where this conflict was being
played out, in the unseen worlds that surrounded them.
She *felt* the importance of Maya's words.

"Joe Calhoun symbolizes your wound because he is a
man," Maya continued softly. "He didn't cause your
pain or your wounding, but because he's a man, he becomes that for you, Akiva. He's innocent in all of this.
I'll be having a similar meeting with him in a little while,
to tell him he's been selected for the black ops mission
with you. Try to see him as an individual, not as the man
or men who wounded you as a child growing up."

Akiva's gold eyes flared with surprise. She'd never
spoken to Maya—indeed, not to anyone—about her
childhood. As she looked into her C.O.'s deep green
eyes, she felt heat flow through her and touch her aching
heart. Yes, she was scarred, deeply wounded by white
men. But how did Maya know?

Akiva thought better of asking. Maya was a medicine
woman of her clan, and one simply did not go up and
baldly ask how she knew a person's mind and heart.
Medicine people often knew the unknowable, for they
could pierce the veils of mystery and see a person's past
as well as her present and future.

Akiva shifted uncomfortably in her chair now that she
knew Maya had seen her ugly, sordid past. Shame flowed
through her, for she didn't want anyone to know the tor-
ment and trauma she'd suffered and endured. The gentleness in Maya's tone ripped off some of the scabs over
that festering wound that consumed her heart and spirit.
Akiva could better keep her defense in place against
someone who yelled at her, than she could against compassion and nurturance. Her life, thus far, had not in-

cluded such things, so she didn't know how to deal with them.

"Your entire life, Akiva, has been a vision quest. I know you understand this."

Wincing, Akiva jerked her gaze from Maya's face to the tiled floor beneath her booted feet. She stared, unseeing, down at her highly polished combat boots, her black uniform blousing along the tops. Gulping, she gripped the arms of the chair. Red-hot pain gripped her heart. Her breathing deepened.

Maya reached out and placed her hand on Akiva's tense shoulder. "I know from my own experience that some people volunteer for such a life, Akiva. They are strong, old spirits who have gone through many, many lifetimes in human form, becoming spiritually strong under adverse circumstances that would normally destroy a person."

Her fingers tightened on Akiva's shoulder. "Much is asked of us when we volunteer for that kind of life mission, my sister. And I do know what I'm asking of you, Akiva. What I ask goes far beyond any military orders, or even this three-dimensional world. You came into this life like I did—to fight the darkness. To bring light back to the world. We are on the front lines of this war between dark and light. We were born and bred for it. We had to have a very tough beginning in order to shape and strengthen us for what lay ahead. I *need* you for this black ops, Akiva. I need your heart, your passionate spirit, your fearlessness and your focus. I know I'm asking a lot of you."

Maya's voice lowered. "But you must see this mission as a vision quest, one that will be brutal on you emotionally and mentally in ways you've never had to deal with before. I know you can handle it. You're courageous. Your bravery often leaves me breathless.'' Maya removed her hand and stood near Akiva, who had bent over in the chair, almost in a fetal position. Maya felt the depth of her pain and closed her eyes momentarily.

''Many are called, Akiva, but few can really answer the call. You're one who can. My bet is on you...that you'll pick up the reins of this mission and give it your heart and spirit. The light burns brightly in you, and your jaguar spirit guide from your great-great-grandmother is with you at all times. Jaguar people never flinch from what is racing toward them. We stand our ground, straight and tall, and we prepare ourselves for the assault coming our way. And deep inside us, Akiva, we know without a doubt that the light—the guardians on that other side of the veil—will protect us, work with us and help us to withstand the blows we're bound to suffer.''

Akiva forced herself to straighten. She felt Maya's warm, throbbing energy surrounding her, like a mother cradling her child lovingly to her breast. The sensation was so foreign to her that it left her a bit in shock—a good kind of shock. Though she'd hunted all her life, she'd never found such protection, such love and care until just now. Lifting her head, her eyes swimming with tears, she saw Maya's softened features waver before her as she looked down at her in those moments out of time.

Speechless, Akiva could only absorb what Maya was giving her. She saw the compassion in her superior's emerald eyes, and the gentle strength that had always emanated from her now filled Akiva. She was starved for such rich and caring emotions, absorbed them hungrily as they flowed through her, touching her wounded heart. Akiva had never talked to Maya of her own spiritual beliefs, or about her jaguar spirit guide, and she was stunned by the knowledge Maya possessed about her. Yet she felt no panic, because Maya had long ago proved that she could be trusted.

Gulping, Akiva forced back her tears as Maya smiled and then quietly moved away. As she stepped back, that warm, loving sensation began to ebb and dissolve, and Akiva grieved its loss. Maya had been energetically feeding her something she had looked for desperately all her life and believed never existed. But it did. Maya had given her hope. Hope that she would not always feel like a person left out on the hill, alone without help or support. For that was what vision quests were all about—facing nature and the spirit world alone, weaponless, vulnerable and open. Akiva never left herself vulnerable, never opened herself up to anyone. And yet, with her compassionate energy, Maya had just shown her that she, too, was deserving of nurturing, of care and protection.

Swallowing against the lump in her throat, Akiva sat there for a long time in silence. Maya walked around her desk, sat down and began to look for the set of orders in the piles of paper on her desk.

"A-all right, Maya. I'll take the mission. All I can say is I'll try." She drew in a ragged breath as Maya lifted her head. For a moment, Akiva swore she saw the face of a black jaguar staring back at her with sun-gold eyes and huge ebony pupils. But as swiftly as she'd seen it, the apparition was gone. So much was occurring that Akiva couldn't quite grasp it all. Something profound had just happened to her, and she knew it had to do with jaguar medicine and healing. Akiva's own jaguar spirit had been given to her long ago. At the time, she had been told that one day she would be properly trained to know how to work with and utilize the vast, transforming power of the jaguar spirit. Right now, all Akiva received from her jaguar guardian was a keen intuition that helped her sense Kamovs. She sometimes would see apparitions, just as she'd seen the jaguar transpose over Maya's face, but that was not often. And now, somehow, whatever energy Maya had transferred to her, was giving her the courage to take the mission—Joe Calhoun and all. A white man. Her enemy.

"Joe's a good person," Maya said, finally locating the orders. She reached for her pen in the pocket on the left arm of her uniform. "Try to see him as an individual, not as one of the men who hurt you. That is the vision quest you're taking on, Akiva." Maya scribbled her signature on the orders and handed them to Akiva. "Here, take these over to logistics, will you? They need to start getting this show on the road. You're now the commanding officer of Black Jaguar Base Alpha—the first base outside the hub we've set up here in Peru. I have every faith that you'll pull off this mission successfully."

Rising, Akiva took the papers. Her heart was beating painfully in her breast. She wondered if she could grow into the job as Maya seemed to think she could. "I don't want to disappoint you," she rasped unsteadily.

"I don't want you to disappoint yourself," Maya whispered, and then gave her a crooked smile. "Learn to trust outside yourself, Akiva. Joe Calhoun is a good person. He's no two-heart."

Again Akiva winced. She'd never realized her C.O. knew so much about her people until now. Two-hearts were people who lied, cheated, manipulated or deceived others for their own selfish ends.

"I'll try to hold that thought," she said, half joking as she moved to the door and opened it. Outside, women were moving quietly up and down the hall of the second floor of H.Q., where the offices were located.

"It's not going to be easy."

Akiva lifted her head and stood proudly in the doorway, as much of her old spirit and strength infused her once again. "Nothing in my life has *ever* been easy. Why should this be any different?"

Grinning like a jaguar, Maya said, "That's the spirit. That's what I want to hear from you. Get out of here. I need you down in logistics to initiate this mission at 1030 today. Start packing."

Akiva nodded, waving the orders in her hand. "I won't let you down, Maya. I promise...."

As she turned and moved down the hallway, Akiva felt her whole reality begin to slowly disintegrate around her. How was she going to make this work? How was she going to stop herself from ripping off Calhoun's head? How was she going to stop that violent, destructive anger she held toward all men?

Chapter 2

"Major Stevenson, I feel like a fox that's been given access to the henhouse," Joe Calhoun admitted, excitement in his deep Southern drawl as he sat in front of her desk. Joe had arrived promptly at 0930, unsure why the commanding officer wanted to see him. Now he knew: he was being offered a plum assignment to Black Jaguar Base Alpha. As executive officer, no less! For a U.S. Army chief warrant officer like him, this was an unheard of gift.

Warrant officers were in that gray area of army ranks— they were no longer enlisted, but weren't full-fledged officers, either. They played an important role in the army, but were outcasts of a sort, accepted neither above nor below them. No one really appreciated what they did militarily, and yet without them, the army helicopter program would die.

Maya smiled. "You Texas boys have a language all

your own, Chief Calhoun. But I'm glad you're willing to give this black ops a whirl.''

He had a tough time sitting still in the dark green metal chair. ''Yes, ma'am, I sure am.'' Joe felt like he was in a dream. As a half-breed Comanche who'd grown up in Texas, he'd long been an outcast. Joe had had a hard-scrabble life as a child, and been the victim of jeers and taunts throughout twelve years of school, where prejudice followed him mercilessly. He felt the army was giving him a chance to prove he was better than the names he'd been called, and he worked longer and harder than any-one else, trying to prove his self-worth.

All his life he'd been told he was worthless, except by his family, who loved him. That love had given him hope to cling to when things got bad at school. Joe worked hard at never making a mistake, because to make one, in his books, was the worst thing he could imagine. It would prove he was a ''dumb redskin'' who was too stupid to learn. He never told anyone of his heritage—ever. Now, as he sat there hearing words he'd never thought possible, it seemed as if all his hard work was going to pay off—he was going to be X.O. of a base! That was mind-blowing to Joe. He could barely sit still because of the happiness exploding through him. Finally, someone was going to give him a chance to prove himself!

''Now…can you tell me a little of how the night ops training went between you and Chief Redtail?''

Furrowing his brows, Joe avoided the C.O.'s penetrat-ing gaze. Clearing his throat, he opened his large, square hands. ''Ma'am, she caught on the quickest of all the pilots when we trained her on the night scope we wear on our helmet to see in the dark.''

Smiling to herself, Maya continued to hold his candid gaze. Just as she'd thought, Joe Calhoun—who had seemed from the start to be a throwback to a kinder, gentler time when women were put on pedestals and treated like ladies—was showing his warm, amicable nature. Maya had seen Calhoun's carefully written reports on the women pilots he'd trained. Oh, he'd been specific about weaknesses and strengths in night ops activities, but nary a word had been said about possible personal problems between himself and Akiva Redtail.

"Joe," Maya said, her voice ringing with authority, "it's very important for me to get the gist of the chemistry between you and Chief Redtail. After all, she's going to be your C.O. at this new base. I have more than a passing interest in how you two might get along." Maya's mouth twisted wryly. "There's a great Texas saying I heard from one of my pilots, who was born there—'you don't drop your gun to hug a grizzly bear.'"

Maya's meaning wasn't lost on Joe. Shifting uncomfortably in the chair, he rubbed his sweaty palms on his jungle-fatigue pants. "Yes, ma'am, I'm familiar with the phrase."

"Good." Maya pinned him with her narrowed gaze. "So, does it clarify the relationship between you and Chief Redtail?"

Joe pushed his long, thick fingers through his short black hair, as he did whenever he was nervous. There was a lock that always rebelled and dipped across his brow. Nervously, he pushed it back. "Ma'am, with all due respect, I *really* admire Chief Redtail. She's the best combat pilot you've got here at Black Jaguar Base, in my opinion."

Maya heard the respect and admiration in Calhoun's soft drawl, but she also saw his struggle to remain positive. Maya knew it was important to get all the cards laid out on the table, to have all the possible problems addressed now—not later, when they were in Mexico, fighting like two cats in a dogfight. Joe's easygoing Texas style made it hard for Maya to think that even Akiva's acidic temper could rile this good ole boy. Joe had, in her assessment, the patience of Job. He was infinitely tolerant, which would well work for him in this upcoming project, as Akiva was none of those things. Maya hoped Joe could provide the necessary balance to make this operation successful.

"I'm in agreement with you, Chief Calhoun, about Akiva's skills. She's the best we've got, which is one reason we're earmarking her for this mission. The other is that in your reports on the pilots, she scored consistently highest on night-scope trials with the Apache. We are in need of two pilots, the best two, because a lot of missions are going to be at night, out over the Gulf. You know as well as I do that flying over a large expanse of water poses potential problems with pilot disorientation. And flying at night, with the scope, is twice as tricky."

Nodding, Joe saw her expression remain hard. He could feel the C.O. casting around for something, and he knew what it was. Joe just didn't want to give it to her. He didn't want to paint Akiva in a bad light. It wasn't his nature to talk negatively of people; rather, he was always upbeat and positive about their strengths, never shooting them down for what they didn't do right, or what their weaknesses were.

God knew, he had his own set of problems to work on, and he wouldn't appreciate someone disemboweling him in public. His father, who was full-blood Comanche, had taught him to speak well of a person, that if he did so, energy would come back tenfold to him as a result. It was easy to eviscerate people, to tear them apart verbally, to shame or humiliate them. Joe had found that out early in his life. And he didn't ever want what had happened to him at school, to happen to others. The stubborn part of him, which was considerable when tapped, was rising to the surface as Major Stevenson continued to stare at him.

He felt like she was looking inside him and reading his mind. Lips pursed, he waited. What did she want? Why did she want to hear that Akiva Redtail practically hated the ground he walked on? Joe had never figured out why, exactly, Akiva disliked him so openly; he had chalked it up to a clash of personalities. Given his easygoing nature, he let her venomous comments and glares slide off him like water off a duck's back, and he didn't take it personally. At least, he tried not to....

"How do you feel toward Chief Redtail?" Maya asked in a low tone.

Brightening, Joe grinned. "She's an incredible combat pilot, ma'am. I really enjoyed teaching her the upgrade on the night optics. She was a pleasure to work with." Joe was, in fact, very drawn to Akiva, but she sure didn't like him, so he kept his desire for her to himself.

"So—" Maya fiddled with the pen in her fingertips and frowned down at it "—you have no problem going on this mission with her?"

"No, ma'am, I don't."

"Not *one* problem, Chief?"

Joe shook his head. "No, ma'am. She's all guts and glory, as we say in the trade. She's already bagged a Russian Kamov. And she's aggressive. That's what it takes out there—we both know that. I'm looking forward to being her back seat, to tell you the truth. I can learn plenty from her."

Smiling thinly, Maya raised her head and stopped thumping the pen against the desk. Joe's expression was so damned easy to read. The guy hid nothing in that square face of his. His gray eyes were wide and earnest. "I don't think it's telling any stories out of school, Chief, that Akiva rides roughshod on some people." Mainly white, Anglo men, but Maya swallowed those words.

Shrugging, Joe said, "I think most combat pilots are perfectionists, ma'am, and they get sour milk real fast when things aren't right. Their lives depend upon the equipment workin' constantly and the crew doin' their job like they're supposed to do. I don't fault her on that in the least. Do you?"

Maya smiled to herself, liking Joe's ability to stress the positive. "I agree with you, Chief." Still, Akiva would wear him down, and Maya wondered how thick Joe's hide really was. How long could he handle her acidic responses to him before he reared up on his hind legs and fought back? That was the fly in the ointment on this mission. It all hinged on Joe's patient, plodding personality, his ability to get along with her, no matter what.

"Ma'am, I feel you're like a huntin' dog sniffin' around for a bone of contention or somethin' here. Are you worried about me bein' able to get along with Chief Redtail?"

"I'm not concerned about you getting along with her," Maya said drolly. "It's the other way around. Akiva has a lot of knives in her drawer, and she's real good at pullin' them out and slicing and dicing, Chief. I just don't want *you* to be chopped up by her when she gets in one of those moods, is all. And I think you know what I'm talkin' about?"

Joe's mouth curved into a friendly smile. "My daddy always said that makin' it in life is like busting mustangs, ma'am. You're gonna get thrown a lot. You gotta expect it. But the key is you get back up, dust yourself off and get right back in the saddle again.''

''Well,'' Maya said with a chuckle, ''that about says it all when it comes to interfacing with Akiva. She's got some…weaknesses, Chief Calhoun. And it's my job to make damn sure you know them going into this black ops, so you're not surprised at the other end.''

''Okay,'' Joe said, stymied. What problems? Akiva had a strong personality, one he admired, but he never considered her penchant for thoroughness and perfectionism to be a problem. It took a strong man or woman to be a combat pilot—that was part of the required package. And he had no problem with strong, confident women. So what was the major hinting at here? Granted, Joe had been at the base only a couple of months and didn't run into Akiva every day, although he wished, on a personal level, he did. Just getting to look at her tall, proud, powerful figure and those penetrating gold eyes of hers made his heart pound with silent need. But this was a busy place, and the training was grueling and ongoing. Joe had his hands full as an instructor pilot on the night optic upgrade training missions, so rarely saw Akiva.

''We have another sayin' in Texas, Major—'Never grumble, it makes you about as welcome as a rattlesnake in camp.'''

''Hmm, I see. Well, you need to know that Chief Redtail isn't all sweetness and light. She's going to need your help and I'm going to need you to roll with a lot of punches she's more than likely to throw your way. Don't take them personally, Chief Calhoun. If the heat in the kitchen gets to be a little much, sit her down with your diplomatic, good ole boy style and talk it out. Akiva can be reasoned with.''

''I'll remember that, ma'am.''

"Good." Maya looked at her watch. "Let's get down to logistics. Morgan Trayhern has just arrived with his second-in-command, Mike Houston, and Akiva should be in the planning room with them about now. We need to go over the assignment."

Leaping to his feet and coming to attention, Joe said, "Yes, ma'am. I'm more than ready for this. Thank you for the opportunity. I never expected this promotion."

As Maya got to her feet and grabbed the clipboard and pen from her desk, she gave the aviator a dark look. "Keep your positive attitude, Chief. You're gonna need it where you're goin'. And I feel you've more than earned this position."

Akiva sat on one side of the planning room and leaned back in the chair, her legs crossed. In the center of the room an overhead projector sat on a table, flashing the first diagram on the white wall in front of them. Two men—both civilians, although she knew they'd both been in the military at one time—stood talking in low tones to one another next to the projector. They'd introduced themselves to her earlier. Akiva had seen them on other occasions at the base, but had never been formally introduced until now. Though she'd arrived right on time for the planned meeting, now that she was here she found her heart beating in panic. Could she really command this mission? More than anything, Akiva didn't want to disappoint Maya. That one fear gave her the resolve to try and make the mission work.

Hearing the door open, Akiva turned to see who had come in. She saw Maya move briskly into the room, clipboard in her left hand. As Chief Warrant Officer Joe Calhoun followed, Akiva's brows knitted and her pulse accelerated. Akiva wanted to hate him. He was a white man. And right now, Calhoun represented all Anglo men to her. Working her mouth, she found a bitter taste in it. Reaching for a paper cup that sat next to her folding chair, Akiva took a quick gulp of the tepid water. When she looked up, she saw Joe Calhoun standing right in front of her, his large, square hand extended.

Akiva choked on the water that was halfway down her gullet. Coming up and out of the chair, she coughed deeply, her hand pressed against her throat. *Damn!* Moving away from him, she finished coughing and turned. Wiping her mouth with the back of her hand, she met his smiling gray eyes. His hand was still extended toward her.

"I just wanted to congratulate you, Chief Redtail." Joe saw her gold eyes narrow with fury. Her cheeks were red with embarrassment. He saw her gaze drop to his hand and then snap back up to his eyes.

"Thanks," Akiva mumbled. She ignored his hand and sat back down, crossing her arms belligerently. She wished mightily that Calhoun would go sit down in one of the chairs on the other side of the room. She didn't want to be anywhere near him.

Joe tempered his disappointment as Akiva refused to shake his hand. Okay, that was fine. He introduced himself to Morgan and Mike, who gripped his hand warmly with obvious welcome. Searching around, he saw a chair nearby and reached for it. As he sat down, he noticed Morgan Trayhern, Mike Houston and Major Stevenson studying them. Feeling heat crawl up his neck and into his face, he saw the quizzical look on the two men's faces, the worry banked in Major Stevenson's eyes. Everyone had seen Akiva snub him. Embarrassed, Joe felt as if he'd done something wrong, but there was nothing he could do to rectify it.

"Okay," Maya said crisply, "let's get this mission planning on the road. Chiefs Redtail and Calhoun, I think you already know Mr. Trayhern and Mr. Houston? Good. Morgan, do you want to start this briefing?"

Morgan Trayhern shrugged out of his dark green nylon jacket and placed it on the back of one of the chairs. Dressed in a pair of jeans, hiking boots and a dark blue polo shirt, he turned and opened up a briefing file. "Mike? You want to give Chiefs Redtail and Calhoun the dope, here?" He handed two sets of information packets to him to give to the warrant officers.

Houston, who was dressed similarly, nodded. He quickly handed out the twenty-page packets on the planned mission. Joe nodded and thanked him. Akiva's belligerent look faded and she actually softened the line of her mouth as he handed the papers to her.

Morgan stood at the projector. On the wall was a map of southern Mexico. "We were able to use satellite infrared to locate this little airport facility. It's hidden deep in the jungle and is completely surrounded by old-growth trees." Flashing his laser penlight, Morgan circled what appeared to be a small pinprick in the map. "This is the exit-entrance point. Many years ago druggies cleared this thousand-foot-long dirt runway for light, fixed-wing aircraft, as well as helicopters. They were using the aircraft to haul cocaine shipments."

Akiva sat up. "You said helicopters? What kind?"

Joe glanced at her. She was now in combat mode, tense and alert, her huge gold eyes narrowed on the map in front of them. Despite her prickliness, Joe couldn't help but admire Akiva. She was six feet tall, big boned, and her womanly body was firmly muscled beneath her tight-fitting black uniform. Joe would never admit it to anyone, because it would be considered sexist by the U.S. Army today, but by damn, she was a good-lookin' woman, with curves in all the right places. She was easy on the eyes, as his fellow Texans would say.

Joe's problem was that he wanted to stare like a slobbering fool at Akiva. She commanded everyone's attention whenever she strode into a room. He liked the fact she wore the bright red scarf of her Apache heritage around her head. Her high, sharp cheekbones and large, slightly tilted eyes gave her the look of a lone wolf on the hunt. That excited him. And yet she'd rebuffed his friendly overtures at every turn. Joe figured she didn't like him at all. Though disappointed, he still absorbed her intense beauty and dynamic energy as she sat up in the chair and pointed to the map.

Mike Houston, who stood next to Morgan, responded to her question. "All civilian types, Chief Re armed military rotorcraft that we can find."

"Good," Akiva muttered defiantly, "becau moving in, we need to know what's out there and a us."

"The closest town, San Cristobel," Morgan said, pointing to the north of their base of operations, "is here. It's a village of about a thousand people, all farmers. The jungle begins just outside their little community. Your base is fifty miles away, so there's no chance that they'll discover you. Few farmers penetrate the jungle, so it's your fortress of protection."

Houston grinned slightly and looked at Akiva and Joe. "I wouldn't bet that people in the village don't know this airport is here, however. So you need to keep on your guard in case someone wanders in someday while hunting for medicinal herbs or whatever."

Akiva nodded and, picking up the clipboard she'd leaned against her chair, she began to make notations on the mission. She respected Mike Houston. He was part Quechua Indian. And from what she had seen of him, his blood was decidedly more Indian than Anglo, which made her trust him more than she would most white men. Though Morgan Trayhern was Anglo through and through, Akiva gave him grudging respect as well. The man owned a black ops company known as Perseus, and he'd done a lot of good for people in trouble around the world. He was one of the few white men she'd seen who was truly good-hearted.

Most Anglos were bastards, in her experience. Sending Joe Calhoun a glance as she lifted her head, Akiva found her heart pounding briefly. Why did she feel so out of sorts around him? she wondered as she watched him write down information on a notepad he held in his large hands. His profile was strong, and for some reason reminded her of the White Mountains on the Apache reservation in Arizona where she'd grown up. The res was a craggy, windswept piece of land, baked by the brutal heat of the sun in summer and freezing cold in winter. Joe's face was craggy, too, with high cheekbones, a chiseled, full mouth, and strong chin.

He was six feet tall, like her, and medium boned, with more of a swimmer's body than a weight lifter's. Most Apache helo pilots were lean and mean looking. Joe was lean and tightly muscled, but he had a kind-looking face, not the face of an aggressor. He didn't fit the normal mold of a warrior, and that stymied Akiva. And yet the army had promoted him to instructor pilot, so he must have the goods or he wouldn't have made the grade to the Apache program. The old maxim of her grandmother—never judge a book by its cover—must apply to Joe, Akiva thought.

She remembered the warmth she had seen in his gray

eyes when she'd met him that first day of training in the Boeing Apache Longbow helicopter. Normally, combat pilots had predatory eyes, reminding Akiva of an eagle in search of its next quarry.

Not so Joe Calhoun. He'd completely thrown Akiva off guard with his friendly, good ole boy smile and demeanor. He was soft-spoken and gentle with her at all times. And unlike most pilots, Joe never cussed. That was a surprise to Akiva, because cursing in the heat and stress of battle was as common as breathing among combat people. And Joe had treated her like a lady, being solicitous and sensitive to her needs as a person, rather than a faceless soldier.

It hadn't taken Akiva long to realize Joe Calhoun was a man of the past, thrown into the present. In her mind he did not fit the combat or instructor pilot mode—at all. And because she couldn't pigeonhole him, he kept her off balance. Only when Akiva could label someone was she able to react in a way that protected her from that person. With Calhoun, there was no slot to place him in, and that unsettled Akiva completely. He'd always treated her with deference and respect. In fact, the admiration in his voice during training was wonderful—but Akiva tried to throw off his praise and warmth just as quickly as he dispensed it. Anglos were not to be trusted under any circumstance.

Yet the worst part was, she was drawn to him! Few men had stirred the flames within her as Joe did. Akiva tried to ignore her quickening heartbeat each time he gave her that gentle smile. Her yearning to know what it would be like to kiss his smiling mouth really shocked her. For all Joe's gentleness, which in itself was a powerful beacon that drew Akiva, he stirred her womanly nature, too. Akiva didn't like being drawn to an Anglo.

No matter how personable Joe appeared to be, some-where within him was the darkness all Anglo men carried. She knew it lurked within him, even if she hadn't experienced it.

She glared at him for a moment. Why did he have to be so damned different? Was it because he was from Texas? She would feel a helluva lot less jumpy if she could only figure him out. Then she'd know what tact to take with him, her well-ordered world would once again fall into place and she could relax.

"And who's the drug lord in the area?" Akiva demanded in a dark tone.

Morgan's brows knitted. He replaced the map with a color photograph of an older man with silver hair. "Javier Rios. He's the kingpin of drugs in southern Mexico. His son, Luis, is a helicopter pilot, and they have four civilian helos that Luis and his mercenary pilots use to fly. The helos have a fixed fuel range and Luis takes his helos to dirt airstrips in various areas along Mexico's Gulf Coast, to fixed-wing planes that load it on board and fly it into the U.S. So Luis's job is as a middleman on these flights."

Akiva stared at the silver-haired gentleman, who stood against a background of whitewashed stucco arches overhung with hot-pink bougainvillea. It was a beautiful villa, the red-tiled patio behind him filled with several pottery urns holding blooming flowers.

Rios's heritage was clearly Castilian, Akiva noted. He was dressed like a patron of old in a wine-colored, short-waisted jacket embroidered with gold thread, a starched white shirt, and a maroon neckerchief held by a gold-and-amethyst clasp. The man's face was wide, and Akiva was sure that in his youth he'd been extremely good-looking. Now his silver hair was neatly cut and a small mustache lined his upper lip. But his eyes made Akiva shiver; a dark brown, they reminded her of the hooded look of a deadly viper getting ready to strike at its prey. Rios's thin lips were smiling, but the smile didn't reach his eyes. It was the lethal smile of someone who knew he had ultimate power over others. A chill worked its way through Akiva, though she tried to ignore it.

"Rios is well regarded in the archeological world," Morgan noted. "He's donated millions to a number of projects over in Italy and is on the board of a number of internationally famous museums. He has a penchant for Rome and loves all things Roman.

"The villa where this photo was taken is just outside San Cristobel. There is an airport near the town, and he routinely flies in and out.

"Javier Rios is a man of old world traditions. Those who know him say he's a throwback to the days of Queen Isabella, when Columbus was searching for the New World. He's highly educated, with a doctorate in history, and he sponsors worldwide workshops on Roman antiquity. His latest project is saving a number of mosaic walls and floors found in old Roman villas in northern Italy that are being threatened by rising waters from a nearby dam."

"What a nice guy he is," Akiva growled sarcastically. "The world probably looks up to him with admiration."

Joe grinned over at her. He liked Akiva's testy humor. Most combat pilots had a black sense of humor; it served to reduce stress during tense situations they often found themselves in. "My daddy always said that if it looks like manure, smells like manure, then it probably is manure."

A sour, unwilling grin pulled at Akiva's mouth. She met Joe's smiling gray eyes, and try as she might, she couldn't stop from grinning at his comment. "I like your daddy. He's a smart dude."

Nodding, Joe felt immediate warmth, soft and velvety, slip around his heart. It was the first time Akiva had actually been spontaneous with him. Maybe being a C.O. was going to change how she related to others. That possibility made him feel good inside.

"My daddy had a sayin' for every occasion," he assured her with a chuckle. Again, Joe saw a spark of warmth in her eyes. Joy deluged him unexpectedly. What would it be like to see that look in her eyes as he kissed her? The thought had heated promise. Joe carefully tucked that desire away in his heart, for now was not the time to pursue it—or her.

Morgan grinned over at Houston. "The world might see Javier Rios as an educated man of immense wealth who supports the arts, but beneath, he's a drug dealer, pure and simple. So, Joe, I think your assessment has cut to the core here. Manure is manure—even if you dress it up and hide it under expensive clothes."

Houston rubbed his chin and studied the two pilots who would be taking the mission. "Rios is a cultured man of letters and principles. He loves bullfighting, and supports the sport financially all over Mexico. At this villa he raises bulls that will be trained for the arena, not only in Mexico, but Spain as well."

Akiva shivered. "The bastard," she whispered tightly. "Treating those poor animals like that…"

"The bulls don't have a chance," Houston agreed. "If one is a little too frisky in the bullring, they drug it to slow it down, so the matador can plunge his sword into the animal's heart."

"And Rios does the same thing," Maya told them grimly. "This dude may look nice on the outside, but he's got a murderous heart. Morgan? Show them a picture of the son, Luis. He's a piece of work, just like his daddy.''

Akiva's eyes narrowed as a picture of Luis Rios flashed up on the screen. It was a color photo of him standing next to his civilian helicopter, decked out in a leather bombardier jacket, starched red shirt, a white silk scarf and tan chinos.

"Chip off the old block, I'd say," Akiva growled, and she gave Maya a knowing look. Luis Rios was drop-dead handsome, with black wavy hair, wide brown eyes, a long, angular face, patrician nose with flaring nostrils and a thin, smiling mouth. In Akiva's opinion he looked every inch the spoiled only child of a superwealthy family.

"This dog'll hunt," Joe muttered, more to himself than anyone else as they studied the photo.

Akiva turned and frowned. "What?"

Joe tipped his head toward her. "Texas sayin'. It means that the son is a sniffer-outer of the first degree." He punched his index finger toward the photo. "I wouldn't trust this guy at all. He's a real predator. I see it in his eyes."

Akiva agreed. "And he's flying a helo. Weapons or not, it still makes him dangerous."

"And," Houston warned them darkly, "he's got three other helos in his little 'squadron.' We don't have any dope on him. The last person the Drug Enforcement Agency tried to put in the Rios camp was discovered. We never found his body. So we don't know that much about Luis or his helicopters and pilots. That's something you'll be finding out as you go along. The Pentagon wants Luis's movements charted. We need to know where he goes, where he sends these choppers along Mexico's Gulf

Coast and what kind of schedule he's got worked up for them.''

"So he's usin' them to haul drugs out of the jungle,'' Joe drawled, "and then off-loading them to fixed-wing aircraft sitting on dirt strips near the Gulf Coast on the eastern side of Mexico? He's pretty sharp for a weasel."

Grimly, Houston nodded. "Yes, he is, Joe. But a helo, if equipped for a larger fuel load, could fly into the Texas border area. And he may be doing that. You're going to try and find this out."

"A helo can dip in and out of a jungle pretty easily," Akiva said. "Just chop trees in a fifty-foot radius and damn near any rotorcraft can drop down, pick up the cocaine and lift it out."

"That's what we think," Morgan said, giving Akiva a look filled with approval. "And that's part of your mission—find the holes chopped in the jungle. That means low-level reconnaissance."

Maya stood up and went over to the two pilots. "You're going to be given one Boeing Apache Longbow gunship and a Blackhawk. You'll use the Apache for interdiction efforts. Use the Blackhawk to start mapping, snooping and finding out what you can around the southern part of Mexico. We expect you to update your maps weekly, via satellite encryption code. You can send them by Satcom to us here, at the main base. The information you begin to accrue will be sent to the Pentagon, as well. With your efforts, we'll start building a picture of Rios's drug trade in southern Mexico."

"And every time he sends a shipment over the Gulf," Morgan said, "you'll be notified by an American submarine crew that's sitting on the bottom of the Gulf, on station, that there is an unidentified flight in process.

They will alert you on a special Satcom channel and give you the coordinates so you can intercept that bogey.''

Akiva's brows raised. "Extreme, dude."

"I thought you'd be impressed," Morgan murmured with a grin.

"I didn't know the U.S. Navy was involved like that," Joe said, amazed.

"Yes, they are. More than you know," Houston said. "The navy sub lies on the bottom for three months at a time. We've been doing this for a couple of years and have a pretty accurate picture of who, what, where and when on every drug-initiated flight. If an American submarine picks up radio traffic or Satcom info, they'll notify you."

"Is every flight a drug flight?" Akiva inquired.

"No," Morgan answered. "There are legitimate civilian flights into and out of Mexico over the Gulf."

"But they file flight plans with the Federal Aviation Agency," Joe pointed out. "And druggies don't."

"Exactly," Mike said with a smile. "Our submarine on station has an hourly updated FAA flight plan file on every aircraft coming out or going into that area of Mexico, so that when they make a call to you, you can be pretty damned sure it's a drug flight."

"What do we do?" Akiva asked. "Shoot 'em down?"

Chuckling, Morgan shook his head. "I wish, but no. First, you're going to follow the same operating procedure you do here—you must identify the aircraft or rotorcraft by the numbers on the fuselage. Your Apache has been downloaded with all the fixed-wing aircraft numbers for Mexico, the U.S.A. and nearby Central and South American countries. If none of them match, then you can assume it's a drug flight."

"At that point," Houston said, removing the picture

of Luis Rios and putting in another photo that showed a single-engine aircraft dropping a load of what looked like plastic bags into the ocean hundreds of feet below, "you are going to scare the hell out of them and make them do one of a couple of things. First, most drug runners don't want to fight. They'll drop their drug shipment in the water and make a run back to Mexico if pressed. If that happens, a Coast Guard cruiser in the area will steam toward that area and pick up the evidence, if it hasn't sunk to the bottom by that time. Secondly, if the plane won't drop its drugs, then it's your responsibility to persuade it to turn back toward Mexico. Do *not* allow that plane to hightail it across the Gulf toward U.S. waters."

"And what do you specify as 'persuasion,' Mr. Houston?" Akiva stared at him.

"Your Apache is equipped with hellfire missiles, rockets and cannon fire. You persuade them to turn by firing in front of their nose."

"Under no circumstance are you to shoot them down," Maya warned. "Same SOP as we practice here, Akiva."

"And if they fire back at us?"

Maya grinned. "Well, then, the game plan changes. If you're fired upon, you are authorized to fire back."

"Good," Joe said with pleasure. "Just the kind of job I've always wanted—defensive countermeasures."

"I hope to hell they fire back."

Joe gave Akiva a knowing look. There was satisfaction in her husky voice when she spoke. He saw the predator's glint in her eyes and knew it well. She was a hunter of the first order, and he found himself more than a little excited at the chance to be in her back seat on these missions. With her three years of combat experience, she could teach him a lot. She was a master at combat tactics.

"That might happen once or twice," Morgan warned, "but they'll get the message real quick and *not* fire. There are no parachutes in those civilian planes, and Rios won't want to lose them and his pilots like that. No, they'll learn real fast not to fire on you."

"What we have to be careful of is Rios finding our base," Joe said. "Once he sees us interdicting his shipments and turnin' them back, he's gonna be one pissed-off dude."

"Yes," Maya warned, "Rios is a man of action. In all likelihood, he'll send his son, Luis, to do the dirty work. And with four helos, they can do a helluva job trying to locate your base. One thing in our favor is that they are civilian helos and don't have the equipment or instruments to easily follow or find you. From the air, your base will be tough to find, which is why we chose it. There is an opening in the trees, but it's about half a mile from your actual base, and you'll have to fly low, under the canopy, to get in and out. Even if Luis spots that hole, all he'll see from above is more jungle, not the base itself."

"But," Akiva said, "if it was an old drug-runner's base, why wouldn't he know about it?"

"Luis can't know everything," Mike said. "There are dirt airstrips all over southern Mexico, hundreds of 'em. Finding your base will be like trying to find the needle in the haystack."

"Still," Morgan cautioned, "you are going to have to stay alert. If Luis ever does find you, he'll come in and kill everyone."

"Worse," Akiva said, "he'll get his hands on the Apache. That could be disastrous."

"Right," Maya said. "So most of your flying is going to take place at night. Both helos are painted black, without insignias of any type. With the Blackhawk, you'll perform daylight combat missions. Combat with the Apache will be night activity only. You fly when the drug runners fly—in the dead of night.

"You don't want to fly near San Cristobel. You'll want to stay out of sight as much as possible. I've worked up a number of vectors that you will fly to and from your secret base, so that no one can get a fix on you and follow you home." Maya handed them each a manual. "Study it. Your lives, and the lives of your ground crew, depend upon it."

Akiva settled the manual in her lap. She felt the thrum of excitement, like a mighty ceremonial drum of her people, beating within her. The more she heard of this mission, the more she knew she was exactly fitted for it. She was the eagle stooping to dive, a sky predator, and with her flawless steed, an Apache Longbow, she knew she could wreak hell on earth in Javier Rios's neighborhood. She salivated at the opportunity. The only glitch in this mission was Joe Calhoun.

Risking a quick glance in the pilot's direction, she noticed that he sat relaxed and at ease in his chair. She saw no predatory excitement in his face or his eyes. He wasn't the kind of combat pilot Akiva wanted. No, she'd rather have had Wild Woman or Dallas or Snake; any of those women had the killer instincts that Akiva herself had honed to such a fine degree. And in their business, they stayed alive because of that steely combat readiness.

Joe Calhoun was an enigma to Akiva. He just couldn't be labeled, didn't easily fit anywhere in her world as she knew it. And yet he was going to be her back seat, the person she had to rely on to keep her safe on these missions. How was she going to trust an Anglo who looked more like he ought to be flying a cargo helicopter than a combat gunship?

Chapter 3

Joe felt like he'd stepped into a hill where rattlers lived, as far as Akiva was concerned. He'd seen the flash of irritation in her eyes when, after the two-hour briefing, Major Stevenson had ordered them to Akiva's office to work out the details of the base operation. Primarily, they were to choose the personnel who would be going with them, three enlisted people who would provide support for them in all respects.

As he followed Akiva into her tiny office on the second floor of the H.Q., he realized it was the first time he'd been in it.

"Close the door," she told him as she pushed several flight reports aside on her green metal desk, dropped her new manuals there and sat down. "Sit over there," she said, pointing to a green metal chair in the corner that had at least a dozen files stacked on it.

Closing the door quietly, Joe walked over to the chair, picked up the files and set them on the floor. He moved the chair to the opposite side of the desk from where she was sitting. Joe sensed her brittleness and distrust toward him. He could tell by her abruptness that she was stressed. But more than anything, he wanted this liaison to work between them.

Joe had to keep himself from staring at her. Akiva could have been a model in some chic Paris show, wearing designer clothes. Her face was angular and classic, with high cheekbones, wide intelligent eyes and a soft, full mouth.

Giving her a lopsided smile, he sat down and said, "You've been here at Black Jaguar Base for three years. I'm sure you've got some ideas of the personnel you'd like to have come with us?" Even as he asked the question, Joe wondered why he'd been chosen to be Akiva's X.O. She wasn't easy to work with—except in the cockpit, where she was all business.

He saw her gold eyes narrow speculatively on him. "Yes, I do have a list of people I want." Her nostrils flared as she waited for his reaction.

Joe sat there relaxed, his hands clasped on the desk in front of him. He was darkly tanned, the color emphasizing his large gray eyes. A lock of ebony hair dipped rebelliously across his wrinkled brow. She wished she could ignore him, but she'd promised Maya to try and make this work. "I'm new at this," she muttered defiantly.

"What? Being a C.O. instead of a pilot taking orders?"

She ignored his teasing demeanor. "Yes." The word came out like a trap snapping shut.

"When Major Stevenson told me I was going to be X.O., I wondered if I had the right stuff to do it." Opening his hands, Joe sat back and said, "It's one thing to be a pilot. Someone's always giving you orders and setting the tasks up for you. It's another to be figuring out the tasks and handin' them out." He gave her an understanding smile.

Joe had long dealt with his own fear of not living up to his assignments. He supposed that had had to do with his childhood. None of his peers had ever expected much of a half-breed. To this day, he lived in terror of someone finding out he'd made a mistake and marking it down in his military personnel jacket, where it would be counted against him later on.

Akiva grabbed a piece of paper and frowned down at it. Joe had a lot less pride than she did. She wasn't about to admit to him her reservations about being a C.O. His sincere humility was a powerful draw to her. He wasn't one of those testosterone-filled studs who snorted and stomped around, beating their chests and proclaiming they were the best pilots or leaders in the world. "You were chosen because of your night optic background."

The words were like an insult being hurled at him, but Joe allowed it to slide off him. "You sit tall in the saddle," he drawled. When he saw her head snap up, and she gave him a confused look, he grinned a little. "Another Texas saying. I guess now that we're gonna be workin' close, you'll get a gutful of 'em. It means that you're the right person to be chosen to head up this mission. It's a compliment."

Why couldn't he be just as nasty and snarling as she was toward him? It would make Akiva's life a helluva lot easier. Anger, prejudice and hatred were things she knew how to battle. His laid-back nature in the face of her prickliness made her panicky inside.

Maya's advice about Akiva's need to leave her prejudice behind in order to make the transition to a C.O.

droned in her head. Damn, forgetting her past hurts was going to be the hardest thing in the world. As she searched Joe's friendly gray eyes and dropped her gaze to his full, mobile mouth, Akiva decided he must have led a rich and spoiled existence. No, he hadn't had life hurled at him like she had. Would he be able to handle this mission as her X.O.?

Wrestling with her anger and anxiety, she choked out, "Thanks...I think...for the compliment."

"You rode horses growin' up, didn't you?" Joe decided that maybe the best tact with Akiva was to get to know her on a more personal level. If he could disarm her prickly nature, it would serve all of them.

"Yes, I did." She scribbled some words at the top of the paper, trying to ignore his gaze.

"My daddy drives an eighteen-wheeler, a big rig, for a living. When I was a tadpole, he said I needed a horse. I remember he bought me this old fifteen-year-old quarter horse called Poncho. The horse had arthritis bad in the knees, but I was five years old and thought I'd died and gone to hog heaven."

Akiva's hand poised over the paper. Whether she liked to admit it or not, she enjoyed Joe's stories; she had since she'd first begun training with him. Even in the cockpit, while he was teaching the upgrade features of the optic night scope to her, he'd told her stories. They always served to relax her, and even now she could feel the tightness in her neck and shoulders beginning to dissolve at the sound of his soft Southern voice.

"Now, old Poncho, as my daddy called 'em, was an old ropin' horse of some repute. But for me, well, I was a greenhorn five-year-old who'd never thrown a leg over a horse before. Every self-respectin' Texan learns how to ride. Texas is a proud state with a long tradition of cowboys and cattle. My daddy was bound and determined to initiate me into Texas ways." Joe saw interest flicker in Akiva's shadowed eyes as she stared across the desk at him. She'd stopped writing to listen. Somehow, his storytelling was a connection with her that was good and healthy. It made his heart swell with unexpected happiness. Still, he knew Akiva would probably take that war ax she wore on her belt to his skull if he even breathed the possibility that he was drawn to her, man to woman.

"Apaches rode horses until they died under them," Akiva said. "My great-great-grandmother rode with Geronimo and was one of his best warriors. I remember stories about her passed down through the women in our family. Apaches have endurance, Chief Calhoun. They would ride up to fifty miles a day, escaping the cavalry. Most of the time there were no horses around. If they found any, they'd steal them and ride them into exhaustion, then get off and keep trotting on foot in order to stay free of the white men chasing them."

"Impressive," Joe murmured, leaning forward. He saw the pride reflected in her aloof face, in the way she held her chin at an arrogant angle. "I don't know that much about your people, but I'd like to learn." And he would, only for other reasons—personal ones. Again he saw her eyes grow more golden for a moment. He was learning by reading her body language what impacted her positively. She was a woman who held her cards close to her chest, giving little away of how she might be feeling inside. Of course, Joe understood why. A combat helicopter pilot couldn't be hanging her emotional laundry out to dry in the middle of a dangerous flight mission.

"I come from very tough stock." Akiva said, then scowled and jabbed her finger at the paper in front of her. "We need to get to work here, Chief."

"Could you call me Joe when we're alone? I don't usually stand on protocol unless I need to."

Her mouth tightened. They were both the same rank. His request wasn't out of line. "Yeah...I guess..."

He was pushing her and he knew it. There was anger in her eyes now, and her mouth was a tight line, holding in a lot of unspoken words he was sure she wanted to fire off at him. "Thanks," he said genially, but with a serious look on his face.

Exhaling loudly, Akiva muttered, "These are the women I want coming with us," and she turned the paper around and shoved it in Joe's direction.

As he slowly read down through the list, Akiva sat stiffly, as if expecting him to fight her on the choices. Yet even as she did so, she realized there was nothing to dislike about the warrant officer; indeed, of the three men who had been assigned to their squadron to train the pilots on the Apache Longbow gunship, Akiva had felt most at ease around Joe.

"This is a mighty good list of people," he murmured, giving her an approving smile. "I've only been here a couple of months, but I'm familiar with all of them."

"Then...you approve?"

"Build the coop before you buy the chickens."

Akiva stared. And then she got it. A half smile threaded across her mouth as she took back the list of people she'd handed him. "It's a good thing I'm a country girl or I wouldn't have a clue as to your country sayings, Chief—er, I mean, Joe...." It disturbed Akiva to say his first name, made her feel too familiar with the kind of man she didn't want to be familiar with.

Akiva saw Joe's eyes lighten considerably as she tried to be somewhat pleasant—which wasn't her forte, certainly. Maya would be proud of her, she realized.

"I knew you were a country girl," he said. "I've seen you down at the mining side of this place, workin' in the garden with Jake Travers and his wife, Ana, whenever you get a chance. Only that kind of woman would be down on her hands and knees, fingers in the warm, black soil. Not a citified type."

"You don't miss much, do you?" The words came out sharp and nasty. Akiva mentally chastised herself. Maya never used such a voice or harsh words with anyone. Akiva had to struggle to learn how to be more like her, since she was a C.O. now and not just a pilot in the squadron.

With an easy, one-shoulder shrug, Joe said, "I like to think I keep my ear to the ground and my eyes peeled." He saw the confused expression in Akiva's face. She really didn't know what to do with him or how to respond to him. That was okay; at least she wasn't spitting bullets at him—yet. Somehow, he had to find the key to Akiva, a way to turn off the venom and nastiness and reach her as a human being.

Without a doubt, Joe knew she had a big heart, because he'd seen it in some situations. Like when she was with the children of the villages that lay around the base of the mountain where their operation was hidden. Akiva would hike down to the villages at least once a week to help the Angel of Death—aka their paramedic, Sergeant Angel Paredes—make her rounds to help the people. The villages were in the middle of the Peruvian jungle, and there was no medical help, no clinic or hospitals, available if someone fell sick. Joe had once gone with Sergeant Paredes, not knowing that Akiva would be joining them. Akiva almost didn't go because he'd tagged along, but he'd cajoled her into staying. He was glad he did, because he got to see the positive, healthy side of Akiva on that day.

She loved kids, big or small. When he had stood back, out of sight, he'd seen her open up to them in a way he'd never seen her do with the squadron. Joe had never seen Akiva smile, joke, gently tease or extend herself as she did with the many children who'd surrounded her the moment they walked into each village. She had hard candy in bright, colorful wrappers in her pockets, and she would hand a piece to each begging child.

Later, Joe had seen her hold babies and children whom Paredes had to work with medically. How gentle and tender Akiva had been with those little ones. Joe had mentally photographed that day into his heart. He was glad he'd seen Akiva let down her armored barriers; it served to remind him that beneath that warrior's facade was a vulnerable woman of immense ability to reach out and love others. And it also told him that her toughness was a protection. He had held back a lot of personal questions he wanted to ask her about her growing up years. Based upon his own struggles as a kid, he knew that events, good or bad, shaped each person during the formative years. His instincts told him that Akiva had had a hellacious childhood, probably one that would have shattered another child. He figured it was her tough Apache blood that had helped her to survive it.

"What are we going to do about medical emergencies?" Joe wondered aloud. He held her stare. "You got any ideas about that?"

"No...I haven't even thought about that...." she admitted. Akiva was proud of Joe for remembering such an important detail. At least he was thinking for the good of all, which Akiva knew wasn't typical of a white male.

"Do you want me to talk to the doc at the medical facility?" he offered.

"Yes, why don't you? We have Sergeant Paredes, but she's the only paramedic here. I don't think Major Stevenson wants to give her up to us."

Joe nodded. "Yeah, I understand why she wouldn't. If a crew member on one of the Apaches gets wounded, Paredes needs to be here to help the doctor do what she can for them."

Akiva sat back and felt herself relax. It had to be due to Joe's quiet demeanor, she decided. Of all the white men she'd ever met, he somehow helped her to let go of most of her protective armor. But Akiva would never let all that armor dissolve. Not ever. White men hurt women; it was that simple. "See what you can find out."

Nodding, Joe said, "Yes, I will, and then I'll let you know what the doc suggests."

"I hate the idea of being out there in the middle of that jungle with no medical resources. Any of us could get hurt. One of the ground crew could get sick.... This is something we need to plan an SOP for."

Joe raised his brows and gave her a hopeful look. "How about if I do the legwork on this problem? Can you trust me to come up with a game plan?" He knew from working with Akiva before that she did not trust him. Trust was something she didn't hand to a man under any circumstances, Joe knew. He watched her wrestle with his request. A good C.O. knew how to delegate. Would she allow him to tackle this one, small element without her micromanaging it?

"Yeah...okay. Do it. I've got my hands full with other stuff right now." Akiva felt a ribbon of heat flow through her when she saw his mouth pull into a smile. She didn't want to feel good because he smiled, but she did.

"What's the ETA—estimated time of arrival—on leaving for Alpha?"

"One week, if we get our stuff together on this."

"Good, I can hardly wait." He rubbed his hands together in anticipation.

Alpha Base was a terrible disappointment to Akiva. She'd flown the Apache Longbow down into the hole in the canopy, skimmed among the towering trees and landed on the overgrown, dirt airstrip near several buildings built out of corrugated tin and poles strung together haphazardly with nails and wire. Sergeant Mandy Cooper, the crew chief for the ground personnel, had flown the back seat with her.

Joe had flown the Blackhawk helicopter, setting it down two rotor lengths away from the Apache. The rest of the base personnel had flown in with him, along with a lot of supplies. He'd joined Akiva as they walked to their new home.

"Not much to it, is there?" Akiva said as she strode across the long, tangled grass, which grasped at her booted feet.

Joe eyed the main building, a hangar. "Bubble gum, paper clips and a lotta prayers, from the looks of it." He purposely walked at Akiva's speed, which was a fast stride. Today she wore that war ax on the belt around her waist, along with a leather scabbard on the other hip that contained a very old bowie knife. From Joe's understanding, Maya had allowed her to wear the weapons that had been passed down through her warrior family. Like him, Akiva wore a side arm in a black leather holster, along with a flak vest, known as a chicken plate, on the upper part of her body. As they crossed the grassy strip, he shrugged out of his own chicken plate and held it in his left hand as he surveyed their surroundings.

There were four buildings, the hangar being the largest. It could easily house both helos, effectively hiding them from prying eyes in the sky. The week before they'd flown to their new home, the Blackhawk had been the workhorse, bringing all the equipment and food that the crew would need to set up housekeeping.

Joe saw the three enlisted women hurrying to catch up with them. The looks of excitement and curiosity on their faces as they trotted across the thick green grass in their camouflage uniforms mirrored how he felt inside. As he glanced at Akiva's profile, he saw the same look on her face, too.

"I'm feelin' like a kid in a candy store," he said with a laugh.

Giving him a sidelong glance, Akiva tried not to allow Joe's laughter to affect her. But it did, in a good way. "We need to split up, take inventory, and then get back together later, wherever my office is going to be. We need to assess what's missing or what has to be done next." Akiva had been told they had a week to come online, ready to start interdiction missions. That wasn't long.

Nodding, Joe erased his smile and closeted his thrill over the assignment. Akiva was all business. He could see the cloak of command settling over her proud shoulders. It wasn't an easy cape to wear, he was discovering, even as X.O. His own job would be to handle the day-to-day workings of the three-woman crew, plus the scheduling of flights. As he saw it, he was to leave Akiva free to do planning and strategy for the missions. More than anything, he didn't want to be one more thing she needed to worry about. The past week, he'd seen the awareness in her eyes of just how much responsibility she was charged with on this mission. In one way, it was good, because that didn't leave her much time or energy to snap and snarl at him. She was too busy with planning.

Approaching the hangar, which was just three walls and a roof of corrugated tin, Joe stopped and looked at it more critically.

Akiva moved onto the hard-packed dirt floor of the building. Spotting several doors on one side, she went over and opened them. *Good.* Behind each, she found a small office. Each held a green, military-issue desk, paper, pens and the necessary things to make paperwork flow. The other crew members would each have an office to work from as well. She left Joe to look around, and continued her inspection of the new base by heading through another door into an alley between the hangar and the next largest building. It would serve as living quarters, mess hall and offices for the three enlisted women, Akiva realized. The sleeping quarters weren't much to rave about, she discovered as she opened a recently erected door in a plywood wall. There were three metal cots with green army blankets and a pillow on each, and that was it. A shower had been built at one end. *Spartan* was the word that came to mind. She noted her and Joe's quarters were at the front, a plyboard cubicle for each.

Moving out of that building, Akiva keyed her hearing to the excited voices of her crew. They were laughing, oohing and ahhing over the facilities. She felt a little of their excitement, but her mind was humming along, assessing, judging and planning. As she left the second building for the smaller one, across the alleyway, she laughed at herself. Maybe Maya was right; maybe she really did have what it took to lead a squadron. Her focus was on keeping her personnel safe, dry and fed.

In the third building, she found all their radio and satellite communications equipment, plus several computers, maps and boards on which to do planning for missions. This was where she would be spending much of her time. Stepping outside the rickety building again, Akiva spotted their electric generator. It had been put into a fairly well-built wooden structure that had a lot of padding to prevent the noise from being heard. An opening for the exhaust had been cut into the top of it. The gasoline needed to run it was in another tank near the edge of the jungle, which was slowly encroaching on the old airport facility. The tank had been painted camouflage colors so it blended in with their surroundings.

Turning, Akiva saw another, much larger storage tank, which held the fuel for the helicopters. Once a week, a Blackhawk would fly in with fuel bladders and refill it so they could keep flying their missions. That helicopter would come from a secret CIA base to the north of them. The CIA would become their main supplier for anything they needed to keep Alpha Base going.

"I'm happy as an armadillo diggin' for grub worms."

Akiva turned and couldn't help but grin. Joe ambled around the corner, his hands in the pockets of his camouflage pants, a pleased look on his face.

"Armadillos?"

"Yeah, those critters that live in Texas and are worse than prairie dogs, leavin' holes all around so folks can stumble into 'em and break a leg. And they're always diggin' for worms and grubs, their favorite dessert."

Joe halted about six feet from Akiva. She was happy; he could see it in the sunlight gold dancing in her eyes as she met and held his gaze. Her hands rested on her wide hips and she had long ago gotten rid of the uncomfortable chicken plate vest. In the black, body-fitting uniform, her womanly curves and stature were obvious. She was a woman of substance, of pride, strength and confidence. Best of all, her full mouth was no longer pursed like it usually was, he noted.

"You like our new home, then." Akiva turned, tearing her gaze from Joe's smiling face. The man's positive outlook on life was diametrically opposed to hers. He was always smiling and joking. She never did either.

"Shore 'nuff," he murmured. "I've got Sergeant Cooper whippin' the women into order over at that second building. I told her to set up housekeeping and unpack their duffel bags."

"Good." Akiva continued studying the way the jungle was hugging the base. She tried to stop her heart from opening up to Joe's sunny presence. Trying to avoid looking up again at his well-shaped mouth, Akiva wondered what it would be like to kiss him. Would Joe be as gentle as he seemed? Or hurtful like every other Anglo man she'd had the sorry misfortune to tangle with? Forcing her mind back to the present, Akiva was unhappy that she was evaluating Joe on such an intensely personal level.

Joe moved to where Akiva was standing with her back to him. He was getting used to how she tried to ignore him. Her thick black hair had been woven into one large braid, tied off with a piece of red yarn and then coiled at the back of her long neck so that it fit beneath her helmet when she flew. Now, as he approached her, she took out the pins holding her braid in place and let it roll down her long, strong spine. The urge to reach out and touch that frayed, silky rope was almost his undoing. He forced his hand to remain in his pants pocket, knowing she'd probably deck him if he tried to touch her. Frustrated, Joe wondered what made her so defensive.

"This is a good place, strategically speaking," he confided to her in a low voice. "The jungle is close enough to really hide us."

"Yes..." Akiva moved away from him. She didn't like Joe's intimacy with her. Giving him a hard look that said *Back off,* she announced, "I'll be in the tack and strat building," and she pointed behind them. "Ask Spec—Specialist—Bradford to get over here and get the computers and communications online."

Joe nodded. "Right away." He turned and headed back toward the hangar. Once again Akiva was all business. But the panicked look in her eyes told him she didn't want him getting that close to her in future. As he made his way with long, easy strides through the tangle of grass, Joe sighed inwardly. What was it about him that Akiva hated so much? She rarely tried to hide the fact she couldn't stand being in the same room with him.

As he stepped into the hangar to hunt down Iris Bradford, their radio communications specialist, Joe tried to stop the ache he felt in his chest. More than anything, he wanted others to like him, to think well of him. He wanted to make up for his youth, spent as an outcast because he had Comanche blood flowing through his veins. He felt a driving need to always look good to his superiors. As a result, he was a hard charger from a career point of view. He saw this X.O. opportunity as a possible gateway to becoming an officer in the U.S. Army someday soon, not just a warrant officer. However, his career was now in Akiva's hands. If she put a bad report in his personnel jacket, she could torpedo his career goals in a heartbeat.

And why? What was wrong with him? he wondered

as he poked his head into the first office, where he found blond-haired, blue-eyed Iris Bradford. She was twenty-three years old and a computer geek from the get-go. Five foot three inches tall, she was slightly chunky, big-boned and, he had learned, of Swedish background. She brightened when she saw him enter the office.

"Sir, I'm looking for the comms. You seen them?"

Joe nodded. "They're over in the last building, Bradford. Why don't you hightail it over there and get that stuff hummin'? Chief Redtail's over there, too."

Flushing with excitement, Iris said, "Yes, sir! This is *so* cool! I love this place! I'm so glad I was asked to be a part of the team." She flashed him a toothy smile, moved past him and then trotted out of the hangar toward the last building in the row.

Joe smiled and looked around the office. He saw a laptop computer on the desk, a printer, a telephone and a small gold plate on the front of the desk that said C.O. This was Akiva's office. Figuring his must be nearby, he left the office and closed the door. The next office over was indeed his. Standing there in front of his desk, where the small gold plate saying X.O. sat, he got chills. Excitement thrummed through him. Finally, the army was giving him a chance to show what he could do. Now his only problem was Akiva.

Chapter 4

Joe wondered where Akiva was. It was 2330, nearly midnight, of their first full day at Alpha. Everyone was in bed in the second building, each in her own plywood cubical containing a cot and metal locker. The C.O. and X.O. cubes were at the front, on either side of the aisle, the enlisted people's to the rear. The light had been doused a long time ago and thin filaments of moonlight threaded through the windows, which were covered with years of grime. As he walked quietly down the aisle toward the door, Joe mentally put cleaning the windows on his to-do list. Just because Navy Seabees had come in here and built them rough living quarters didn't mean the place was livable. From a cleanliness perspective it was a disaster.

Exhaustion pulled at him. Stuffing his hands into the pockets of his camouflage jacket, he headed out the door. Overhead, foglike clouds were gathering, due to the high humidity. The scream of monkeys and the hooting of

owls drifted out of the darkened jungle as he walked
across the flattened grass between the living quarters and
the communications building. He had a hunch Akiva was
still over there in the planning room, working out the
myriad details of their upcoming flights, which would
start as soon as they could get organized at the base.

Opening the rickety door as quietly as he could, he
entered and stood just inside it. The Seabees had divided
the room into three sections—the comms center, a meeting space where flight planning could be held, and a
small cubicle with a desk in it. There were no doors on
the partitioned-off areas, and he saw dim light flooding
out of the smallest cube.

He moved to the office, stood in the doorway and felt
his heart wrench. Akiva was sleeping over the flight
maps, one arm beneath her cheek, the other spread across
the table, a pencil hanging limply in her long, thin fingers. At some point she'd unraveled her braid, and her
hair cloaked her shoulders like an ebony coverlet, the
reddish highlights glowing in the light of the fluorescent
lamp on the plywood table that served as a desk.

Hungrily his gaze swung back to her face. In sleep,
Akiva looked incredibly vulnerable and beautiful. Joe
was sure she had no idea how attractive she was to men.
Although she never wore makeup, just the chiseled, patrician quality of her features would make any man look
at her twice. Her full lips were soft now, and parted in
sleep. Black strands of hair flowed down her temple, covering her ear and curving along her clean jawline. The
bright red cotton scarf she wore across her brow highlighted her copper skin and black hair, presenting a dra-
matic picture.

Whether he wanted to or not, he needed to wake her
up. Akiva had to get her sleep in order to keep going,

and napping like this wasn't very restful. Gingerly, Joe slid his hand along her proud shoulder, the black uniform felt smooth beneath his fingers.

"Akiva?" he whispered. He squeezed her shoulder gently.

Akiva's brows moved slightly. Her mouth closed and then opened.

Heart speeding up, Joe found himself mesmerized by her soft, lush-looking mouth. What would it be like to lean down and caress those lips with his own? The thought was like a lightning bolt of fire and heat coursing through him and settling hotly in his lower body. Grinning to himself, Joe knew if Akiva had read his thoughts, she'd deck him. Rightfully so. Again he squeezed her shoulder, and deepened his voice.

"Akiva? Come on, time to wake up. You've got to get some good shut-eye, gal." The endearment slipped from his lips before he could stop it. Consarnit! Joe knew Akiva wouldn't take kindly to such familiarity. Had she heard him?

Groaning, Akiva heard a male voice somewhere in the folds of her fuzzy awareness. She also felt a hand—a man's hand—on her shoulder. Ordinarily, she wanted no one to touch her, for as an Apache woman, her body was sacred and not privy to idle touch by anyone without her permission. In her sluggish sleep state, however, her protective walls were no longer in place. The low, husky tone of the man's voice seemed like a warm stream flowing into the cold winter of her heart. He'd called her "gal," in a deep, intimate, caressing tone. The sensation was delicious—and surprising. Akiva had never felt such warmth flowing through her and she wanted badly to languish in the feeling. The man's touch was nurturing. Akiva had never experienced that with any man.

Again she heard her name called. This time she snapped awake out of habit. Sitting up, she blinked.

Joe released her shoulder and stepped back, knowing full well that Akiva would not like him touching her. Her eyes were slightly puffy with sleep, and half-open, with a drowsy look in their gold depths. Her black hair slid around her shoulders like a soft, silky shawl, and he ached to reach out and touch those vibrant strands to see what they felt like between his fingertips.

"What? What's wrong?"

"Whoa, nothing's wrong," Joe said, holding up his hands as she swung around. He could see the sleep leave her abruptly. Her eyes were narrowed and alert now, the gold depths penetrating. Inwardly he longed for the woman who had seemed so innocent and approachable while she slept. That woman was now hidden away once again beneath Akiva's massive armor plating.

Blinking rapidly, Akiva stared at Joe, who stood relaxed before her. His head was cocked to one side, his gray eyes hooded, with a look in them Akiva could not decipher. One corner of his mouth hitched upward.

She sat back in the creaky chair. "Everything okay?" she croaked, then cleared her throat. She tried desperately to shove the sleep away from her in order to think clearly.

"Everything's fine, Akiva. I just found you over here. I'm hitting the rack. I think you should, too." Joe gestured toward the table with maps spread across it. "This is no place to sleep. We need good, restful sleep. Come on, let's go."

Ordinarily, Akiva would have fought him. But Joe's voice was low and coaxing, like a hand caressing her in a very gentle and nonthreatening way. He was right: she needed a good night's sleep.

"Yeah, okay... Thanks..." She rose to her feet and rubbed her face tiredly.

Joe stepped aside and said, "I'll have Spec Dean wake us at 0600."

Feeling vulnerable because she was still wrapped in the last remnants of sleep, Akiva nodded. She watched Joe give her a slight smile, turn and leave. For a moment, as she stood there in the silent room, she missed his quiet strength and gentleness. Shaking her head, Akiva sternly told herself he was an Anglo and few of them ever had such attributes. Yet as she stood there alone, she realized that she hungered for Joe's nurturing nature, now that he was gone. Never had she felt such a driving urgency. At a loss to explain it, she sighed in frustration. How could she be so drawn to Joe? He was Anglo. Her enemy.

Turning, Akiva switched off the light, not wanting to waste electricity. Stumbling from the darkened room, she let her eyes adjust before walking to the door. The moonlight was like thin, diluted milk as it filtered through the glass panes of the grimy windows. As she sighed and rubbed her eyes, Akiva knew she had to get some decent sleep. Being a C.O. was hard work. Much harder than she'd ever anticipated. And tomorrow was another day with Joe...a man she did not want to work with or be around. Yet one she was beginning to need with the hunger of a lone wolf wanting a mate. It was a terrible cosmic joke—on her.

"Well," Joe said as he knocked lightly on the planning room door, a cup of coffee in hand, "what do you think?" It was late afternoon and Akiva was sitting at the planning table, several flight maps spread out in front of her. She was in her usual uniform, the bright red headband in place, her hair black and straight around her shoulders. Joe was glad she wore her hair down; it made her look incredibly beautiful.

Akiva turned. Her eyes narrowed. Joe was in his black flight uniform and was holding out a cup of coffee toward her.

"Dean got the coffeemaker going?" she asked, hope in her voice.

"Yeah. How about that? Would you like some?"

Akiva wanted coffee. But she didn't want to accept it from him. She saw the hope burning in his eyes. All day, in small, subtle ways, Joe had tried to be helpful, and yet stay out of her way. He wasn't dumb; he knew she really didn't want him around. Akiva eyed the coffee, wanting it desperately. But if she took it, Joe would think it was a sign of peace between them, and that's not how she felt.

"No...thanks. You go ahead and drink it." Again, that sense of incredible nurturing cloaked her. It was from Joe, Akiva realized, without a doubt. Her heart dropped with anguish. She desperately wanted that warmth from him, but wavered when she remembered her past experiences. She was torn, knowing that if she reached out for that warmth she craved, she'd be reaching out for him. Akiva could not have what he offered without accepting Joe's presence in her life. The realization was paralyzing to her. It filled her with a fear she could not sneer at, run from or face. At least not yet.

Joe shrugged and sipped the coffee. "Dean makes a mean cup of java."

"Smells good," Akiva admitted hoarsely. She turned her back on him and looked at the maps. Hearing him come closer, she tried to tell herself to stop soaking up his presence like a thirsty sponge. Was she so hungry for intimacy? So empty that even the remotest human warmth touched some dark, frightened part of her and made her feel almost out of control? Akiva had never experienced the overwhelming emotions she experienced now. It was as if Joe was creating a tidal wave of powerful, surging need in her—need that only he could fulfill. How was that possible? Akiva had always felt herself impervious to men and whatever crumbs they offered. Joe, however, was offering such a rich banquet, vital and nurturing energy that she wondered how she was going to stop herself from reaching out and consuming it like a starving wolf.

"How is the planning going? You're looking at potential flight routes from here, over the Gulf and back?"

Sighing, Akiva nodded and picked up the plastic protractor, tapping it against one of the colorful maps. "Yeah. Trying to figure out flight routes. We can never take the same one twice. Someone might be watching us. I'm trying to devise five different flight strategies, depending on where we meet up with a druggie, and how to fly that pattern back here to the base."

Joe stood quietly. "Mind if I take a look at what you've come up with so far?" His heart thumped hard in his chest. He knew Akiva was a hands-on manager, not one to give up territory or duties to others unless she absolutely had to. Oh, she'd been more than happy to have him, as X.O., handle all the things that needed to be reckoned with in setting up Alpha. But when it came to the serious stuff of planning interdiction, she'd made it clear she didn't want him nosing around.

Mouth thinning, Akiva scowled and put her hands over her notebook, where she'd been scribbling ideas. *Damn.* The last thing she wanted was Joe here. Why couldn't he just leave her alone? The more mature side of herself said, *Because he's the X.O. He has a right to be here.*

Besides, he might have some good ideas that you could use. The immature part of her, the wounded side, won out. Her voice became clipped. "I'll let you see them when I'm done. Don't you have other duties that need attending to?"

Wincing inwardly, Joe tried to tamp down his impatience and frustration. In an instant, he had seen Akiva put up her defensive guard; it was in her voice and in her stiffening body. Looking around, he saw that Iris Bradford had left the building. They were alone.

"Tell me something," Joe said in a low, soothing voice. "Am I green lookin', with scales and a set of horns on my head?"

Stunned, Akiva twisted around and stared at him, her mouth falling open. Joe was leaning languidly in the entranceway, his brows furrowed, his eyes dark and searching. "What?"

"Did I grow horns and a tail? Is that why you don't want me within ten feet of you at any time? Am I some virus you're afraid will infect you through casual contact?"

Akiva was shocked by his brazenness. Maybe she had misjudged him; she had thought Joe was a beta male, not an alpha one. She stared up at him, stunned speechless. The silence thickened between them. Gulping, she realized that if she spoke the truth, he could, by military regulations, have her strung up for dereliction of duty because of prejudice. And she wasn't about to let that occur. But if that was Joe's intent, she didn't sense it. There was nothing in his face or his voice that indicated he intended malice toward her. No, what she heard from him was hurt. Hurt that she was leaving him out of the loop, that she didn't need him around at all. And also, there was a gentle persistence in his tone clearly meant to create dialogue to get past the defensive anger on her part.

Her heart twinged with guilt…and another emotion that she refused to look at. Her gaze snapped away and then back to Joe.

"We're alone," he told her. "I would never bring this up within earshot of anyone, Akiva."

Lips pursed, she growled, "Look, I'm new at this…being a C.O. I don't know how to lead, I guess. And right now, all my attention is on our mission and flights."

"Understandable," Joe rasped. "And I haven't had any training to be an X.O., either, so maybe we're both floundering around, unsure and on shaky legs with our new assignments?" He saw her eyes fill with fear and uncertainty. "I know I'm feelin' that way." Well, that wasn't really true, but Joe decided the white lie might create some camaraderie between them—and perhaps create an opening with Akiva. There was no sense in accusing her. She'd only shut down and retreat inside that cool, icy tower. That was the last thing Joe wanted.

"Uh, yeah…" Akiva searched his hooded gray eyes. Her ability to read men was deadly accurate; she could smell them intuitively a mile away. And if her all-terrain radar was working correctly, she felt Joe trying to offer her an olive branch of peace. Her heart said to take it. Her mind screamed no. Torn, she shrugged.

"Let me… I'll be done with my preliminary flight paths probably by tonight. How about you look at them then?"

Nodding, Joe sipped the coffee, though he no longer tasted it. "That would be fine. Thanks. I gotta go. Spec Dean and Ferris have got the helos in the hangar, and

they're going to begin working on the big rig for us. They
have to go through normal pre-mission checks on it.''

"Good. Fine...fine..."

Joe saw the indecision in Akiva's gold eyes. He saw
her being pulled between her desire to be civil toward
him and something else. What was that other thing? He
sensed it more than saw it in her body language. It was
as if she wanted to explain herself to him for some reason. "I'll see you later," he said, and turned on his heel.

"Better catch your sun rays today to keep that tan,"
Akiva called, trying to be friendly. "There's a lot less
sun here, I think, than what we had back in Peru."

Stopping, Joe twisted around and gave her a quizzical
look. She'd already turned her back to him and was bent
over the maps once more. Confused by her words, he
took a sip of coffee and then headed to the door. What
had Akiva meant by that statement? Was she just trying
to be pleasant? Maybe she was feeling bad about the way
she was treating him and was trying to be social. Heartened, he took her off-the-wall comment as a white flag
of truce—at least for now. His heart lightened with each
stride, because Joe felt as if they'd taken a step together,
in the same direction, for the first time.

Joe had asked the enlisted women to share the mess
duties, taking turns being responsible for each day's
meals. Spec Susan Dean, their ordnance person, had been
given extra duty as chef today. She hailed from the
Bronx, and had a distinct nasal twang to her voice. As
they sat at the benches and tables in the dining area, she
quickly served them their first dinner at Alpha. Dressed
in her camos, her olive-green T-shirt damp with sweat,
she zoomed around, passing out aluminum trays filled
with the delicious smelling spaghetti she'd whipped up.

Joe sat on one side of the officers' table and Akiva sat opposite him. She was smiling at Susan, who was singing an Italian song in high falsetto as she served them their meals. It was 1800 hours, and Joe was glad to see everyone pulling together. This was going to be a tight team, and he was proud of the enlisted women, each of whom had pulled double duty today serving outside their trained area of expertise.

Susan set trays in front of Akiva and Joe. Her green eyes danced with pride. "There you go, Chiefs. My mama, who is a killer cook, gave me this recipe. Enjoy!" She turned and quickly went back to the makeshift kitchen for trays for the others.

Akiva grinned and picked up her fork. She risked a glance across the table at Joe. The black uniform he wore accentuated his black hair and darkly tanned features, making him look dangerous to her. Akiva couldn't pin down exactly what it was about Joe Calhoun that drew him to her, only that her silly heart was always thumping a little when he was in the vicinity. A rebellious lock of black hair dipped over his broad brow. She had the maddening urge to push it back into place. Stunned at her spontaneous feelings, Akiva scowled and forked the fragrant spaghetti into her mouth.

"Pretty good," Joe called to Susan, who was just sitting down to eat with her friends. "I almost feel like I'm back in New York City sittin' at an Italian café."

Susan glowed at the compliment as she dug into a huge pile of spaghetti. "Thanks, Chief."

"With this kind of food," Akiva said, turning toward the other table with a smile, "we'll survive. Nice job, Dean. Keep it up."

"Yes, ma'am, you bet I will."

"Hey," Spec Robin Ferris, the software expert, called,

"I'm next! It's my turn in mess tomorrow." She gave Susan a triumphant look. "I'm makin' chicken and dumplin's for dinner. How about *that?*"

Akiva grinned. "No food fights, ladies. We're all looking forward to your kitchen skills. Now, let's eat. We've got a night of work ahead of us."

The collective groan rose from the enlisted table. Akiva turned back and saw Joe watching her. He nodded and gave her an approving look, as if to say, *Well done.*

Glowing from the unvoiced compliment, Akiva turned her attention to eating. She was starved. Fortunately, Susan had made the most of their limited supplies, which consisted mainly of canned vegetables and meat.

"Things are lookin' good," Joe said in a low tone as they ate. "It's all comin' together around here. You can feel it. Good vibes, thanks to you."

Akiva's heart swelled at his sincere compliment. She nodded, but continued eating. Susan had somehow found flour and yeast and baked some homemade rolls. "Yes, it's looking good." She felt hopeful, despite her terror of being a bad C.O. She appreciated Joe's comment because it made her a bit more confident about being a leader. Even though there was only five people involved, to her it was a daunting task filled with land mines she could step on, and Akiva didn't want to do that.

Taking a roll, Joe sliced a pat of butter from the white dish before him and slathered it across the top. "Did you get those flight plans done?"

Nodding, Akiva wiped her mouth with her paper napkin. "Yes. I'll give them to you to study tonight. We'll go over them at the planning office tomorrow at 0800."

"Good. I'm anxious to see what you've come up with." And he was. Joe admired Akiva's intelligence and her combat experience. She didn't look real happy about him nosing around in her plans, however, even if she spoke the correct words any C.O. would say to an X.O.

"Yeah…well, don't knee-jerk on me, okay? I'm new at this."

Chuckling, Joe put his empty tray aside. After he wiped his own mouth, he wadded up his napkin and dropped it on the tray. "Like I'm going to jump down your throat or something? Scream and yell? Is that what you expect from me?"

"I'm just not used to working with…well…men. Women think a certain way. We see things differently than you. I'm used to working with my own gender, that's all."

"Three years down here with an all-woman crew would make a person get used to a certain way of thinking and seeing things," Joe agreed. "I guess I never thought of it from that perspective."

"You wouldn't. You're a man." *Oh, damn!* Akiva rolled her eyes as she saw Joe react to the insult. His eyes widened at first, and then she saw hurt in their gray depths. Guilt ate at her. "I didn't mean that like it came out," she muttered darkly so that only he could hear. It was the closest thing to an apology that he was going to get from her.

Joe settled his elbows on the table, his cup of coffee between his hands. "I'm looking forward to being taught how women think in strategic and tactical terms, Akiva. I know you can teach me a lot, and I'm willin' to learn. You ladies have forged a whole new concept about war and interdiction down here, and a lot of people need to learn from your experiences."

Oh, great. Now I really feel bitchy. Akiva didn't like herself at times, and this was one of them. Joe had been gentle and nonthreatening. He'd just given her a sincere

compliment, and she'd jumped on him and bitten two big
fang holes into him. Yet he was taking it in stride and
turning a negative into a positive. Rubbing her furrowed
brow, she growled, "Do me a favor and take the best
that women offer, and not the worst...."

"You're under a lotta stress," he said confidentially
as he sipped his coffee, his gaze on the table of enlisted
women behind Akiva. The laughter and good-natured
talk among them melted the tension. Yet Akiva was staring darkly down at her food, her brows furrowed. He also
noticed there was a high, pink flush to her cheeks. Son
of a gun, she was blushing! Joe sat there absorbing her
response. Grinning a little to himself, he felt his spirits
buoy. If she was blushing, it meant she felt badly over
the acidic comment she'd just fired at him. That made
him feel better. "Learning to be a leader is tough stuff,"
he added sympathetically.

"Yeah? Well, from the looks of things, Calhoun,
you're doing a much better job as X.O. than I am as
C.O." Blowing a breath of air in frustration, Akiva gave
him a pleading look. "You're right, I am stressed out.
I'm feelin' Maya breathing down my neck. I can hear
her voice in the back of my head saying, 'Well, are you
online yet? When's the first mission ready to roll?'"

Joe stopped himself from reaching out to touch Akiva's hand, which was resting near her tray. She'd
bunched it into a fist. Right now, he knew she needed to
be held, if only for a moment, to make the big, bad world
go away temporarily, and give her some breathing room.
"I don't think Major Stevenson would expect us to be
gunnin' and runnin' so soon." He offered Akiva a
skewed smile as he set his coffee cup down between his
hands. "I just think you want to do a good job for

her…for all of us. And I'd say that's the earmark of a good leader—the fact that you care."

Whether she wanted to or not, Akiva desperately needed someone to confide in. Back at the base, she had her tight circle of friends, her confidantes. Out here, she was cut off from everyone. She couldn't talk to the other women here; the gulf between enlisted and officers was like the Grand Canyon. As a fellow officer, Joe was someone she could confide in, but it was so hard. To open up meant to trust him, and she just couldn't do it. Yet when she gazed into his warm, lingering gray gaze, her heart expanded with such a powerful feeling of trust that it left Akiva momentarily breathless.

Opening and closing her fist convulsively, Akiva stared down at her tray. To look into Joe's dove-gray eyes was like spotting a shimmering rainbow after a hard rain. She simply wanted to lose herself in his gaze. That shook her deeply. No man in her life had ever affected her like this. Not ever.

She tried to stop herself from speaking, but the words slipped from between her pursed lips. "I—I really miss my friends back at the base…being able to talk to them…."

Joe saw the battle in Akiva's narrowed golden eyes. He saw her waver and almost trust him enough to open up to him. Sitting there, he realized he was holding his breath, hoping she'd do exactly that. When she didn't, he knew why: there wasn't a basis of trust between them.

"Maybe," he suggested gently, "over time I'll prove I have a good ear and can listen." He patted his shoulder and grinned a little. "And a shoulder to cry on, if you need one."

Chapter 5

"Bogey painted on radar five miles ahead," Joe warned Akiva, who was flying the Apache gunship toward their intended target. It was dusk; the horizon was darkening as they flew east over the calm waters of the Gulf. Tension sizzled through him. This was their first mission after taking a week to get Alpha online. The call had come in from the American sub sitting somewhere offshore, reporting a fixed-wing aircraft speeding over the water toward the U.S.

Akiva sat in the lower front cockpit of the Apache, the cannon directly beneath her flight boots as she flew. "Roger," she answered in a clipped tone. All her attention was on flying the swift gunship. Its shaking and trembling felt comforting to Akiva. She was relieved to get back up in the air and do something she knew she was very good at: hunting down drug aircraft.

What worried her as she kept gazing across her instrument panel was Joe Calhoun. She'd never flown a combat mission with him before. How good was he? Could he see trouble coming soon enough to warn her? Because she wasn't sure, Akiva watched her HUDs—heads-up-display screens—more than she would ordinarily. They were two square monitors in front of her, highlighted with colorful lines that told her in symbolic form what Joe was seeing from the rear cockpit, directly behind her.

Akiva moved the optic night scope into position over her right eye, flipped up the lid, then looked into it. The scope gave them a tremendous advantage, especially in combat, providing a huge amount of information. Akiva wasn't sure if there was any "enemy" around, but Luis Rios and his fleet of civilian helicopters was never far from her mind. The son of the drug lord was known to be aggressive and spontaneous. She sure didn't want Luis Rios to show up right now, even if his civilian helos weren't rigged with weapons. Besides, helos had only a certain fuel range, and their time would be spent intercepting fixed-wing aircraft over the Gulf. That didn't mean Luis couldn't wait on shore and attack them. That possibility nagged at Akiva. If Luis had his helo fleet retrofitted with larger fuel tanks, he could become a deadly threat to them over the land mass.

"Four miles," Joe said.

Akiva nodded. She saw the same blip on the screen. The HUD display shifted as Joe asked for a conformation of the type of aircraft it was. Instantly, it showed a profile of a twin-engine Beechcraft.

"Three miles..." Joe wiped at a dribble of sweat working its way down the side of his temple with a quick movement of his Nomex-gloved hand. His eyes were intent on the HUDs. At the same time, he was watching other equipment for any signs of trouble. Below them, at five thousand feet, the darkening waters of the Gulf looked peaceful. He sat in the upper cockpit, which rode piggyback style above the first one. His seat was closest to the rotor, and the familiar shaking as the blades whirled was something he enjoyed. The specially designed helmet he wore effectively cut out all the noise.

"Got a lot of cumulus up ahead," Joe warned. Over the Gulf, they had discovered, thunderstorms popped up suddenly and with a violence that he'd only seen in West Texas. Although the Apache was an all-weather helicopter, able to fly in fog and deteriorating IFR—instrument flight rules—conditions, a thunderstorm was something to be avoided if possible because of the massive up and down drafts of air that could literally toss an aircraft—any aircraft—around like a toy. The Apache was not a huge helicopter; sleek and streamlined, it was designed for combat. It would be like a wooden rowboat thrown on the mercy of a raging sea if it had to enter a thunderstorm to chase down the bogey ahead.

"I don't *like* storms," Akiva growled. Her gaze flicked to the thin green radar arm arcing across one of the HUDs. "That bogey doesn't, either."

"Yeah," Joe confirmed, "he's dropping elevation. He's going to try and go under it. Think he knows we got a fix on him? He's acting like he does."

"I don't know. This is our first mission. We got a big learning curve ahead of us. Just stay alert."

Grinning, he drawled, "Don't worry. I want something nice put in my personnel jacket when this is all over. Not 'Joe Calhoun sunk the Apache out in the Gulf.' Wouldn't look good, would it?"

His dry sense of humor during the tense moment got inside Akiva's normally unflappable facade. Chuckling outright, she muttered, "Calhoun, I've come to think that you will live and die for that personnel jacket report."

It felt good to hear Akiva laugh. It was the first time Joe had heard her laughter, and it warmed him immeasurably as he sat in the tight, narrow cockpit, the nylon harnesses biting deeply into his shoulders and across his thighs. ''Your laugh is like water runnin' over rocks at one of my favorite places on earth—Yosemite. Three miles...''

There was no time to absorb his huskily spoken words, though. Akiva was surprised at the unexpectedly intimate tone in his voice in that moment. Whether she wanted to or not, her heart accepted his compliment, for it was a beautiful one. She'd been to Yosemite National Park and had stood at the foot of the waterfall he was probably talking about. It was a grand waterfall, dropping a hundred feet, with rainbows shimmering through its spray as the sun moved across the sky. Enjoying the comparison of her laughter to the water singing on the rocks, she smiled a little.

''Two miles...you oughta be able to get a visual on him....''

Akiva lifted her head, her eyes moving to slits. She gripped the cyclic and collective, guiding the Apache smoothly in a descent toward the waters of the Gulf. The light was fading rapidly now, but she could see the dark, looming, cauliflower-shaped thunderheads directly ahead of them. Lightning flashed within the clouds, illuminating them momentarily as the bolt zigzagged through it.

''Yeah...'' She strained to look downward, searching for the plane. If it was a drug flight, the pilot probably wouldn't have his red and green flashing lights on, not wanting to be seen. Under FAA flight rules, all planes had to have lights on in order to be detected, so other aircraft wouldn't accidentally run into them. Of course, the Apache didn't have running lights on, either, but they were a military aircraft on a mission.

"I got 'em!" Joe said. "See 'em? Eleven o'clock, Akiva."

She cocked her head and peered through the cockpit Plexiglas.

"Roger. I see him."

"Hang on...gonna see if I can read the numbers on his fuselage." Joe picked up the pair of night-vision binoculars and aimed them down toward the fleeing plane. It was flying at a thousand feet, almost hugging the surface of the Gulf. In the dusky light, it was hard to read the numerals on the cream-colored fuselage of the twin-engine plane.

"I don't think he knows we're shadowing him," Joe murmured. He got the numbers and scribbled them down on the knee board strapped around his right thigh. Setting the binoculars aside, he quickly typed the numbers into his computer and sent the inquiry via satellite to deep within the Pentagon, where such aircraft numbers were stored.

"No, he doesn't—yet. Did you get the numbers?"

"Yes, ma'am. I've already inquired. Hold on...." Joe watched his right HUD light up with a response. He grinned savagely. "Wal, this good ole boy ain't on the FAA flight plans or register at all. How about that? I think we got a druggie on our hands, Chief Redtail."

Again she felt his warm, easygoing teasing dissolve some of the tension accumulating in her shoulders and neck as they chased the other aircraft. They were flying at fifteen hundred feet, directly behind its tail—a position called an aircraft's "six." There were no sideview mirrors on a plane, so the pilot wouldn't know they were there. Most civilian aircraft did not have the radar on board to alert them that another aircraft was shadowing them so closely.

"Good," Akiva said tightly. "Let's rock 'n' roll.... You'd better strap those binoculars down so they aren't flying around the cabin. You could get a broken nose," she warned as she gripped the cyclic and collective a little tighter.

"Already done," Joe assured her. "Ahm such a good-lookin' guy that I don't think a broken nose would hurt my looks, do you?"

Akiva couldn't help but laugh. "Do you always joke in tense moments?"

"Jest my nature, Chief Redtail."

Shaking her head, Akiva growled, "You surprise me every day, Calhoun."

"Good," he chortled, feeling her take the Apache to a higher speed, surging ahead of the fleeing Beechcraft. Joe enjoyed Akiva's flying ability; she was smooth as silk. The Apache was a living extension of her, shaking and trembling around him as she aimed the nose of the gunship a good half mile ahead of the drug plane.

The night was darkening. The water looked shiny and black below, except when a bolt of lightning flashed, reflecting across it.

"That dude is runnin' without lights. Shame on him. The FAA will fine him right and proper," Joe muttered.

"The least of his worries. Arm the cannon."

"Online," he murmured, flipping a switch and watching his HUDs. "You want to fire across his nose in warning?"

"Yes." Akiva smiled grimly. "But first we're gonna scare him a little."

Joe didn't have time to ask how. Akiva whipped the agile gunship around so that they were now facing the

Beechcraft racing toward them. She hovered the Apache at one thousand feet, directly in line with it.

"Flip on our running lights," she ordered tightly, her gaze locked on the aircraft barreling toward them. Akiva would bet the pilot wasn't that alert; he'd be more concerned about skirting the thunderhead to their right and staying out of any possible up or down drafts that would smash his aircraft, like a mosquito struck by a flyswatter, into the Gulf waters just below.

Her mouth twitched as she saw the plane.

"Half mile," Joe warned, tension in his voice.

"Sky chicken, Calhoun. Relax."

He'd automatically tensed. What if the pilot didn't see them? What if he was too busy dodging and ducking drafts and air turbulence? Would he see their green and red running lights? Joe's eyes widened. From where he sat above Akiva, he saw the Beechcraft come hurtling out of the surrounding darkness.

"Quarter mile..." he choked out. *Come on! See us!* Joe didn't want a midair collision. He'd heard the pilots at the base talk of playing "sky chicken." It was a game where a pilot would fly directly at another aircraft, never banking to the right or left. One of the pilots—the "chicken"—would have to give way at the last moment or there would be a head-on collision. Gulping, Joe sucked in a breath.

The Beechcraft loomed close. He could see the twin propellers spinning, the cream-and-orange design across the rounded nose. He braced himself and gasped.

At the last possible moment, the pilot of the plane saw them. Instantly, he banked sharply to the left and downward.

Akiva chuckled darkly. "Gotcha, you son of a

bitch…'' Instantly she followed the plane down toward the water.

Joe's helmet banged the side of the cockpit as Akiva suddenly swung the gunship around. He was amazed at her swift response as she torqued the craft to its limits, twisting the helo like a hawk swooping in a dive after its scrambling prey.

Shaking his head, he hung on, feeling the immense press of gravity against him during the steep, tight turn. The Apache screamed in protest, shaking even harder. As Akiva pulled the helicopter out of the dive, she notched up the speed to match the Beechcraft's, which was now barely two hundred feet above the water's calm surface. Just the way the pilot was flying the plane indicated he was rattled. He'd lost his direction and was now flying due north, not east as before. Akiva brought the Apache up next to the Beechcraft, close to the pilot's side, so he could see that they were there.

"Call him on the radio," Akiva ordered tightly.

"Roger." Joe quickly placed the call, using at least ten different radio frequencies, one after another. It could be that the pilot had his radio off, as well as his lights. As Joe glanced out at the pilot leaning over his instruments, he shook his head. "No response, Akiva. I think he's got his radio turned off."

"Pity…. Hang on and warm up that cannon."

"Yes, ma'am."

For Akiva, this was old hat. She'd turned back many a helicopter and fixed-wing aircraft back in Peru. The only difference now was that instead of jungle below her, there was water. She kept herself on high alert, because water disorientation was nothing to fool with. She wasn't used to working over water and wanted to avoid the hazard.

Akiva felt the cannon beneath her feet shake the gunship. Joe had fired off a couple of rounds to make sure it was working properly.

"We're hot," he told her, satisfaction in his voice.

"Roger. Get ready to fire across his nose. I want this guy to realize we want him going *back* to Mexico."

"Right on…" Joe tensed as Akiva brought the gunship up and over the Beechcraft and then settled slightly ahead of it.

"Fire."

Finger on the trigger, Joe fired a short burst. He could see the red tracers arcing about twenty feet in front of the plane's nose.

Instantly, the Beechcraft turned and headed west—back toward Mexico.

"Whooee! That good ole boy must be ex-military! He got your message, Akiva. In big red letters." Joe whooped with glee once more.

A smile tugged at Akiva's mouth. "Yeah, he knew what firing across his bow meant. Let's just follow him to shore. Once he's there, we'll peel off and use corridor C to make our way back to Alpha."

"Roger that." Joe grinned. "Nice huntin', Akiva. I learned a thing or two from you tonight."

Akiva didn't answer. She was all business now. The plane was fleeing at top speed, gaining altitude to a thousand feet and heading back toward the land mass of Mexico, which she could see painted on the screen of her HUD.

"Just keep your eyes peeled for his friends. We don't know if he's making a call for help right now on his radio."

"Roger, gotcha. I'm on it." Joe frowned. He knew his business in the back seat. Why did Akiva have to remind him each time? Was it because she didn't trust him? Yes, he realized that was it. He watched the green radar hand sweep back and forth across the screen, but it remained blank, indicating no other aircraft were in the vicinity.

In another thirty minutes, the Beechcraft flew back over the Mexican coast. At that point, Akiva raised the Apache to ten thousand feet and flew back toward the base, using one of the five flight routes she'd worked out to get back to Alpha without being traced or followed. Joe relaxed a little in the cockpit. Looking at his watch, he saw that only an hour had passed since they'd sighted the bogey.

"Amazing how time flies when you're havin' fun," he noted. "One hour. It felt like ten minutes."

Akiva nodded and felt some of the tension draining out of her. "Yeah, it's an amazing thing. When you're in combat, time seems to speed up."

"Adrenaline," Joe agreed.

"Keep an eye out for more bogeys."

He frowned. Of course he was doing that. "Right," he murmured, "I'm always scanning the HUDs, Akiva. I'm not off in dreamland, believe me. It's my butt in this gunship, too. I don't want to be jumped or surprised any more than you do."

"I'm still the commander," she snapped. "And if anything happens, it will be my butt in the sling first." Frowning, Akiva locked the cyclic for a moment and moved her hand upward. With her fingers, she wiped the sweat away from her eyes. Tension was still thrumming through her and she knew the adrenaline in her bloodstream was making her feel this way. Unlocking the mechanism, she wrapped her fingers around the cyclic and continued to fly the gunship manually. Off to their left, thunderheads continued to billow and grow. Frowning, she glared at them. Thunderstorms were no good, and it looked like they would be playing tag around them quite often on these missions. That was one thing she hadn't counted on, and it left her uneasy.

"Do you want me to tell you I'm scanning once a minute?"

Her temper rose. The adrenaline was fraying it. Clamping her lips together, she counted to ten and hoped her voice wouldn't be charged with annoyance as she replied, "No, Mr. Calhoun, you don't have to give me minute-by-minute updates on the fact that your eyes are glued to those HUDs in front of you."

Joe felt her anger. He was angry, too. She didn't trust him at all. Well, once they got back to Alpha and on the ground, he was going to confront her.

It was another thirty minutes before they landed back at Alpha. Joe waited patiently outside the hangar as the three-woman ground crew pushed the Apache back into the hangar so it couldn't be seen. Akiva stood talking to the crew chief about a few software glitches, her Nomex gloves in her left hand and her helmet resting against her hip beneath her left arm.

The darkness was complete at Alpha, except for the dim light cast from the hangar, where the crew was putting the gunship to bed for the night. It would be refueled immediately, the ordnance replaced and checks run on the software, because no one knew when the next call from the American sub would come in.

The air was humid and unmoving as Joe waited. They would have to go to the planning shack to fill out their flight reports next. He'd talk to her about their problem in there, where they'd be alone and out of earshot of the busy ground crew.

Rubbing his jaw, he pulled off his helmet. The cool air felt good on his hot, sweaty head. Holding the helmet by the chin strap, he saw Akiva finally turn and walk toward him. Though her face was dark, he saw a gleam from her narrowed eyes. The way her mouth was set, he knew they were going to mix it up good once they were alone in the shack.

Joe opened the door for Akiva. It was just the way he was; he believed women should have doors opened for them. When he stepped aside to let her into the dimly lit room, she cut him an acidic look. Grimly, he followed her in and made sure the door was shut. The third room to the left, where there were two metal folding chairs and a makeshift desk of plywood set on wooden crates, was to be their report room.

Their booted feet echoed as they entered. Joe carefully set his helmet on the floor near his chair. Grabbing the white form that all crews had to fill out after a mission, he sat down opposite Akiva. The fluorescent overhead light made her copper skin look washed out.

Flicking her a glance as he pulled a pen from his left shoulder pocket, he saw fear in her eyes. Why fear? Over the coming talk they would have? He could feel the tension around her. Her long, thick braid, which lay across her proud shoulder and down the front of her black uniform, was frayed from the humidity. Tendrils of hair around her face softened her angular features, and Joe felt his heart lurch in his chest. More than anything, he wished Akiva wouldn't dislike him so much. Settling down, he scowled and filled out the report in precise, printed letters.

Quiet descended upon the room. Akiva wrote quickly, but neatly. She shot Joe a glance and saw his brow was furrowed. That lock of black hair dipped rebelliously over his perspiring brow, and she could feel his unhappiness. Their first confrontation was coming.

Akiva warred within herself. She was a C.O. How would Maya handle this? Akiva knew she'd been riding Joe when she shouldn't have. He was as well trained as she was, and she had no business bugging him constantly about his duties in the Apache. Licking her lower lip, she put the report aside.

Joe set his report aside, too. He slowly folded his hands in front of him and leveled a benign look at her across the table.

Akiva glared back. Her hands rested tensely on her long, curved thighs beneath the table. "Well?" she snapped. "Let's get this over with."

Joe's mouth crooked. Not exactly the way a good C.O. would start off a conversation. He searched her gold eyes, which were thundercloud dark with suspicion and distrust—toward him.

"Okay," he rasped, "let's." Opening his hands and keeping his voice low and nonthreatening, he said, "I know my duties in the Apache. What I need to know is why you don't trust me to be your back seat."

Stunned that he'd hit her point-blank with the real essence of their problem, Akiva froze momentarily. Rage moved through her like a rattler moving toward a prey. Trying to wrestle with her anger, she hissed, "I don't trust *any* man, so don't think you've been singled out!"

Joe absorbed her anger. It was like a slap in the face to him. "Whoa, just a minute. I don't buy that. You aren't like this around Mike Houston. You treat him with respect." Gazing into her angry eyes, he added, "That's all I need from you—respect."

"Mike Houston is different!" Akiva said as she suddenly stood up, her hands flat on the surface of the table.

She glared down at Joe, hoping to intimidate him into stopping his search for the real reason she didn't trust him.

Joe sat very still. Akiva's voice was grating. Her nostrils flared and she was breathing hard, as if he were physically attacking her. And through the anger, he still saw the fear in her eyes. Why fear? Mind spinning, he tried to figure it all out, but couldn't. Worse, they were still coming down off the adrenaline high of their combat mission, and he knew neither of them was particularly stable at this moment.

He stared up at her, her words echoing through his head. "Houston is different than me? How?"

"You don't get it, do you?" Akiva straightened and wrapped her arms tightly across her chest. She saw the confusion in his eyes. If she told him of her prejudice, he could put her on report and her career would be over. It was that simple.

"Okay," Joe muttered, "he was an *officer* in the army. I'm only a warrant officer. Is this what it's all about? Rank?" Joe knew it could well be that. He saw Akiva's face grow cold and stubborn-looking. Her full breasts rose and fell quickly beneath her black uniform. She stood there tensely, as if expecting him to throw a punch at her. Of course, he would never do that, but she looked like a boxer in a ring, ready to take a blow she expected was coming.

And then it struck him. "Wait a minute..." He rose out of his chair. "Wait..." And he quickly went over in his mind a conversation she'd had with him a week earlier. Holding out his hand toward her, his voice thunderstruck, he said, "Houston is part Quechua Indian, right?"

Shocked, Akiva stopped breathing for a moment. She avoided Joe's searching gaze. Right now, she hated his ability to stay in emotional control when she was out of control. Nostrils flaring again, she rasped, "Yes, he is. So what?"

"And you're Native American."

"Apache and Lakota Sioux. So what?" She saw his eyes turn pensive at the discovery and his mouth flex. He was putting it together, and that scared the hell out of Akiva.

"The other week," Joe said, softening his tone in hopes of defusing the tension between them, "you said something about me getting enough sun to keep my dark tan." He jerked back the sleeve on his uniform to show her his flesh.

Akiva glared at him. "I was just making conversation."

Joe stood there, his mind clicking over the entire scenario. "No...no, I don't think you were. I think I know what's at the heart of this problem between us." He lifted his head and squarely met her glare. Now the fear was real in her gold eyes. He watched as Akiva's mouth thinned, the corners pulling inward.

"You've got an ax to grind with white men, don't you? I never believed it when you said you had a problem with men in general." He wiped his mouth with the back of his hand and held her unsure gaze. "I see now...it's *white* men. And you're Native American." Joe saw her react as if his words had been bullets. Her eyes widened momentarily. And he understood the fear in their depths, because what he had just suggested was prejudice—one thing the army wouldn't tolerate. She wasn't about to admit it to him, though. He could see it in the jutting of her jaw and the way her mouth was set.

He laughed. It struck him as utter irony because, for

once in his life, not owning up to his Indian heritage had created a bias against him.

Akiva stared at him.

"This is too funny!" Joe chortled. He yanked at the closure around his neck, the Velcro giving way, and pulled open his uniform so that Akiva could see his entire chest and torso. Beneath his uniform, he wore nothing.

"Look, will you?" he entreated, gesturing to his exposed skin. "If I was a *white* guy going after a suntan, would there be tan all over my body? You want me to strip completely out of my suit and prove to you that my color isn't just from the sun?"

Gawking and stunned, Akiva stared at his well-shaped chest, which was carpeted with thick black hair. He'd exposed himself down to his navel. Gulping, she watched as he shrugged out of the sleeves and exposed his full upper body.

"Look, will you? Do you see any tan lines on my shoulders? My neck or my chest? Don't you think there would be? And check out my back, too." Joe turned so that she could see all the way down to his hips, where his uniform hung.

Akiva saw the powerful muscles of his broad shoulders and the deep indentation of his spine. Again she gulped. As Joe turned around, jamming his arms back into the sleeves of his uniform and pressing the Velcro closed down the front, she felt shock flowing through her. And when he lifted his head to catch and capture her gaze, she saw a glint in his eyes she'd never seen before. He was no longer smiling. Now his mouth was pursed.

"Just for your information," he began in a low, emotional tone, "this so-called suntan you think I have isn't one at all. The color you see on my hands—" he held them out to her "—is all *over* my body, Akiva. I'm half

Comanche and half white. What you mistook for a tan is from my daddy's side of the family. He's a full-blood Comanche.

"I think I've got it figured out now. Your prejudice is toward *white* men. Mike Houston is part Native American, so he's safe…someone you can trust because he has Indian blood in his veins just like you do."

The silence swirled thickly between them. Joe lowered his hands and moved his jaw, trying to stop the emotions from overwhelming him. "You don't trust Anglos. Okay, I can live with that," he continued. "And I know you're never going to admit that to me, because army regs aren't too nice about prejudice. They don't tolerate it."

He saw her drop her gaze to the table. The suffering he saw in Akiva's face nearly knocked him over. For an instant, Joe felt all her armor falling away. He kept his voice low because he didn't want to fight with her; he wanted to repair whatever the problem was.

"I'm Indian, too. Part Comanche," he repeated. "Maybe that's what you need to know in order to trust me in that cockpit with you, Akiva. And if it is, now you know the truth. I know my job in the Apache. My butt's on the line up there just like yours is. I don't want to get blown out of the sky, either. But you can't keep asking me every few minutes if I'm doing my job. I kept you well informed up there on that flight. I didn't screw up. I was on top of things."

The shock, like a lightning bolt, was still moving through Akiva. She stood there for a long minute, digesting his words. As she forced herself to look up at him, she saw that Joe wasn't angry with her. That surprised her. Instead, she saw him wrestling with finding a way to reach her.

Her heart hammered violently in her chest. She slowly

unwound her arms and let them drop to her sides. Closing her eyes, she took in a ragged breath and then exhaled it. Opening them, she saw the hurt in his face, and at the same time saw him struggling to connect with her. He was part Comanche! That revelation stunned her. What she'd thought was a dark tan was really due to his Indian genes. Joe carried the blood of Native Americans within him...just as she did. In her heart, that made him a friend, not a foe.

Rubbing her mouth with her fingers, she tried to find the right words to reply. "You've acted more like a C.O. in this little confrontation than I have," she admitted hoarsely.

"Akiva, I *care* about you." Joe opened his hands, his voice pleading. "I'm not interested in the army knowing anything about this conversation. I'm not your enemy. I never have been and never will be. I'm someone you can trust, if you'll just let me show you that. But if you don't let me, how can I? Trust is something we've got to have in that gunship cockpit, or it will kill us someday as we're battling one another instead of looking at our instruments or out the cockpit windows. We both know that."

Nodding, Akiva moved her fingertip around on the unpainted plywood in front of her. "You're right...." Her voice was choked. She swallowed against the lump forming in her throat. She had treated Joe without respect. He, on the other hand, had maintained respect throughout their confrontation. What did that say about *her?* Akiva was humiliated, and she had no one to blame but herself.

"I—owe you an apology...." she told him thickly, and raised her chin to meet his hooded gaze.

"I don't want your apology, Akiva," he pleaded hoarsely. "What I want is to earn your respect, your trust...."

Her heart filled with pain. Joe's pain. She'd treated him poorly. And yet, like a knight, he had treated her with gentlemanly respect and care. Oh, she felt his care, all right. She heard it in the quaver in his roughened tone. And she saw that mysterious look in his eyes that made her feel a little weak, a little shaky. It wasn't a bad feeling. No, it was a good one—so nurturing that she hungrily absorbed it.

Lifting her hands, she whispered, "As an Apache warrior, I've shamed myself before you. I haven't kept the warrior code—to protect all people, to care for them and be honorable at all times." Bitterly, she looked away. "I've failed you by behaving in a dishonorable way." Also, Akiva realized that the issue *wasn't* really Joe's heritage. Her *real* problem, her darkness, revolved around men in general, and her distrust of them. Worse, her fear of men glared fully in her face because of her growing feelings toward Joe, no matter how hard she tried to ignore her heart.

Joe saw the suffering in Akiva's face and knew she meant every word of what she said. She was more than contrite. "Listen, we're both tired. We're exhausted from this long runnin' battle of settin' Alpha up. Let's just bury the hatchet on this one, shall we?" He managed to lift one corner of his mouth as he saw her head snap up, her eyes flare with surprise at his suggestion.

Pointing to the leather-covered ax head she wore in the belt around her waist, he said in a teasing tone, "So long as you don't use that on me when you're pissed off, I think we got nowhere to go but up, gal. Fair 'nuff?"

Chapter 6

"Hey, Akiva..." Joe stuck his head into her open door along the hangar bay. She was sitting at her desk, doing the thing she hated most: paperwork. This morning, her black hair was long and free. In the past month, Joe had come to enjoy seeing her like that. The only time she wore her red scarf about her head was when she was going into battle. Otherwise, her hair was a beautiful black cloak about her squared shoulders. "You gotta see this. Come on...."

Akiva looked up to see Joe grinning idiotically, his hands on the doorjamb. He was dressed in his body-fitting, olive-green T-shirt and his camouflage pants. The look on his face sent a sheet of warmth through her.

Akiva put down her pencil and shoved the map aside. "What?"

"Ahh, come on.... If I told you, it wouldn't be a surprise." As he wiped from his brow the sweat he'd worked up in the hangar while helping with maintenance on the Apache with Spec Dean, he saw Akiva's gold eyes narrow. Since their confrontation a month ago, he'd seen Akiva lessen little by little the amount of armor she wore around him. She showed it in small ways, but he was grateful for anything other than the icy demeanor she'd maintained before. Every once in a while her delicious mouth would curve faintly in a slight smile when he teased or joked with her. And that was something Joe had discovered: humor got to Akiva. It was the only doorway that gave him entrance to her, and he used it often.

Looking at her wristwatch, Akiva saw it was 1130. It was Sunday, and the sky was a misty, milky-blue color with the usual low-hanging clouds hugging the jungle treetops around the base. "Almost lunchtime."

"Hoo doggies, it sure is," he muttered, straightening and looking at his watch. "Well, shucks, gal, let's grab a sandwich from the mess hall and take it with us, then."

"Where are we going?" Akiva asked, glad to be leaving her desk. Being C.O. meant being hounded by too much paperwork. She didn't know how Maya stood it. Akiva disliked the time it took. She would rather be flying. Coming around the desk, she met and held his dancing gray eyes. Ever since she'd realized Joe carried Native American blood in his veins, she had stopped being so hard on him. And to give him more than a little credit, he had graciously dropped the topic completely. He was more forgiving than she deserved, Akiva knew.

Joe moved away from the door as she stepped through it. Out in the hangar, all three women were working on the helos. The maintenance on them was constant, especially in this humid climate. Looking outside, Akiva could see sunlight beginning to pierce the canopy here and there. Joe stood with a smile on his face as he looked at her. Akiva swallowed. That smile always made her feel good. If she was honest, she'd have to admit that Joe was a wonderful addition to this group. The enlisted women doted upon him, loved his good-natured way with them. He was a good bridge between them and Akiva.

"You look like a man on a mission," she muttered in a low tone as she approached. Pushing thick strands of hair behind her shoulder, she saw his eyes widen momentarily, and the look in them changed. Her heart responded automatically. Akiva tried to ignore it, but Joe wasn't easy to ignore—not with his husky laughter floating through the hangar, or his Texas drawl reaching her office as she worked. Yes, Akiva liked his presence, but wasn't sure she wanted to admit that to herself.

"I am," he said wickedly. "Come on, I got somethin' to show you."

Hesitating, she said, "What if we get a call?"

Joe pulled the cell phone from the clip on his web belt and held it up for her to see. "Bradford's over at comms. She'll call us." Tucking the phone back on his belt, he led her outside the dark confines of the hangar. "Actually, Dean found it yesterday and told me about it a little while ago. It's about a quarter mile from here. I thought you might like a break from all that paperwork that's choking you."

Akiva gave him a grimace. "You've got that right. Paperwork sucks. Give me a mission anytime." She walked in long strides past the group of buildings. In the distance, she could hear monkeys screeching, and parrots, well hidden in the dark jungle vegetation, calling to one another.

"Hold on a sec," Joe told her, and he trotted into the mess building.

Akiva smiled to herself. Joe seemed like such a little

boy sometimes, so exuberant about life in general. It didn't take much to get him excited and for that dancing laughter to shine like sunlight in his gray eyes. Pushing the toe of her flight boot into the red-colored soil, she shook her head.

Joe came out again with a sack. Holding it up, he said, "Lunch for two. Ferris has the duty. She's made some mean chicken sandwiches with pickle relish."

Akiva nodded and walked with him as he rounded the last building and headed off toward the jungle. "This isn't too far away, is it, Joe?"

"No...not far. I know, I know, you're worried about a mission call comin' in."

"Yes..." They'd been flying one or two flights a day, nearly every day. The flight patterns had been changing weekly as the drug-running pilots tried to find a way to get across the Gulf without the Apache interdicting them. So far, with the American sub's help, they'd turned back a total of fifty-five flights in the first month of actual air ops. Akiva was proud of their total. She could almost feel the building frustration of the drug lord as his flights were blockaded. No matter what plan the Rioses launched, she and Joe had stopped it. Satisfaction laced through her as they headed down a familiar path into the jungle.

"This is the way to our laundry stream," she said to Joe as she followed him closely down the trail, which was damp with fallen leaves. Akiva watched where she placed her feet; roots often popped up or were hidden by the leaves and could easily trip a person. As they moved deeper into the jungle, she spotted the small stream of clear water, a shallow creek about twenty feet wide. Dean, in her exploration of the place, had found it, and this was where everyone did their laundry.

More than once, Akiva had come down here with Joe, where, on her knees, she'd leaned over the stream and beaten her clothes with a rock to clean them. He'd often joked that they had the most modern gunships on the face of the earth and what were they doing? Going back to the Stone Age to wash their clothes. Of course, Alpha wasn't a fully functioning base. It was an experiment, and such social amenities as a clothes washer and dryer were not possible. Not until the crew proved that the base could work.

Here and there sunlight filtered through the thick trees and brush of the rain forest. This jungle was easy to walk through compared to the one Akiva knew in Peru, which was a nearly impenetrable green wall. As she followed Joe down the path, she heard him begin to hum a tune. He always hummed when he was happy, and he usually hummed some Texas ditty that was funny. Sometimes, to break up the tense atmosphere and the urgency that often hung over the base, he'd start singing in his deep, Texas voice while working on one of the helicopters. It always lightened the atmosphere, and for that, Akiva was grateful.

"Joe? How much farther?" she asked, hurrying to keep up with him. They were past the laundry area. Here the path was covered with fresh grass that had not been tamped down by foot traffic. The path itself began to disappear as they moved along the stream, which widened considerably and deepened, too.

As she walked behind Joe, Akiva admired his broad back, appreciated his athletic build and the way he moved.

"Just a little farther," he called encouragingly over his shoulder. Akiva gave him a dark look of misgiving. He grinned at her. "Have faith, gal. Just keep followin' me."

When they were alone, Joe often called her "gal." It was a Texas endearment, although he didn't think Akiva realized that. Still, he cherished the moments of privacy they had—which were few and far between. She let him call her that, and the fact sent Joe's heart soaring. If they weren't flying a mission, they were usually at the base doing maintenance to keep the Apache flying, or they were trying to catch some sleep between flights, which could happen at any time. Most of them so far were at night, but now, that pattern was changing. That worried Joe, because it meant they could be detected a lot more easily by their enemy.

Swinging downhill, he skidded on the damp leaves along the stream. The terrain descended steeply for about a hundred feet, then smoothed out below. He turned and saw Akiva hesitate at the top of the leaf-covered hill strewn with bushes. She was looking at the waterfall tumbling into space to her left. Enjoying the expression of awe on her face as she perused the view, he called to her above the roar of the water. "Hey! Come on down! The view's even better from here." And he stretched his hand toward her.

Akiva skidded and slid down the steep hill. The soil had a clay base, and she felt like she was gliding on ice. Just as she made it to the bottom, both feet flew out from beneath her and she gave a cry of surprise. Joe was there to catch her. When his strong arms closed about her, Akiva gasped.

Joe buoyed her up and hooked his arms beneath her. She felt his hands, strong and warm, wrapping around her torso as she struggled to get her feet beneath her once again.

Gasping, she gripped his thick wrists to steady herself. Wildly aware of her back resting against his broad chest, his entire body like a bulwark steadying her own, she quickly pulled away. Everywhere his body had touched hers, she felt a burning sensation. It was a startling feeling, but not a bad one. As Akiva brushed herself off and avoided his gaze, she felt nervous and very shy. Straightening, she turned away from Joe altogether and looked at the waterfall plunging down the hill.

At the top was a huge black rock, cutting the stream into two distinct forks that merged again halfway down as the water tumbled downward. The mist rising from the round pool at the bottom floated upward like fog. Sunlight piercing the jungle canopy flashed through the mist, creating a beautiful, breathtaking rainbow. Akiva couldn't help but gasp with delight.

Joe inched closer to where she stood, her booted feet apart to keep her from falling on the slippery clay near the pool. "Purty, ain't it?"

She gave him a sideways glance. His Texas drawl always soothed her. "Yes…mind-blowing. I never expected this…." And she gestured to the beauty around them. The pool was circular and about the size of an Olympic swimming pool. All around it were trees of varying heights, with bromeliads and orchids hanging from their branches, or tucked into forks.

"Smell the orchids?" Joe asked with satisfaction. He savored the surprise and happiness in Akiva's face as she absorbed the peace and beauty of the spot. Setting down the sack that contained their lunch, he added, "As I said, Dean found this by accident the other day and she told me about it. I wanted to go check it out myself, and I figured, you bein' Indian, you'd like this place as much as I do."

Inhaling the faint, spicy fragrance that wafted around the pool, Akiva realized it was from the colorful orchids

dotting the area. "This is incredible, Joe. Just fantastic!"
She turned and smiled at him. He was regarding her
through half-closed eyes, a thoughtful look on his face.
"Thanks…I'm glad you hauled me away from my desk.
This is worth it."

"Good." He reached out and briefly touched her upper
arm. "Come on, let's eat and enjoy this little respite from
our duties. I think we've earned it." He found a large
black rock, worn flat with time, that would easily seat
two people and keep them dry from the damp ground.

Joe had deliberately touched her. And when his fingers
had met her firm arm, he'd seen Akiva's eyes flare with
surprise…and then some other emotion. It was one he
hadn't expected to see, and it took him by surprise.

Hope glowed brightly in Joe as he sat on the rock and
opened the sack to hand Akiva her wrapped sandwich.
She sat down, her back near his. The rock wasn't that
big, and it forced them into a closeness he didn't mind
at all. But did she? He watched like a starved dog as she
pulled the wrap off her sandwich with her long and grace-
ful fingers. Joe wondered what it would be like if Akiva
touched him that way. Lately, since their truce, she was
opening up to him, a little more each day. To Joe, it was
like watching some rare, gorgeous flower begin to open,
a petal at a time. Of course, he didn't share this thought
with Akiva. She always seemed unsure of herself as a
woman around him. Frowning, Joe decided to take a huge
risk. As he bit into his sandwich and allowed the music
of the waterfall to embrace them, he waited for an opportunity to spring his question.

Akiva munched her sandwich, but her attention was on
the rugged beauty of the waterfall. She absorbed Joe's
closeness and felt a camaraderie with him that she'd
never experienced before with a man. Gesturing toward

the water, she said, "Has anyone made this the official bathtub for the group?" It would surely beat the tepid and sometimes cold showers they took every morning back at their quarters.

"No, but as C.O., you can issue an order to make it such," he said. "I think the ladies would like comin' here to take a bath." The water was clear, and the pool was about six to ten feet deep, as far as Joe could see. There was a sand and gravel bottom—much better than algae-covered rocks, which would make it slippery and hazardous.

"It will be a pleasure to write this order," Akiva chuckled.

Taking a deep breath, Joe decided to change topics. "You know, when I was growin' up, my daddy never said much about his Comanche blood. You, on the other hand, got lucky and were raised in the ways of your people, weren't you?" Joe twisted to look in her direction. This was the first time he'd tried to talk to her about such a personal topic. Would Akiva join in? Or would she shy away like the wild mustang he saw her as?

Her brows dipped and she looked down at her half-eaten sandwich. His heart raced a little with anticipation. Joe hungered for a more personal connection with Akiva. Would she allow it? He wasn't sure, but he had to try. His heart drove him to it.

"My people…" Akiva began, her voice mirroring her bitterness. "My father was Lakota, Joe. My mother was Apache." She snorted softly and took another small bite of her sandwich.

Joe waited. He'd heard the instant tension in her voice.

"I'm not one to profess great intuition or anything, gal, but I hear a lot of pain in your tone." How badly he wanted to turn and slide his arm around her drooping shoulders. Mention family to Akiva, and she seemed to shrink before his very eyes. It wasn't something Joe expected, so he felt like a man who had just discovered a claymore mine beneath his boot—if he moved, it would explode and kill him. Something drove him to take that chance, though. His heart thumped as he saw Akiva's profile soften. Ordinarily, she would draw up her armor and not allow him in. This time, something was different. He could feel it.

"Yeah…well, what is it my grandmother said once when I was a spindly kid of seven? She said my mother marrying a Lakota man was like throwing cold water on a hot fire. Apaches are known to be strong-willed, warrior people. And the Lakota are a Plains tribe who have lost their matriarchal way. They've become a nation of ego-tistical males who no longer respect their women as they did before."

"And so you were a child created out of the love of this water and fire?"

The huskiness of Joe's voice slid quietly into her heart, soothing the anger that she felt toward her family. Akiva heard the care in his tone. She was desperate to talk to someone, and since all her friends were back at the Black Jaguar Base, she felt overwhelmed with the need to share on a personal level. She'd had no one to confide in for the last six weeks. Since their confrontation, Joe had proved in so many ways that he could be trusted. Yet Akiva was afraid. It was a natural reaction, she supposed. Her distrust of men started when she was very young.

Finishing off the sandwich, she moved lithely to her feet, went over to the pool and knelt down on one knee. Sifting her hands through the tepid water, she washed them off. Then, standing, she wiped them on her thighs and turned to look at Joe. He was studying her, with a gentle expression on his face that she'd come to think must be pity for her. Akiva didn't like that, but her need to talk and share overrode her reaction.

"My mother said I was born into hell. A white man's hell. The Apaches don't believe in hell. We believe that when you die, your spirit moves on to a good place." She gestured around the area. "A place of beauty and serenity and goodness, like this place." She took a step closer to him and watched his face for any signs of disagreement or disinterest. Joe sat relaxed, one leg beneath him, his arms resting on his broad thigh. The warmth she saw in his eyes made her go on as she approached and then sat back down on the rock. This time, her hip just grazed his knee.

"She said that about you? That you were born into hell?"

Nodding, Akiva sighed. "My father had fetal alcohol syndrome—FAS. It's a well-known disease that's rampant among Indians. If a pregnant woman drinks liquor while carrying her baby, the baby is born with genetic defects, usually mental ones. My father had a real short fuse, was mentally unstable and would beat the hell out of me if I even breathed wrong sometimes...." Akiva glanced at Joe through her lashes to see what effect her admission had on him. What she saw she didn't expect. Anger instantly flickered in his darkening gray eyes. But she didn't feel it pointed toward her, but rather toward her father.

"That's a rough start," Joe said quietly, and he choked down the building rage he felt.

Giving a short, explosive laugh, Akiva tipped her head back and let the sound tumble out her mouth. It was absorbed by the roar of the waterfall. "I was born on the Red Rock Apache Reservation in the White Mountains of Arizona. My father wanted us to go north to live, to the Rosebud Reservation, where he came from. So two days after my birth, my mother packed us up and left with him.''

''You grew up on a Lakota reservation?'' Joe saw the play of emotions clearly across her proud copper features. He also saw the living hell in her eyes, and that shook him deeply. It was the first time Akiva was allowing him the privilege of seeing her simply as a human being— not a warrant officer, not as a gunship pilot or a C.O., but as a woman who was hurting deeply from her scarred past.

''I grew up in hell,'' she told him wryly. Sighing, Akiva crossed her legs and rested her elbows on her knees. Her voice sounded faraway even to her as she continued. ''I was the Apache brat on the res. I was different. I didn't belong. The Lakota kids teased me mercilessly— but that is the way of many Indians. They find out if you're weak or strong. If you're weak, they'll eat you alive and destroy you. But I wasn't going to let that happen. They could pull my braids all they wanted, taunt me that my mother was an Apache whore, and throw pebbles and sticks at me as they followed me around like a wolf pack at school, or on the way home.'' Her eyes flashed with anger. ''They were too cowardly to face me one-on-one like a warrior would. They always came after me in a group—both boys and girls. They thought there was strength in numbers....''

Akiva grinned slightly. ''What they didn't count on was my great-great-grandmother's warrior blood on my mother's side of the family. Na-u-kuzzi, Great Bear, was Geronimo's best warrior. She was my relative. I have her blood in my veins.'' Lifting her head proudly, Akiva held Joe's troubled gray gaze. ''One day, I'd had enough. One of the boys, Jerry Crow Boy, had thrown a pretty hefty stick at me. It hit me in the shoulder and hurt me. I felt a rage that day that just exploded—like a ten-ton nuclear bomb going off inside me, Joe. I picked the stick up, gave the Apache war cry, then turned and charged into that group of kids. I was swinging that stick as hard as I could.''

Chuckling darkly, Akiva laced her fingers together and said, ''They scattered like a pack of cowardly dogs in all directions. I went home that day feeling victorious. I held on to that stick—it became my war club. When I got home an hour later, some of the parents had already driven over to see my dad, and told him what I'd done. Of course, they left out the fact that Crow Boy had struck me first.''

Akiva tapped her right shoulder. ''Under my uniform here is a two-inch scar that stick had opened up. Of course, my father didn't care that I had blood all over my blouse from being hit by Crow Boy. My mother wasn't home at the time. She worked at the school as a secretary.''

Joe's stomach clenched. He knew from the look on Akiva's face, and the sound of her voice, that he wasn't going to like what she was going to tell him. ''So, what did your father do? Did he hear you out? Listen to both sides of the story first before acting?''

Snorting, Akiva flashed him a wicked look. ''Him? One thing you find out about Indian nations is that they're still fighting the battles they fought a hundred or more years ago between one another. I was the Apache whore's kid. I didn't count in Lakota eyes. I was the enemy. In my father's twisted reality, all Crow Boy had done was count coup on me. In his eyes, and with the urging of the other kids' parents, he saw Crow Boy's actions as honorable.''

"What?'' Joe couldn't keep the anger out of his voice.

"Yeah,'' Akiva murmured acidly. "Well, that was fine. I learned about counting coup the Plains Indian way. My father beat the tar out of me for attacking Crow Boy and his gang. He sent me to my room without dinner. I remember sitting in there, crying and wondering what I'd done wrong. I knew a lot about Lakota people, because he was always telling me stories of his people and downgrading anything Apache. He didn't like my Apache side. He saw it as a flaw, something to be ashamed of.''

Keeping his mounting rage in check, Joe began to understand why Akiva always had her armor in place. "I can't imagine why he did that to you. You were a little girl, scared and alone…. You needed to be held, not hurt. You needed to be protected, cared for, not beaten….''

The wobble in Joe's voice opened up her heavily guarded heart as nothing else could have. Akiva sat there and felt the hot sting of tears at the back of her eyes. Lowering her lashes, she muttered off-key, "Indians are tough on their kids. It's the way it is.''

"No,'' Joe rasped unsteadily, as he searched her suffering profile, "it's not. My dad never laid a hand on me. Oh, I got punished for what I did wrong, but he never killed my spirit or tried to break me the way your father tried to break you.''

Lifting her chin, Akiva gazed at him through her lashes again. Joe's face was alive with emotions. She saw the anger, the sympathy and something else burning deep within his stormy gaze. Somehow, just sharing her past with him was helping to heal her, and Akiva didn't understand why. Suddenly, her pain oozed out of her, like pus from an infected wound. As she shared more with him, Akiva began to feel as if the pressure of her painful past was easing. She could feel herself being freed from it once and for all.

"My mother came home, saw what had happened, and the next day left my father. She took me back to the Red Rock Reservation, where we lived with my grandmother. But after the divorce, my mother fell for an alcoholic white man." Akiva's lips tightened. She picked at the flaking black stone they sat upon. "He was a math teacher who taught on the res."

"Sounds like you went from the frying pan into the fire?" Joe guessed grimly as he saw the set of her mouth. Akiva dipped her head in answer, the silken coverlet of her black hair sliding across her shoulder and partially blocking his view of her haunted features.

"Yep," she sighed. "Because he was a raging alcoholic, no school officials in their right mind would hire him. But things are desperate on a res, so he got hired even though he was drunk out of his gourd half the time at school. I was ashamed of him. I was angry at my mother. My only safe place was with my grandmother. When my mother remarried and we went to live in res housing, I tried to spend most of my time at my grandma's home instead."

"And how did your stepfather get along with you?"

"Let's just say it wasn't pretty. I was eight by that time and I was a tough little kid. My grandmother let it be known that he was not to hit me. She was a pretty formidable warrior," Akiva told him. "She had the blood of warriors in her veins, and she was the one who gave me back my spirit, my pride in who I was. She helped me to connect with the long line of honored Apache women warriors I came from."

"And your mother?"

Shaking her head, Akiva whispered painfully, "She was beaten to a bloody pulp by that Anglo bastard once a week.... And when I was there, he beat me, too."

Wincing, Joe rapidly began to put the picture together as to why Akiva didn't trust men in general regardless of their skin color. Scowling, he picked up a damp leaf and methodically began to tear it into small pieces. Feeling her anguish, Joe looked up. Akiva was sitting there like a frozen statue, her eyes dark and distant. She wasn't here with him any longer, she was in the past, reliving that terrible nightmare of her childhood. Dropping the pieces of leaf, he rubbed his hands on his thighs. If he didn't, he was going to turn around and hold her, because that's what Akiva needed right now. To be held and to know that she was *safe*.

His mind clicked along at lightning speed over the incidents of the past six weeks with her: what she'd said, how she'd reacted to certain things he'd done or said. Her past was never far away from her. Not really. But was anyone's?

"Your grandmother gave you pride in being Apache?"

"Yes. She healed me with her jaguar spirit medicine. My stepfather kept beating me up until I was eleven." Akiva touched the leather-covered hatchet that hung from her web belt. "She threatened to use this war ax on him if he touched me again after that. She'd seen what my Lakota father had done to me—the scars on my body— and she swore to my mother and to him that if she saw one more scratch on me, she'd scalp him with the ax." Akiva's eyes glittered. "And she meant it, too. My grandmother was a warrior woman—the only living one on the res at the time."

"Jaguar medicine? My daddy vaguely mentioned this thing about animal medicine once or twice, but that's all

I know about it.'' Joe asked, puzzled. ''I've heard of wolf medicine, eagle...but jaguar?''

''Jaguars used to roam the Southwest.'' She noted his confused look. ''Did your father teach you about spirit guides?''

''No...he didn't. I'm afraid he wasn't tied to his people or the natural world. He never shared much of his beliefs with me. I do know that he comes from a long line of warriors, though.'' He shrugged. ''Maybe that's why I fly an Apache now. Instead of a horse, spear and bow, I have a helicopter with a cannon, rockets and missiles.''

''Each of us, whether we're Native American or not, has guides. These are spiritual beings who are much more evolved than we are. They love us unequivocally, no matter how bad we are, no matter how many mistakes we've made.'' Akiva shrugged. ''In the Christian faith, they are called angels, but to us, who are of an earth-based religion, they are spirit guides who come in many shapes and types. Jaguars were considered the most powerful spirit guide a person could have. An Indian with a jaguar guide is a great warrior who battles the dark side to bring light and harmony back into our third-dimensional world.''

''And you have such a guide?''

Akiva bowed her head. ''Yes, I do. I feel him around me at times of danger. I feel his thick, soft fur against my body, helping me, protecting me. I've never been trained how to use him, but I know he's there. I see his help strongly with regard to my intuition, in knowing when the enemy is near.''

''That must be a good feeling,'' Joe murmured, wishing that his father had taught him of his heritage. He liked the idea of such a spiritual protector being around in time of danger.

"It is." She tapped her head. "Sometimes I hear him whisper in my ear. It isn't in language—just a telepathic urge or emotion that is imprinted upon my mind. I always listen to his wise suggestions. He's helped me know when Kamovs are around. He's saved my life and the lives of other pilots with his warnings of danger to me." The corners of her mouth tipped wryly. "Only when I don't listen to him do I get into trouble."

Chuckling, Joe nodded. "I could sure use someone like that whispering to me. I'd probably avoid a lotta the potholes in life that I've stepped in with great regularity."

She smiled tentatively. "I know you have spirit guides. You just aren't in touch with them, is all. But you can be. All you need to do is desire it. Desire is intent, and intent draws the spirit guide closer to you. Just open up your heart and feel her."

"I'll try that the next time I'm in hot water," Joe promised seriously. He was glad to have this opening with Akiva. She was allowing him access to her as a person by sharing her private life with him. His heart ached for her.

Akiva eyed him for a long time, the silence strung gently between them. "You must have medicine people in your blood somewhere," she said finally.

"Why?"

"Because you're healing me. I never thought it was possible...until now..."

Chapter 7

"Luis, come, look at my latest acquisition." Don Javier Rios sat at his huge, carved mahogany desk, which was placed at one end of his den. His son, tall, dark and with looks that made the *señoritas* swoon with desire, stood looking out of the French windows, his hands in the pockets of his expensive tan pants.

"Come…" Javier pleaded. He picked up a three-foot-long sword from his collection, held it between his hands to show his son as Luis turned and walked toward him.

Luis knew what was coming. His stomach was in knots, his irritability and frustration barely in check. "What is it, *Patrón?*" For as long as he could remember, he had called his father *Patrón*, not Papa or Father. Because of the brilliance and wealth of his academically esteemed father, Luis had grown up in a movable household, on many continents.

"Look," Javier said, with deep pleasure resonating in his voice, "a Roman short sword. The one that was at auction in Europe. Is it not beautiful, my son?'' He held it up toward Luis as he came to a stop in front of the massive, carved desk.

Taking the sword with careless abandon, Luis looked at it more closely. "This is authentic?" Of course it would be. His father had great renown in archeological circles for his academic knowledge of the Roman era.

Chuckling, Javier, who was dressed in a starched white shirt and a black neckerchief, picked up a Cuban cigar from a nearby burgundy leather humidor. "Of course it is. Britain, 30 A.D." He picked up the snippers and clipped off the end of the fragrant, thickly rolled cigar. There was nothing like a Cuban cigar anywhere in the world, and Javier cherished each one he smoked. His thick gray brows rose as he dug for a silver lighter in the pocket of his tan slacks. Lighting the cigar, he puffed on it contentedly, the thick white smoke curling upward around his head. He watched as his only son gingerly inspected the weapon. Oh, he knew that Luis, who was twenty-seven and still very young, didn't have his love of all things Roman. In fact, Luis cared little for antiquity at all. His son was in love with his helicopters. Flying was his passion. Javier watched his thin, dark brows bunch as he ran his fingers carefully and respectfully along the dull, aged blade.

"This one has seen some fighting," Luis said. "A lot of nicks in it." Glancing up, he saw his father's light brown eyes settle on him, his mouth firm above his gray, meticulously shaped goatee and square chin. Luis knew what was coming. Inwardly, he tried to protect himself against it.

Javier rolled the Cuban cigar around in his mouth. "I'm having Alejandro create replicas of it. Exact replicas, for the next spectacle. Just think, Luis—my Roman soldiers will be carrying a replica of the real thing.'' And he punched his square index finger toward the sword in his son's hands.

"Your soldiers will be well prepared in the arena,'' Luis teased lightly as he gently set the sword back on the desk in front of his father.

Gazing down at the ancient weapon, Javier studied the handle, which was made of brass and had once been wrapped, he was sure, in leather. In the heat of battle, a man sweated heavily. Without leather around the handle, the weapon would slip or fly out of a soldier's hand.

"I am thinking seriously of having my leather maker create a handle for this short sword. Do you think that wise?''

Luis moved his feet restlessly. "Yes.''

"Why?'' He saw his son scowl and once again jam his hands into the pockets of his slacks.

"The sword would not be easy to hold without some kind of grip on it.''

"Very good!'' Javier exclaimed. He sat up and puffed once more on the cigar, then placed it in a crystal ashtray nearby. Running his large hand across the sword in a reverent gesture, he whispered, "Think of who might have owned this sword, Luis. What did he look like? Was he a tribune, in charge of many soldiers? A centurion, responsible for his hundred-man phalanx? Perhaps a general? Why…even Caesar himself!'' His voice softened in excitement as he delicately touched each nick in the blade. "How many battles was this sword in? Did the man who owned it die with it in his hand? What battles did this sword see? It was excavated at a Roman garrison site in England. Other objects were carbon dated for 30 A.D. That was a time when Julius Caesar was widening the Roman Empire, and he was pushing out the Celts and

Druids, slaughtering them, to bring Britannia beneath the yoke of Roman rule.''

Sunlight poured through the French windows at that moment, and Luis lifted his head and watched the golden glow spill into the long, rectangular room. This was his father's Roman room, a place where he spent a good part of every day. At age sixty-five, Javier found his passion for all things Roman had pushed their other business aside. He'd given Luis free rein to begin to handle the other empire he'd built over the last fifty years: his cocaine trade. For the most part, he allowed Luis to manage it alone. However, Javier had a penchant for thoroughness and details, which was what had propelled him to the top of the trade in southern Mexico; he didn't overlook anything.

''You'll spend the next month wondering who owned that short sword,'' Luis told him genially.

''Ah, yes, my destiny, is it not?'' Javier allowed his hands to rest on the million-dollar artifact.

With a slight smile, Luis nodded. ''It is, *Patrón*.''

Sighing, Javier picked up the cigar and leaned back in his burgundy leather chair. He puffed on it, the white smoke swirling and reminding him of the wisps of clouds that always hung over the jungle surrounding his estate just outside San Cristobel.

''It has come to my attention, Luis, that in the last sixty days we've had fifty-five flights turned back from crossing the Gulf. I've talked to some of the pilots. We pay these men top money to fly the cocaine to the States.''

Stomach tightening, Luis stood very still. His father's deep, rolling voice continued in a thoughtful manner. The *patrón* was not a man who gave in to his emotions. No, he saved his passion for his beloved Roman artifacts, which he'd collected nearly all his life.

"I asked Señor Bates, who has been in our employ the longest. He was in the U.S. Air Force at one time. I asked him *what* is turning you back. Why are you not completing your runs to the U.S.? He told me there is a black military helicopter, without any markings on it, that comes out of the night and fires across the nose of his aircraft. Señor Bates, having been in the military, knows that this is a warning to him. That if he does not turn back, he will be shot down with the next rounds being fired. So—" Javier shrugged "—he comes back here. Back to one of our dirt airstrips, our cocaine undelivered. Our people waiting for the shipment are very unhappy, Luis. Now, I know you have tried to reroute these flights up through Mexico and into the Southwestern U.S. to other dealers, but my son, this is an escalating problem. You need to solve it."

Taking another puff on the cigar, Javier placed it back in the ashtray. Weaving his fingers together, he placed them against his flat stomach. "Our main dealers along the Gulf Coast are angry. They're threatening to use our competitor in Colombia instead, if we can't get these shipments out to them in a timely manner."

"I know, *Patrón*." Running his hand through his dark, long hair, Luis could not keep the frustration out of his voice. "I share your worry."

"What *is* this black helicopter?"

"Bates says it's a Boeing Apache gunship."

"U.S. Army?"

"Yes."

"But...no markings on it?"

"It's probably a spook gunship on a covert mission,"

Luis grumbled. He took the chair set off to one side of his father's desk and sat down dejectedly.

"So, we have the CIA in our backyard?"

Shrugging, Luis muttered, "It looks like it. I have men from San Cristobel looking around the jungle area. So far, they've come up with no leads. I've started sending my other three helicopters to follow the plane flying our Gulf Coast route, to see if we can spot or trace this Apache."

"I see...." Javier ran his fingers lightly over the sword. "Could this Apache be from another country other than the U.S.? What if one of the other drug lords bought it and is trying to hurt our business?"

"It's possible, *Patrón,* but doubtful. The U.S. is not going to let just anyone buy such a machine. It is state of the art, the best gunship in the world. They're very careful who has them."

"And what do you think?"

Grimacing, Luis shot his father an irritable look. "That it's spook-related. It's U.S."

"But the army...?"

"Why not?" Luis growled. "The Pentagon is financing a huge military buildup in Colombia right now, trying to destroy the drug trade there. They throw all kinds of money, equipment and military trainers at the Colombian government. Why not send this combat gunship to hunt us?"

"Do you think this Apache is part of that effort?"

"I don't know, *Patrón.* I lay awake at night trying to beat answers out of my brain, and I don't know—yet."

"So," Javier said softly, "you must have a plan to catch this Apache. Yes?"

"Yes." Luis sat up. "I've been working with Bates on the fifty-five incidents. I've tried changing the routes—where and when they leave Mexico and fly the Gulf. Every time, no matter what route I've chosen, that black helo shows up. I've changed times, places, and nothing works. They seem to know when we leave. It's uncanny."

"Do we have a mole in our organization who is feeding them this information?"

Luis shook his head. "No, because I'm the only one who tells which plane and pilot to leave, and from what airstrip, as well as what route to travel over the Gulf." He tapped his head. "It's all up here, *Patrón*."

Nodding, Javier stared down at the short sword. "Yet they do not shoot our aircraft down. Do you think that odd?"

"Yes and no. Bates said if it's a U.S. gunship, they're probably under orders not to fire because if they make a mistake and shoot down a civilian plane, there will be an international incident. No, they want to keep their cover, keep their anonymity and keep nipping at our heels." Opening his hands, he added, "I've routed fifty percent of these shipments north instead of over the Gulf. Our dealers are still getting the stuff, just not as quickly as they'd like."

"Yes, but if we continue to swamp the Southwestern border of the U.S. with these FAA-unauthorized flights, then they will do something about it." Javier stroked his goatee in thought. "Increased flights overland are going to net us a very swift response from border patrol and you know that."

"Yes, *Patrón*, I do."

"And trying to get the cocaine across the Gulf on boats is very hard," Javier sighed. "The U.S. Coast Guard is too vigilant. They are waiting for us. No, we've got to

get those flights across the Gulf going again, that is all
there is to it.''

Luis moved uncomfortably in the leather chair. The
sunlight drifting into the room had disappeared. Outside,
wispy white clouds over the jungle were moving lan-
guorously across the morning sky and blotting out the
sun.

"I do have a plan, *Patrón*.''

"Ah. Yes?'' Javier sat up, his brows arched expec-
tantly. His mouth twitched. "You are such a good son,
Luis. You are always thinking. I'm very proud of you.''

Squirming inwardly, Luis said, "*Patrón*, it is a risk. A
huge one.''

"Yes? What is the plan?''

"I'm having the four helicopters armed with machine
guns and rocket launchers.''

Javier frowned. "If you arm them, then you'll be going
after this Apache?''

"I *have* to, *Patrón*.''

Tapping his thick, square fingers on the polished surface of his mahogany desk, Javier thought for a moment
before he spoke. He saw the anger and frustration in his
son's face. Luis had always looked so much like his
mother, God rest her soul—especially his eyes, and his
long, narrow face. But those chocolate-colored eyes had
an eagle's merciless glint in them. Javier knew Luis's
square jaw and broad forehead came from him, as did
his intense, aggressive personality. Marguerite, Luis's
mother, had died in childbirth, leaving him to be raised
solely by his father, so Javier's influence had dominated.

Don Rios still grieved for his lost wife. She had been
ethereal and beautiful, more like the mists that formed
and shifted above the humid jungle than flesh-and-blood
human. She had been delicate and her health fragile.

When Luis was conceived, she had been joyous, and so had Javier. He had been totally unprepared to lose his wife, who held his heart so gently. It was the most bittersweet moment in his life when the doctor came out of the delivery room and told him sadly that his wife was dead, but that he was the proud father of a son who would carry on his name and empire.

Giving Luis a dark look now, Javier asked, "Do you not think that if you fire upon this gunship, it won't fire back at *you?*"

"Absolutely, *Patrón*. But our plan is to jump it—all four helicopters, from four different directions, all at once."

"It's my understanding the Apache has the most sophisticated radar system in the world. What makes you think the crew won't know you're coming?"

Shrugging, Luis got up and thrust his hands into the pockets of his slacks once again. "I know we're going up against one of the most deadly military helicopters in the world. But I'm doing my homework. I'm finding out more information. I have my lookouts posted in the jungle now, to alert me if they see or even *hear* a helicopter in their area. Somehow, we must find out where they are flying out of, where they're based."

"Yes," Javier agreed heavily, "if you want to kill a snake, you chop off its head." He picked up the short sword and made a swift, chopping motion to emphasize his point.

"I understand, *Patrón*." Halting, Luis ran his fingers across his recently shaved jaw. "I'd give *anything* to know who the hell they are...."

"Well?" Akiva asked as she came over and stood by Joe and Spec Robin Ferris. Ferris, who was their software

technician, had been working on a group of cables that
snaked along the left side of the Apache. In the last five
days, HUD screens had been blinking off and on, and
she was trying to run down the problem.

It was very hot in the afternoon, with high humidity.
Joe was in his camouflage pants, his olive-green T-shirt
damp with sweat. Akiva was in her army uniform as well.
They all stood looking at the opened panel.

Ferris sighed. "Ma'am, I'm not having any luck so
far." She placed her short, slender fingers on the thick
bunch of cables that were bound together and laid flat
within the panel. "I've been doing checks all morning,
and I'm finding nothing so far."

Akiva stared at the cables. Many panels on each side
of the Apache fuselage housed white wire cables. Each
cable was protected by waterproof sealing. "Humidity?"
That was always a problem back at the Black Jaguar
Base, which was also set in jungle terrain. Air vapor, over
time, would condense into small droplets of water that
could get into the wiring and potentially short out a system. The problem was finding out where it was occurring.

Ferris shrugged. "That would make sense, ma'am."

"We've been running diagnostics," Joe told her. Ordinarily, Akiva never came out to the hangar to check on
maintenance. That was his area of responsibility. To keep
the base running, she had her hands full with paperwork
alone—paperwork he knew she hated. As Joe studied her
profile, his heart speeded up. Ever since their talk down
by the waterfall a month ago, their relationship had subtly
but continuously changed—for the better, as far as he was
concerned.

As Akiva reached forward and brushed her fingertips
across the thick cables, Joe stepped back a little to give
her room. He saw her brows knit as she continued to

explore the two feet of exposed cables, which looked like bunches of spaghetti tied together.

"This is all damp," she muttered, rubbing her fingertips together.

"It's like that all the time," Ferris told her. "This is worse than back in Peru." Pointing out the hangar opening, she added, "We have ninety-percent humidity all the time, ma'am. It rains almost every afternoon, and maybe three nights a week. I dry off the cables regularly, particularly just before a mission. But there's nothing we can do about this high humidity."

Akiva nodded and glanced at Joe. Her pulse leaped when she found his gray eyes trained on her. Instantly, her heart opened to him. Trying to ignore her feelings, she muttered, "Okay, Ferris, keep following down the leads. It's probably humidity. That's the only thing that makes sense."

"Yes, ma'am...."

Akiva gave the young enlisted woman a slight smile. Ferris was twenty-two, with dark blond hair, green eyes and with a triangular shaped face. Akiva knew Ferris was their best software technician at the base, and if anyone could track down a problem, it was her. "I know you can find that gremlin for us."

"I will or else," Ferris promised fervently.

Joe turned and walked with Akiva as she left the area. "Hey," he said in a conspiratorial tone only she could hear as they headed back toward her office, "how about a spontaneous moment?"

She gave him a dark look. Joe was grinning. Her spirits lifted because of the intimate smile he shared with her. Halting at the door of her office, she said, "What's the matter, have I been working too hard? All work and not enough play, Calhoun?"

He liked her ability to tease him in return; that was a new facet of Akiva that she had started sharing with him since their gut-wrenching talk at the waterfall. "Something like that." Rather proudly he confided, "I got Dean, who has mess duty today, to make us a special dessert. I want to share it with you. Got ten minutes?"

"You're impossible," Akiva muttered. She turned and looked at her desk, which was strewn with paperwork that begged for attention. Between flying two missions a day, plus all the other demands on her time, Akiva had found that she was getting behind on the paperwork.

"Ten minutes," Joe pleaded. He saw her golden eyes become shadowed. Joe knew she was working eighteen hours a day nonstop, without proper rest or sleep. She was trying to learn to balance her C.O. duties against her mission duties. And right now, she needed a little time off.

Though he ached to reach out and touch her, he kept his hand at his side. Since their talk, the idea of kissing her, of pulling Akiva into his arms and holding her, to give her that sense of safety she'd never had with a man, was eating him alive. He knew he could open up a beautiful new world to her. More than anything, Joe wanted to be the one to share that discovery with Akiva.

"Oh, all right... I shouldn't..." Still she hesitated, looking at the papers that begged for her attention.

"Hoo doggies! Come on! You won't regret this...."

Chapter 8

"Ta-da!" Joe brought out his surprise from the mess kitchen. As he rounded the corner of the plywood wall that separated the kitchen from the dining area, the still-warm dessert in his hands, Akiva gave him a quizzical look.

"Sit down," Joe entreated. "We're gonna chow down like hawgs at the feedin' trough, sweetheart." With a flourish, he placed the dessert on the rough-hewn picnic table. "This is my mama's recipe for cheesecake," he informed her proudly. "Over the past few weeks, every time the spooks choppered in our supplies, I've been wranglin' with those good ole boys to get me the ingredients." He rubbed his hands, then headed back to the kitchen to retrieve paper napkins, flatware and an opened can of cherries in thick red sauce, which he set down next to the cheesecake.

Stunned, Akiva managed a slight smile as she sat down opposite him. The cheesecake was delicious looking. Her mouth watered. With another gleeful flourish and a boy-ish grin, he cut the cheesecake and placed two pieces on paper plates, then spooned several dollops of the cherries on top.

"Now, the only thing missing," he told her conspir-atorially, sitting down opposite her, "is whipped cream. My mama would pile a ton of it on top." As he handed Akiva one of the plates, their fingers met and touched. Joe's hand tingled pleasantly from the contact. He saw that slight smile on Akiva's mouth. "You *do* like cheese-cake, doncha?" He stopped, realizing he never thought to ask Akiva that question.

"Oh, yes, I love cheesecake," she murmured, and picked up her fork, hardly waiting for Joe to do the same. "This is a wonderful surprise, Joe." She cast him a dark look. "You're a first-class scrounger. Cheesecake isn't on our menu."

Grinning from ear to ear, Joe felt heat tunnel up his neck and into his face as relief rushed through him. Akiva slid the first bite into her mouth. He watched as she closed her eyes and chewed slowly, savoring it thor-oughly. His heart speeded up again as he saw the ex-pression on her face change to one of utter pleasure. Joy flowed through him. Anything he could do to make Aki-va smile, to lift the weight of the world off her shoulders, if only for a moment, made him feel damn good. He was always looking for ways to give her a time-out, to play instead of work.

Digging into his own piece, he drawled, "This is heaven come to earth, gal. My mama's cheesecake is known throughout West Texas and the Panhandle. She's won all kinds of county and state prizes for it."

Opening her eyes, Akiva said, "I can see why! This is delicious, Joe. Really..."

Pleased, he murmured, "Consider it a gift from the heart. Mine to yours." He cut off another small chunk and popped it into his mouth, relishing it thoroughly.

A gift from the heart. Akiva bowed her head and tried not to think about his words, which had been spoken with husky sincerity. They were alone in the mess hall. It was midafternoon, with hazy sunlight shining through the clean windows of the building. For a moment, Akiva felt nothing but happiness, her heart soaring as she absorbed this unexpected moment with Joe. How many times had she wanted to just sit and talk to him, as they'd done that day at the waterfall? She was starved for conversation, but there was never time, and they were rarely alone. The base was small and there were people around them almost all the time.

Lifting her chin, she watched Joe as he ate voraciously. "One thing about you," she announced with irony in her voice. "There's no secret to how to get to you—through your stomach."

Chuckling, Joe said, "What's that old saying? A way to a man's heart is through his stomach?" He raised his right hand. "Guilty as charged, gal."

She laughed and continued to cut small chunks of the cheesecake, relishing every little bite. "You are going to share the rest of this with the women?"

"Shore 'nuff. But this came out of the oven two hours ago and I wanted you to have a piece when it was still slightly warm. That's when it's best—all the flavors are at their peak."

"Do you cook?" Akiva tilted her head and watched his gray eyes light up with pride.

"Sure do. When I was a whippersnapper, my mama shooed my little butt into the kitchen and told me I wasn't

gonna be one of those Texas good ole boys who didn't
know how to cook for hisself.''

"She taught you well," Akiva murmured, laughter
lurking in her eyes. She studied Joe closely. He was a
good-looking man, and best of all, he had one hell of a
sense of humor. Akiva truly appreciated that about him.

"My mama's a wise woman. My daddy was gone a
lot on long hauls with his eighteen-wheel rig, drivin' back
and forth across the U.S. almost weekly. I always looked
forward to seein' him, when he drove in.''

"That's not a life I'd like," Akiva murmured. She took
her fork and stabbed a cherry that had fallen off the
cheesecake, then slid it into her mouth.

"What?"

"One parent missing for most of the week. Didn't you
miss him?"

"Oh, sure I did. But when he came home, he more
than made up for his being gone.''

"How?"

Joe finished off his cheesecake and put the plate and
flatware aside. He got up and went to the coffee dis-
penser, which sat on a box near the wall of the kitchen.
Pouring two cups, he said, "He made sure we had time
together. Mama saved all my schoolwork in a pile on the
coffee table near his chair. He'd sit with me and go over
everything—the grades, the exercises, and any problems
I had with stuff. I wasn't real good in English, so he used
to spend time showing me how to diagram sentences.''
Coming back, he sat down and slid one of the thick white
ceramic mugs over to Akiva.

"Thanks." She took the cup and sipped the coffee, her
gaze never leaving his face. Just listening to Joe talk,
hearing the stories he wove, always made her feel good.
Akiva could feel the stress draining out of her neck and

shoulders. She felt a sense of lightness when she shared these precious, stolen moments with Joe.

"One of the things his dad—my grandpappy—did was to make sure he was well schooled in English. Being Comanche and all, the old man had real problems getting and holding a job. So he taught my father English so he'd never have the same problems all his life."

Nodding, Akiva said, "Yes, it's a familiar situation. Was your grandfather's native tongue Comanche, with English as a second language?"

"Yep."

"Do you speak Comanche?"

Shaking his head, Joe said, "No...I don't. My dad said I needed to learn English, not our old language. Now, I'm regretful about that, after talking to you about your life as a Native American. I've missed a lot...." He brightened. "But Spanish was like a second language in our household, because we lived on the poor side of the tracks, with the Latinos. I was speaking Spanish more than any other language, except at school."

"And I learned Spanish as a second language on the res," Akiva noted. "Apache first, then Spanish, and finally English. And I still retain some of the Lakota, but I'm really rusty at it now."

Joe gave her a searching look. "What was it like growing up on the Red Rock Res? Was it better for you than the Lakota one? Did life settle down for you?"

Joe saw her gold eyes dim with memories. Her slender hands tightened momentarily around the cup. Knowing full well he was traipsing into her personal life once more, Joe held his breath. Akiva had no idea that he'd planned this whole thing to get a few minutes of quiet, uninterrupted time with her. She also didn't know that he'd ordered the three enlisted women to stay away from the mess for an hour so that they could talk. Of course, the women thought they were talking about business, but Joe wasn't going to tell them differently.

With a wave of her hand, Akiva said, "In one way it did. My mother was home with all our relatives who lived on the res. She felt better. But that lasted about six months. When I was nine, she married that Anglo teacher."

"Your grandmother, though," Joe said, "seems to have played a key role in your life. She did protect you from him and his bouts of drinking."

Grimly, Akiva sipped her coffee. "My grandmother saw what was going on and told my mother that I was going to come and live with her. She'd come over to my parents' house one evening and found me with a bloody nose and a black eye. My stepfather was roaring drunk, yelling and screaming at us. He was mean when he was drunk, Joe. All I could do—all I wanted to do—was run and hide." Her mouth quirked. "Only there was no safe place to do that. If I went to my room and closed the door, he'd smash it open with his foot and drag me out into the living room. My mother would try and protect me, and then he'd slap her around."

Joe shook his head. "I'm sorry, Akiva. I really am."

He reached over without thinking and laid his hand over her fist, which was resting on the table. Moving his fingers gently across hers, he worked her clenched fingers loose. Giving her cool, damp hand a tender squeeze, he looked into her face. The moment he'd touched her, he saw some of the darkness leave her wide, golden eyes. She was so beautiful to him. With her thick black hair hanging like a cloak around her shoulders, she made him ache to hold her and give her that sense of safety she so richly deserved.

Akiva froze inwardly as Joe picked up her hand and held it in his warm, dry one. Every time she talked about the past, she broke into a sweat. It was an automatic reaction, she knew; the past was never far away from her, emotionally. Yet his spontaneous gesture calmed her pounding heart, and she felt the adrenaline dissolving. His touch was magical. Healing. As she stared across the table at Joe, and saw his face alive with anger and pain— the pain she'd suffered as a child—something old and dark broke loose within her tightly armored heart.

Time slowed to a halt between them, like sunlight dancing on woven strands of gold. She felt her heart opening as his rough fingers caressed hers. The look in his stormy eyes made her feel a thread of happiness that was foreign to her. She *liked* Joe touching her. It made her feel safe. Protected. Hungering for more of that feeling, Akiva stared, confused, into his eyes.

"What's happening?" she asked unsteadily as she looked down at their hands.

"Nothing that isn't good, gal," he whispered rawly. He lifted her hand in his larger one. Akiva's full attention was on the way his fingers grasped hers. "You deserve some goodness in your life, Akiva. I'm sorry for what happened to you. I can't imagine you, a little girl goin' through that kind of hell... I wish—well, if I'd been there..."

Warmth and happiness suffused her unexpectedly. Akiva pulled her hand free, a bit frightened by what she was feeling. Wrestling with the happiness throbbing through her chest and warming her lower body, she sat there, hands in her lap beneath the table. The tender flame burning in Joe's gray eyes nearly unstrung her. There was nothing, absolutely nothing, to dislike about this man. And that scared her.

"My grandmother beat you to it," she managed to reply in a strained tone. "That night, she took me out of the house and told my parents they had shamed themselves, that no one should ever lift a hand to strike a child."

"Good for her," Joe rasped. Right now, Akiva's head was bowed and she was looking at her hands, buried beneath the table. Her high cheekbones were suffused with pink. The moment he'd touched her hand, he'd seen the corners of her drawn mouth ease, some of the pain she carried dissolve. And he'd seen something else—something so gossamer and fleeting, he wasn't sure if he'd made it up or not. Had he seen desire in Akiva's eyes? For him? Or was he imagining it because that's what he wanted—for her to like him…perhaps even to desire him? Oh, Joe knew that was a far-fetched dream of the young romantic still stuck inside him. He was an idealist at heart, and he held out hope for the hopeless.

Joe knew Akiva didn't trust men in general, and Anglo men in particular. The fact that he was part Indian was helping her accept him. And little by little, he'd felt the walls she held up to keep him out dissolving. Now, he sensed those walls were nearly gone, and it was a heady, scary moment for him. If he said the wrong thing, Akiva would shut him out once more, he knew. And that was the last thing he wanted. Somehow—Joe wasn't sure exactly how—he had to keep asking the right questions, keep the dialogue alive between them. This was one of many times when Joe felt inept as he floundered mentally and emotionally, casting around for the right words to keep that nurturing connection with Akiva strong.

"And so she brought you to her home?"

Nodding, Akiva lifted her hands. She pushed the last

of her cheesecake, uneaten, toward Joe. "Here, you finish it. I've lost my appetite."

Scowling, he whispered, "I'm sorry, gal. I didn't mean to upset you like this...."

"It's old news, Joe. Past history." She shrugged, as if ridding herself of that dark past. "I don't know what's going on, but every time I sit with you and talk about it, I feel like whatever I say or share with you is lightening a load from my shoulders." She gave him a confused look. "I can't explain why that's happening. It's never happened to me before."

He pulled the plate toward him. If the truth were known, he'd lost his appetite, too. Still, he picked up his fork and dug into the cheesecake, because if he didn't, he was going to reach over and pick up Akiva's hands, which were now clasped on the table in front of her.

"What we have," he said in a low tone, holding her uncertain gaze, "is somethin' special, gal. Somethin' that's being built over time. I like it...whatever it is...and I hope you do, too?" He held his breath as he saw Akiva's thin black brows gather. She looked up toward the ceiling, as if searching for words. Afraid, he felt a frisson of anxiety in his chest. His heart beat a little harder.

"Look," he counseled, "don't worry about us, or where this is goin'. We've got a mission and a base to run. That comes first. It's always first." Joe forced himself to eat the cheesecake, but he didn't taste it as he watched the play of emotions cross Akiva's face. Did she realize how devastatingly beautiful she was?

"Y-yes...the base. And our mission. It always comes first, Joe." Akiva didn't know what else to say. "I—well, frankly, my relationships with men haven't been anything to write home about."

"Based upon your early childhood, how could they be?"

"It's a trust issue," Akiva muttered.

"I know that."

She gave him a narrowed look. "I always feel like you know more than you're telling me. Sometimes I feel like you're reading my mind...." *Or my heart*. But Akiva didn't say that.

She saw Joe's mouth pull into that tender smile he sometimes gave her when they were alone. Akiva had come to cherish that special look. When she found herself wanting to slide her hands across the table to touch his, touch him as he'd just touched her, she was startled. What was going on here? What magic was at play? Stifling the urge, because Akiva was not one to brazenly go after a man or share her feelings with him, she sat quietly.

With a one-shouldered shrug, Joe finished the cheesecake and set the plate aside with the other one. "Maybe because I had a normal childhood and you didn't, and I can see the wounding it did to you?"

"I hate dragging my childhood around with me to this day. I try to get rid of it, but it's like an infection—it just stays with me."

"But your grandmother helped you in many ways, yes? That braid you always wear. I heard someone back at the Black Jaguar Base say once that only Apache men or women who passed all the tests of warrior training could wear it?"

Touching the slender braid hanging from the center part of her hair, Akiva said, "Yes, that's so."

"Your grandmother, it sounds like, gave you back your self-esteem, your confidence as a person."

His insight was always surprising, because Akiva never expected any man to have that ability to look into her heart and soul. Joe did on a regular basis. She was slowly getting used to it, but it still left her feeling slightly off balance. She knew so little of him in return. Yet she hungered for these rare moments of privacy with him.

"My grandmother held a ceremony with the local medicine woman. She brought the pieces of my shattered spirit back to me. Nowadays, it's called shamanism. She was able to help heal wounded souls who had lost pieces due to the trauma they'd endured.

"About a month after that ceremony, I began training to become a warrior like my great-great-grandmother. My grandmother gave me the war ax and the bowie knife I now carry on missions. She instilled in me the pride of our people—our toughness and endurance, and the fact that we never surrendered to the U.S. Army. We are the only nation who did not bow beneath the white man's heel. Oh, I know the Anglos' history books say different, but I believe the stories passed down to me."

"What kind of training did you go through?" Joe asked curiously.

"My grandmother had an old paint mustang that was probably well into his twenties. She taught me to ride. Not only to ride, but to do what we call a running mount and dismount." Gesturing with her hands, Akiva said, "I'd be at a full gallop, Joe, and with a signal, my grandmother would tell me to dismount. I'd grab the mustang's mane, swing my leg over his back, hit the ground running, then release his mane and keep running."

"Whew...that sounds tough."

"It was. I ate a lot of desert sand and rock before I got the hang of how to do it." She laughed, the memories flooding back to her. "Once I got that down, my grandmother had the mustang brought into a round enclosure made of brush and limbs tied together with ropes. It was probably as large as a small house. The horse would gallop around and around the edges of this enclosure and my grandma would stand in the middle, using a whip to keep the horse moving at high speed. She then told me to run toward the horse, grab his mane and fling myself up on his back.''

Joe's eyes widened. ''And you did?'' That was an amazing feat of agility and physical strength. He saw Akiva smile broadly, with pride, for the first time. And when she smiled, her chin tilted at a confident angle, his heart pounded. How incredibly beautiful and soft she looked in that moment.

''Oh, yes. It took a lot of tries. I'd usually stumble and fall in the deep, soft sand of the enclosure. Or I'd grab the mane, but not grasp enough of it, and I'd go banging into the horse and be knocked off my feet, into the dirt. My grandmother would laugh, then tell me to get up, dust myself off and try again. Finally, after a lot of bumps and bruises, I got the hang of it.'' Akiva smiled in fond memory of those times. ''Every day after school, after I got my homework done, I'd do running mounts and dismounts. The next test was to run five miles, then ten, fifteen and twenty, across the desert with a mouthful of water—and not swallow it as I ran.'' Her eyes glimmered as she saw her statement register. Joe's eyes widened considerably as he thought about what she'd just said.

''That sounds impossible,'' he muttered. ''Hold water in your mouth and *run* twenty miles?''

''Yep.'' Pleased, Akiva added, ''The last test—and there were fifteen of us who took this warrior test at the time—involved running twenty miles. Only that time we ran ten miles on the flat terrain of the desert, and the last ten climbing a mountain, where the medicine woman waited on top. We had to climb it, kneel down at a hole she'd dug and spit the water we'd carried into it. If we managed to do that, then we were awarded the third braid of a warrior.''

"Whew…" Joe muttered, impressed. "I never knew… I mean, that's *somethin'.*''

"There's more," she said. "After that came training with the weapons of our people. I was taught how to throw a war ax and wield a bowie knife with deadly accuracy at both a still and a moving target. My grandmother then had me learn how to do it from the back of a galloping mustang.''

"Did you use a bow and arrow?''

"Oh, yes. And a spear, too. When Geronimo was running from the U.S. Army, dodging the brigades trying to capture him, his people were either riding or trotting on foot more than forty or fifty miles a day through the hot desert. If a horse died of exhaustion or lack of water, they got off and continued on foot at the same pace. Most horses were taught to eat cactus, which was peeled for them by my people, so they didn't get spines in their mouths. Those that wouldn't eat it died of dehydration.''

"And Geronimo and his people lived off the cactus as a source of water?''

Nodding, Akiva said in a low tone, "My people are tough, Joe, with strong spirits. No matter how you beat us down, we will come back. We will stand and face you. And that is what my great-great-grandmother did. She was one of Geronimo's best warriors.''

"Before I met you, I didn't know Apaches had women warriors.''

"Of course they did. We're a matriarchal people. If a woman was good at something, she did it. If she took the tests of the warrior and passed them, then she wore the third braid. There was no gender difference to us.'' Akiva opened her hands, excitement in her low tone. ''My grandmother wore the third braid. My mother did not. But I brought pride back to our family once again, and I felt good about that.''

''And well you should,'' Joe declared, thoroughly impressed.

''At the ceremony when I became a warrior, all of my family was there, except for my stepfather. My grandmother made a speech to everyone. She held up her own war ax and bowie knife and announced that I would carry the family honor forward into this century, that I was now the warrior in the family.''

Akiva smiled softly and allowed her hands to drop back to the table. ''That was the greatest moment in my life, with everyone shouting, clapping and calling my name as my grandmother handed me those weapons. I wanted to cry for sheer joy, but I didn't. I stood there, tall and proud, though at twelve years old, I was pretty gangly. Five foot ten inches tall, I towered over all the other kids. My grandmother said that my great-great-grandmother had been six foot tall, an unheard of height among our people, especially back then. She predicted that I'd grow to six feet, too.

''The medicine woman who came forward to speak on my behalf, and who gave me the name Akiva, told me that I would carry on the family honor and make everyone proud. Not only my family, but the Apache nation.''

''Heavy-duty stuff,'' Joe murmured. He saw the glimmer of pride in Akiva's eyes. More than anything, he cherished the openness that now existed between them. She was talking to him as if he were her closest friend and confidant. Yes, he'd like to be that to her—and more. But for now, Joe was more than grateful for what existed between them. Another part of him hungered to connect with his own Comanche heritage. He was learning more every time Akiva shared her life on the res with him. It was a gift to him.

"Is that why you joined the army? To learn to fly?"

Akiva nodded. "I was a warrior, plain and simple. My grandmother told me that my horse would be an aircraft. That like my great-great-grandmother of old, I would be on the front lines battling darkness and making room for the light. The medicine woman told me that I now had my great-great-grandmother's spirit guide and guardian—a jaguar. That that was what had made Na-u-kuzzi so brave, heroic and powerful."

"Guides... Yes..." Joe recalled Akiva telling him about them earlier.

"Spirit guides come in various forms from Mother Earth and nature." She gestured to him. "You said you didn't know who your spirit guardian is?"

Shaking his head, he said, "No...I don't."

"Do you ever dream of a certain animal? Insect? Reptile?"

Rubbing his chin, he thought for a moment. "Well, yes..." He chuckled slightly. "I remember that, as a kid growing up in West Texas, from time to time I'd dream of a jaguar, too. Only this wasn't the gold kind with black spots. She was always black. She had huge gold eyes and a shiny black coat, and as she moved in my dreams, I could see a rainbow sheen on her coat. She was beautiful."

Akiva studied him in the silence. "I'm very impressed. Then you, too, have a jaguar guide." That confirmed to Akiva that Joe was truly a warrior for the light, just as she was.

From under her shirt, she pulled out a leather thong

that she wore around her neck at all times. On the end was a small leather pouch, stained and darkened over time from perspiration. With her fingers, Akiva opened up the dark leather bag and showed him what was inside.

"This is a jaguar claw that my great-great-grandmother was given by Geronimo. He, too, had a jaguar spirit guide. One time, when the U.S. Army nearly surrounded him and his people, my great-great-grandmother turned her mustang and rode back and attacked the entire column, scattering them in disarray. She then rode off into the mountains, so was never harmed or captured by the white men. Geronimo, when she caught up with them, rewarded her with this.

"He wore two claws. It is said that he had a black jaguar and a gold one as his guides. He was a medicine man of great powers."

Akiva held the claw up for Joe to look at. The obviously old, blackened claw had been pierced at the top, the hole threaded with a smaller leather thong.

"Wow," Joe whispered, "this is mighty special, Akiva."

"Do you know your guide's name?" Akiva demanded as she placed the claw back into the pouch and pulled the drawstrings closed.

Shaking his head, Joe said, "No. My daddy never exposed me to Comanche traditions like your grandmother did. I'm sorry he didn't. I'd like to know the history of his people as well as you know yours. Now I wished he had. I feel like I know only half of my family history." Before he'd met Akiva, Joe had shrugged off his Native American inheritance, seeing it only as something that caused prejudice against him; a blight on his youth. Now, seeing Akiva's strength and pride, he was hungry to connect with his past.

Nodding, Akiva slipped the medicine pouch beneath the green T-shirt she wore. She never wore a bra, so the pouch settled naturally between her breasts beneath the fabric. "I don't think I'd have survived to adulthood without my grandmother, or the knowledge of my people."

"I agree. Your grandmother must be a tough old buzzard." Joe grinned. "She saved your life and gave you back your sense of selfhood. Who you were—and are."

"And someday, you need to go to your father's people and find out more about who you are." Akiva gestured to his hand, which lay on the table. "A part of you is Anglo, but the copper-skinned part of you, the Comanche, needs to be heard and embraced, as well. You need to know your family history, for it all counts. It makes you who you are now. And it's good to know what road you have traveled, and why you are where you are today."

Joe grinned again. "Well, this old dirt farmer Texas boy knows he's got miles to go compared to you. I'm *really* impressed, gal. You've always been a real special person in my eyes. And hearin' all this, well, I'm speechless. There aren't too many modern-day warriors around, but you have earned every bit of your status."

Absorbing the respect and pride in Joe's voice, Akiva folded her hands. "Among my people, warriors are in place to protect those who cannot defend themselves. We don't make war to make war. We defend the weak when they're attacked."

"Much like what we're doin' right now on this mission," Joe observed.

"That's right," Akiva said, satisfaction in her tone. "A true warrior is honor bound by history and tradition. We don't kill for the pleasure of it. We don't jump into fights just because we *can* fight. There has to be good reason for me to get involved. That's why I like the army, and flying the Apache. What we are doing is honorable and right. People's lives will be better because of what we do.''

"No disagreement there.'' He smiled, then saw Bradford coming to the mess door. Glancing down at his watch, he saw that their precious hour was over. "Looks like it's time to start cookin' up dinner,'' he observed wryly. Giving Akiva a wink, he said, "Let's do this again. More often? I like talkin' and sharin' with you. How about it?''

"Yes,'' Akiva said, turning as she heard the door opening, "I'd like that.'' As she rose, she resumed her mask of C.O., though she cried silently at the loss of the openness she'd just enjoyed. Bradford entered and said hello to them, then hurried to the kitchen and her mess duties, and Akiva sighed inwardly. As she moved away from the table, she saw Joe picking up the plates and flatware. He could have left them for Bradford to clean up, but he didn't. Warmth stole through her heart. He was such a strong part of the team. He didn't see himself as something special. No, he worked daily, just as hard as everyone else.

As Akiva pushed open the door and stepped into the humid warmth of the late afternoon, she felt so much lighter. Happier. How long had it been since she'd felt like this? As she walked between the buildings back to the hangar, she could only recall two other times: when her grandmother had honored her in front of her nation, as she'd earned her warrior status, and again when she had her gold wings pinned on her uniform when graduating from flight school in the U.S. Army.

Slowing her stride, Akiva looked around at the wispy

clouds and the slanting light of day. The monkeys were screaming once more, their shrill voices carrying out of the shadowy jungle. The birds were quieting their calling as day began fading once again. The happiness she was feeling now was different. It was light, euphoric, and her heart felt as if it were an opening blossom within her chest.

Reaching up with her fingertips, she touched the area between her breasts. Joe's smile lingered in her heart. His deep Southern voice caressed her. And more than anything, where he'd touched her hand, her skin still tingled. In that moment, Akiva had never been happier. Or more afraid.

Chapter 9

"I've got a bad feelin'," Joe said over the intercom as they flew over the Gulf. The reassuring vibration of the Apache soothed him to a degree as he narrowed his gaze on the HUD, which showed two drug planes fifty miles offshore, heading on a direct track for Florida.

Tightening her lips, Akiva glared at the black night sky, which was crowded with thunderstorms on all sides. Lightning flashed almost constantly, causing them to lose their night vision, which was imperative in the use of their night optic scope, for precious minutes at a time. "I hate thunderstorms," she muttered defiantly. "I'm having trouble with my night vision. Are you?"

"Yeah," Joe said grimly. It was 0200, and they'd been torn out of a deep, badly needed sleep for this second mission. The first had occurred at 2100. On that mission, they'd turned a drug plane around and flown back to Alpha, arriving at 2300. They'd hit the sack, exhausted.

And then a second call came in from the American submarine, reporting two bogeys.

All around them, thunderheads were building rapidly. Akiva was flying the Apache between them because it would be a fool's undoing to fly through one. Besides the possibility of getting hit with fifty thousand watts of electricity from a bolt of lightning, the up and down drafts were violent enough to slam the Apache around and out of control.

Consequently, they were having to dodge and duck, flying around or under the storms. They had been told there was a front approaching—a mass of cold air hitting the highly humid warm air rising from the Gulf—making conditions unstable as hell. The Apache was bouncing around, sometimes lifting fifty to a hundred feet in seconds as it hit an invisible air pocket. Akiva was doing her best to keep the gunship stable, but Joe knew it was impossible under the circumstances. The harnesses bit deeply into his shoulders and thighs. He'd tightened them to a painful degree because if he left them loose he'd be bounced around in the cockpit. His job required that he keep his gaze steady and pinned on the HUDs for incoming radar information in order to give Akiva up-to-the-second briefings on where and how to fly.

"They're down on the deck, right over the water," Akiva muttered. "Both of 'em. This is new, Joe. The tactic is new. Two planes going out at once."

"Yeah." He chuckled darkly. "I think they've figured out there's only one of us, and if they throw two drug planes at us, we can chase only half the cargo. The other plane can escape and make it to the U.S. coast. They're not dumb boxes of rocks like I thought."

Grinning savagely, Akiva said, "No...they aren't." Her arm muscles were tight and her fingers gripped the collective and cyclic. The winds were chaotic, and the Apache was being buffeted constantly. Flying at ten thousand feet, they were racing to get ahead of the two planes in order to meet them and turn them back. Rain slashed and hammered at them relentlessly. Sometimes they ran into hail, which made Akiva very uneasy. The Plexiglas windshield at the front of the Apache was hard enough to withstand a direct hit from a 20mm cannon, but the sides weren't. Hail, if large enough, could potentially do a helluva lot of damage to her Apache, and that worried her. One huge ball of hail, about the size of a softball, hurtling at hundreds of miles an hour into their two-hundred-mile-an-hour Apache, could spell disaster if it hit the side of one of their cockpits, or worse, struck an engine and rendered it useless. She didn't want to think about such scenarios, but she had to, because any of them could happen. Worse, an engine could explode, and the fire might not be able to be put out by the built-in extinguishers. If that happened, the whole gunship could blow up, or fire would eat into their cabins, or the Apache could spin out of control. None of those possibilities were good. Her gut felt like it was weighted down with stones.

"These good ole boys drivin' these two planes are flyin' them like military pilots would—wingtips a hundred feet apart."

"They probably are ex-military," Akiva said.

"Russian? American?"

"Who knows? We're getting ahead of them. Tell me when I can drop altitude."

"Roger." He wrote down some numbers on his knee board, then punched a few figures into the computer and watched the info pop up on the right HUD. "Begin descent now to five thousand feet." A flash of lightning illuminated the cockpit, destroying his night vision.

''Damn...'' He cursed softly, rubbing his eyes and blinking them rapidly.

Akiva heard Joe curse. That wasn't like him. He rarely uttered a nasty word. The tension was thick in the cockpit. The whine of the twin engines above them was comforting to Akiva. She glared at the bulbous cumulus clouds that rose in thick towers, probably up to forty thousand feet, on either side of them. Flying between two huge thunder cells like this was next to lunacy, but they had no choice.

Listening to Joe's quiet instructions, Akiva nosed the Apache downward on a glide path that would eventually bring them alongside the fleeing drug planes. First they had to get the fuselage numbers, check them against aircraft flight plans filed with the FAA, and then check another computer to see if they were known drug carriers. If they were indeed drug flights, as Akiva suspected, then she and Joe could fly ahead of them and try to fire to turn them back. But not until then.

The descent between the roiling, grumbling thunderheads increased in roughness. The cyclic between her legs wrenched from a sudden downdraft. The Apache groaned, and they dropped like a rock. Gasping, Akiva wrenched back and tried to steady the gunship. The engines whined loudly in protest.

''Heck of a roller-coaster ride,'' Joe muttered in a worried tone.

Perspiration dotted Akiva's bunched brow as she intently studied her flight instruments. In weather like this, especially over water, pilot disorientation was very real. A pilot had to believe her instruments and not what her eyes, or the sensations in her body, were telling her. The brain could easily receive mixed signals because of all the tossing around in the cockpit; while her inner ear was in a state of imbalance, it could send misinformation to her brain.

They finally reached the deck—pilots' jargon for right over the water—and hovered a hundred feet above the choppy surface. Akiva knew from experience that water directly beneath a thunderstorm was in turmoil, the waves often reaching five and six feet high, with the white spray thrown skyward. To her left were the two aircraft.

"You got them in sight?" she demanded tensely.

"Roger," Joe answered, binoculars raised to his eyes. Again, lightning flashed around them, and he jerked.

"Damn, that was close!"

"No kidding." Akiva worriedly looked around. Rain slashed unrelentingly, making visibility almost impossible. Lightning was dancing all around them. They were now skirting the bottom of a monstrous thunderstorm. And the foolish pilots in the airplanes were heading directly beneath it. That was stupid. The chance of a massive downdraft slamming them into the grasping waves below was very real. Only a pilot running a drug flight would take such a chance. Unfortunately, Akiva and Joe would have to follow them.

Akiva waited impatiently for Joe to get the information they needed. It was tough, but he had night-vision binoculars and should be able to pick up the numbers off the fuselage no matter how dark it was.

The Apache hit another air pocket and surged upward. Hissing a curse, Akiva wrenched back the collective and steadied the craft. The whitish light of a nearby bolt of lightning exposed the two planes, which were less than five hundred feet from them. In this kind of weather, that was too close; the possibility of air collision was very real. But it couldn't be helped.

Sweat rolled down Akiva's temples. She pressed her

mouth into a thin line, her narrowed eyes focused on her instruments.

"Got 'em!" Joe crowed triumphantly when the information on the planes came back. "Both drug planes. These boys aren't even botherin' to change their numbers! They're getting brazen."

"Good," Akiva growled, and she powered up to take the Apache well ahead of them, intending to stop them.

Just then, a flash of light exploded around Akiva. She uttered a sharp cry. Blinded, she gripped the controls. The Apache shook violently. The engines dropped in power, then suddenly surged. Over her headset, she heard Joe give a shout of surprise.

It was over just as quickly as it had happened.

Stunned, Akiva looked around. Gasping, she said, "Joe! Where're our instruments? Where's—"

"Lightning hit us, Akiva."

The Apache was acting sluggish. Akiva looked at her blackened instrument panel. The software on board the Apache was backed up by a secondary system, but it clearly wasn't bridging the gap.

Her mind spun. The wind was slamming at them. Lightning had hit them! Right now, Akiva didn't care about the druggies. She looked around at the dark, malevolent sky. The rain was so bad she couldn't see below her to figure out how close she was to the Gulf waters.

"Hang on," Joe gasped, "lemme see what I can do to fire this software back up...."

"Hurry," Akiva ordered through clenched teeth. She stared at the dark instrument panel, mentally willing it to show her just the basics of her flight. Desperately needing the altitude indicator and several other major instruments that could get them safely out of here and back to base, she waited. Mouth dry, she licked her lower lip. Light-

ning was heavy now, dancing constantly around them.
She could smell the burned wiring in the cockpit.

"Do we have a fire?" she demanded.

"No…not that I can see. I think the lightning struck
and burned some of the wiring in the panels."

She dropped the Apache back to the deck. Below,
maybe a hundred feet or less, she could see the white
tops of the angry sea.

"I'm turning back, Joe. Screw the drug interdiction.
We're in trouble."

"Roger that. Hold on…."

Suddenly, Akiva's main instrument panel flickered in
front of her. Green light flashed, then disappeared.
"No!"

"Hold on…." Joe repeated, his voice strained.

"Do whatever you did before," Akiva begged. "I
need my instruments, Joe. We're flying blind." She could
fly by the seat of her pants but over water and in a thunderstorm, with visibility almost nil, she knew her brain
and inner ear could skew her perceptions and cause spa-
tial flight disorientation. If that happened, they could be
flying straight into the water and not even know it until
it was too late. She desperately needed those instruments!

"Just…one more…sec…"

The instruments flared to life, the green lines much
fainter than they should be, but visible. "Yes! Yes,
they're on!" Instantly Akiva corrected their flight path.
She had indeed been heading down toward the water,
totally disoriented. Her heart was beating hard in her
chest. Sweat was coursing down her rib cage beneath the
uncomfortable chicken plate she wore. The Apache was
getting slammed repeatedly by strong drafts as they tried
to hurry out from beneath the massive thunderhead. Her
teeth jarred. The harness bit savagely into her shoulders.

"We're blind, deaf and dumb," Joe informed her unhappily. "I can't get any of our weapons online. We have no radar...nothing. You're gonna have to fly on instruments to the base, Akiva."

"Great," she whispered angrily. "I hate thunderstorms."

"Yeah," Joe said sympathetically. He looked around. With the rain teeming down, it was impossible to see far. Only when lightning illuminated the sky could he hope to spot other aircraft.

"Keep your eyes peeled," Akiva warned. "You're our only radar now."

"I dunno who'd be out on a night like this," he joked. Wiping the sweat off his brow, he pushed the night scope back against his helmet and locked it in place. With the computer out of commission, the scope was of no use. And with lightning dancing around them, his night vision was destroyed.

"You okay?" he asked Akiva in a low, stressed tone.

"No. How about you?"

"No."

"At least we're honest with one another," she joked darkly, her lips lifting slightly.

"This isn't a time for heroics. Let's just muddle back to base ASAP."

"No argument from me."

As they flew out from beneath the thunderhead, the rain began to let up. The jarring was not as intense, and Akiva was able to steady the Apache's flight. They were less than ten miles from the shore.

Joe spread a map across his knees and took out a penlight. "You want to take corridor C back to Alpha?"

"Yes. It's the fastest. I don't trust these instruments to stay online. I just want to get back as soon as we can."

"Roger that." He scowled, wrote down the latitude and longitude and quickly scribbled out the math for her. Giving Akiva the flight direction, he kept a hand on the map.

They were flying the old-fashioned way—how planes were flown long before the advent of computers and automatic pilots. Joe looked around. Between the massive cumuli clouds hanging out over the Gulf, the night sky was dotted with stars. The rain had stopped, and so had most of the jarring.

They were flying at five thousand feet now, and he looked down out of the cockpit. There was the black expanse below them that he knew was the Gulf; it looked like slick black glass on this moonless night. As he looked up, he blinked. Was he seeing things? They were less than five miles from shore. Rubbing his eyes, he looked again.

"Akiva..." he said hesitantly, "I think I'm seein' something dead ahead of us...but I'm not sure. Damn, my night vision is shot. Do you see any black things above the jungle? In the night sky, about ten o'clock?"

Busy flying and watching her instruments, Akiva jerked her head up for a moment. She'd feel a helluva lot better being over land instead of water. If she had to set the Apache down, she could. On water, it would sink, and so would they. "What?" She peered, eyes squinting, toward the area Joe had mentioned.

"Am I seein' things, gal?"

Every time he called her that, his voice dropped to a caressing tone that made Akiva feel wonderfully safe and protected. She liked the endearment, and she was getting up her courage to tell Joe that. But to admit it meant admitting that he held emotional sway over her, and Akiva was afraid of that. She was a real coward, she had

GET 2

HOW TO GET YOUR 2 FREE BOOKS AND FREE GIFT!

1. Peel off the MIRA sticker on the front cover. Place it in the space provided at right. This automatically entitles you to receive two free books and an exciting mystery gift.

2. Send back this card and you'll get 2 "The Best of the Best™" novels. These books have a combined cover price of $11.00 or more in the U.S. and $13.00 or more in Canada, but they are yours to keep absolutely FREE!

3. There's no catch. You're under no obligation to buy anything. We charge nothing – ZERO – for your first shipment. And you don't have to make any minimum number of purchases – not even one!

4. We call this line "The Best of the Best" because each month you'll receive the best books by some of today's hottest authors. These authors show up time and time again on all the major bestseller lists and their books sell out as soon as they hit the stores. You'll like the convenience of getting them delivered to your home at our special discount prices . . . and you'll love your *Heart to Heart* subscriber newsletter featuring author news, horoscopes, recipes, book reviews and much more!

SPECIAL FREE GIFT!

We'll send you a fabulous surprise gift, absolutely FREE, simply for accepting our no-risk offer!

5. We hope that after receiving your free books you'll want to remain a subscriber. But the choice is yours – to continue or cancel, anytime at all! So why not take us up on our invitation, with no risk of any kind. You'll be glad you did!

6. And remember...we'll send you a mystery gift ABSOLUTELY FREE just for giving "The Best of the Best" a try.

Visit us online at www.mirabooks.com

BOOKS FREE!

Hurry!

Return this card promptly to GET 2 FREE BOOKS & A FREE GIFT!

The Best of the Best™

▶ DETACH AND MAIL CARD TODAY! ▶

Affix peel-off MIRA sticker here

YES! Please send me the 2 FREE "The Best of the Best" novels and FREE gift for which I qualify. I understand that I am under no obligation to purchase anything further, as explained on the opposite page.

385 MDL C6PQ

(P-BB3-01)
185 MDL C6PP

NAME   (PLEASE PRINT CLEARLY)

ADDRESS

APT.#   CITY

STATE/PROV.   ZIP/POSTAL CODE

The Best of the Best™ — Here's How it Works:

Accepting your 2 free books and gift places you under no obligation to buy anything. You may keep the books and gift and return the shipping statement marked "cancel." If you do not cancel, about a month later we will send you 4 additional novels and bill you just $4.24 each in the U.S., or $4.74 each in Canada, plus 25¢ shipping & handling per book and applicable taxes if any.* That's the complete price and — compared to cover prices of $5.50 or more each in the U.S. and $6.50 or more each in Canada — it's quite a bargain! You may cancel at any time, but if you choose to continue, every month we'll send you 4 more books, which you may either purchase at the discount price or return to us and cancel your subscription.

*Terms and prices subject to change without notice. Sales tax applicable in N.Y. Canadian residents will be charged applicable provincial taxes and GST.

If offer card is missing write to: The Best of the Best, 3010 Walden Ave., P.O. Box 1867, Buffalo, NY 14240-1867

BUSINESS REPLY MAIL
FIRST-CLASS MAIL   PERMIT NO. 717   BUFFALO, NY

POSTAGE WILL BE PAID BY ADDRESSEE

THE BEST OF THE BEST
3010 WALDEN AVE
PO BOX 1867
BUFFALO NY 14240-9952

NO POSTAGE
NECESSARY
IF MAILED
IN THE
UNITED STATES

decided, on the emotional front. Oh, Joe was helping her climb a lot of walls she'd put up regarding men, and lately she had found herself desperately wanting to tell him that her heart took off with happiness every time she shared those rare private moments with him, or when he flashed that silly, tender smile of his and called her "gal."

Forcing her attention back to the present, Akiva peered through the darkness toward the coastline of Mexico. Compressing her lips, she studied the horizon, and then the darkened night sky pinpointed with blinking stars.

"I...yes...there's *something* out there, Joe. But I can't ID it. Can you?" Her hands automatically tightened around the controls. Whatever it was, it was *flying*. That wasn't a good sign. "There's no aircraft running lights on them."

"Roger," he told her grimly. "Let me see if I can get a fix on them with our night binoculars." He lifted them to his eyes. Everything appeared in various shades of grainy green, from very dark to very light.

"What?" Akiva demanded. She felt her heart begin to pound with dread. Something wasn't right. They never saw aircraft while coming back off a mission. This part of Mexico was nothing but wild, uninhabited jungle.

"Gal," he rasped tensely, "I'm looking at *four* helicopters comin' straight for us. And I see weapons on 'em. Rocket launchers on the skid mounts."

"Damn!"

Joe sucked in a slow, ragged breath, fear eating at him as he continued to watch them racing toward them. "And they know where we are, so that means they've got some kind of radar aboard those civilian helos."

"They're civilian?" Akiva's mind spun with possibilities. Right now, with their software fried, they had no weapons with which to protect themselves. They were, in essence, sitting ducks that could easily be shot out of the sky. Heart racing, she felt fear shoot through her, along with a rush of adrenaline that heightened all her senses.

"Roger that. All civilian. And," Joe growled unhappily, "they fit the ID of Luis Rios's four rotorcrafts, if I don't miss my guess."

"Okay, we're taking evasive action. I'm not sitting here letting them get a fix on us!" With that, Akiva sent the Apache skyward, its nose pointed straight up and clawing for air and altitude.

Joe hung on. "I'll try and keep you informed of their positioning," he told her. Oh, how he wished he had the software up and running! The Apache software was the most sophisticated in the world. Not only would it ID the four civilian helicopters, it would choose from an array of weapons and tell him which should be targeted first, second, third and fourth. Now, he had none of that information at hand.

"They're starting to spread out in a fan formation," he called to her, and gave her their positions. Right now, he was smashed back against the seat as the Apache continued its vertical climb.

"They don't know we aren't armed," Akiva told him.

"Yeah, but they're gonna find out real soon," he warned her.

Sweat trickled into Akiva's eyes, and she blinked rapidly. "I've got to get us over land." Wrenching the cyclic and pushing on the rudders with her booted feet, Akiva swung the Apache toward shore. Because the Apache could climb so rapidly, she knew she'd beat the other helos at their own game. Wrenching the power to redline, she heard the engines howl as she drove the Apache straight for the coast.

"Rockets fired! Eight o'clock!"

Joe's voice was tight with fear. Akiva snapped her head to the left. She saw two rockets heading up—directly at them.

Did the rockets have the ability to track them? Some did and some didn't. With a curse, she banked the Apache steeply, out of the target zone. "See if they follow us!" she gasped to Joe.

The gunship howled as the engines torqued, moving into a steep dive away from the approaching rockets.

Slammed around in the cockpit, Joe couldn't keep the binoculars up to his eyes. His helmet smashed into the Plexiglas. Cursing softly, he gripped the field glasses.

"No! No, they ain't bird-doggin' us!"

Relief shot through Akiva. Thank the Great Spirit! Mind racing, she saw the landfall coming up rapidly. Bringing the Apache out of the sharp bank, she leveled the helo out at two thousand feet. They were too low and too vulnerable to attack this way.

"Bogeys at six o'clock. They're gonna climb our tail rotor...."

"Roger." Akiva took a deep breath and again gunned the Apache to redline, hoping to climb up and out of the deadly situation.

"Two more rockets comin' in! Ten o'clock!" Joe barked.

Whipping the Apache around so that she could see them, Akiva hissed, her lips drawing away from her clenched teeth. The Apache surged valiantly beneath her hands and feet as she guided it up, up, up into the night sky. The engines screamed at every inch of air purchased.

The rockets hurtled toward them, their red-and-yellow trails glowing.

She heard Joe take in a breath of air. Her entire body jerked in spasm. Eyes widening, she watched the rockets come directly at them, closer and closer. Using every bit of combat knowledge she'd ever accrued, Akiva threw the Apache into another steep, banking dive. Only this time she headed straight for the helicopter that had just fired the rockets.

The rockets flew past, no more than twenty feet away from them. Joe let out a yell of triumph.

Akiva held the gunship in a tight turn and then straightened it out for level flight—aimed directly at the helo, which was less than a mile away from them. "I'm going to get this son of a bitch," she rasped between tight lips. "Hold on."

Joe braced himself, hands pressed against the narrow cockpit, legs spread on either side of the floor pedals. "What—" He didn't get to finish his question. Because he was sitting in the upper cockpit, he had a far better view of what was going on in the sky around them than Akiva did. She was hurtling the Apache directly at the helo. The pilot in that helo had to be scared out of his mind. Joe sucked in a gasp. Was Akiva going to hit him?

Within moments of collision, Joe gave a shout, thinking they were going to smash into the other chopper. At the last possible second, the civilian craft banked violently to the left. Akiva jerked the nose of the Apache up. The two helos passed within sixty feet of one another.

Jerking his head around, Joe pulled the binoculars to his eyes.

"Where's the rest of them?" Akiva yelled. "Dammit, tell me their positions!"

Joe knew she was, in effect, flying blind. Aircraft without wing and taillights were dark apparitions against the night sky. She could no more see them than he could without the help of the special binoculars. And worse, the other helos had radar on board, so they knew where the Apache was flying and could target it.

Akiva was jerking the Apache around, trying to make it a hard target to fire at. They were over land now. Joe was wrenched around repeatedly from side to side as he frantically searched the night sky around them.

"I don't see 'em!"

"I need an escape plan, Joe," Akiva rasped. "We can't lead these bastards back to Alpha. I'm low on fuel. Start thinking of where we can land. I'll be damned if we're leading them home!"

Joe gripped the map. He jammed the binoculars between his arm and body because if he set them down, they'd fly around his cockpit like a projectile and possibly knock him out or smash into the instrument panel, doing more damage. "Hold on...."

Suddenly, the *ping, ping, ping* walking up alongside the Apache caught Akiva's heightened attention. Cursing savagely, she saw bullets from a machine gun ripping into them, the sparks of the projectiles—red tracers—arcing behind. Out of the corner of her eye, she followed the tracers back and saw the dim silhouette of a helo no more than half a mile away. Cursing, she brought the Apache up into a high, swift climb to escape. The bullets continued to lace into the thin skin of the Apache.

Wrenching the gunship around, Akiva pulled it into an inside loop. This was a maneuver no other helicopter in the world but the Apache could do. Looping would get the gunship up and out of firing range, but would also afford her the chance of coming down on the bogey's six, where she could shoot at it. The only problem, she thought, as she pulled the shrieking Apache into the loop, was that they had ammunition, but couldn't fire it.

It didn't matter. Akiva had a plan.

Joe hung on. There was nothing else he could do as the Apache swung into a powerful inside loop. The rotors thumped and beat hard as the helo swung in a circle. As they came out of it, Joe could see Akiva maneuvering to get behind the helo that had fired at them. His lips parted, and he braced himself with his hands and feet.

Within seconds, Akiva situated the Apache behind the helo. Eyes slitted, she powered up the gunship. In moments the combat helicopter was within a hundred feet of the other helo's rotor blades. The other pilot didn't even know she was there. Good. "Hold on, Joe."

That was all the warning he got. His eyes bulged. He felt the Apache dropping—directly down upon the rotor assembly of the unsuspecting helo. Letting out a yell of surprise, he could do nothing but go along for the ride. What the hell was she doing? Joe watched as Akiva lowered the gunship quickly and precisely.

Within seconds, a shudder went through the Apache. Joe yelled again, feeling the impact. Sparks and fire erupted beneath the landing gear of the Apache. The gunship shuddered drunkenly.

Akiva gave an Apache war cry as she sank the cannon—the huge gun assembly that rested directly beneath her booted feet, between the landing gear—into the helicopters rotor blades. In seconds, the heavy metal smashed the thin rotors and cracked them.

Instantly, Akiva lifted the gunship upward and away. As she did, she saw the other helicopter floundering. Its rotors were chopped up, no longer able to keep it in the air. She grinned savagely. She had timed the attack so that the useless cannon would strike the bogey's blades and shatter them. Without blades, that chopper was going down. And indeed, as she watched with satisfaction, she saw fire break out on the rotor shaft.

"What the hell!" Joe yelped. There was a sudden explosion in the other craft, less than five hundred feet away. Flames, yellow and orange, lit up the night sky. He raised his gloved hand to protect his face.

As she moved the Apache away from the flame, a lethal smile curved Akiva's lips. "I used the cannon to tangle his blades."

Joe was breathing raggedly. "That was some kind of risk...."

Chortling, Akiva said, "Yeah, but what do you do if you don't have guns, Calhoun?"

Shakily, he put the binoculars to his eyes, searching for the other three helos. The Apache was screaming along at roughly two thousand feet, the jungle racing by below them. "I can't see 'em," he gasped, twisting frantically to the right and left.

"We're gonna get shot down if we don't set down," Akiva said raggedly. "We need a landing place, Joe. I'm going to try and outrun them, set the ship down, egress and then blow this helo up."

His mind raced as he considered her decision. "You want to land and try to make a run for it? Escape into the jungle? Work our way back to Alpha?"

"Yeah. You got a better plan? I'm all ears." Her heart was pounding wildly in her chest. The tremble of the helicopter heightened.

Joe rubbernecked constantly, trying to find the other three helos he knew were pursuing them. Unfortunately, without their sophisticated radar operational to show him what was out there waiting to kill them, their rear was just as vulnerable to attack. "No, it's a good plan. Let's try to get to within a hundred miles of Alpha. That's a long walk, but one we can make."

"That's what I figured." The Apache shook around Akiva. She didn't even have engine instruments online to tell how the helo had fared, but her hearing told her that the bullets had done damage. "I only have fifty pounds of fuel left. We're gonna have to sit down soon."

"I know." Then Joe spotted the helos. "All three of 'em are hanging back about four miles, on our six. I think you scared 'em off for now."

"For now," Akiva said grimly, relief sheeting through her. Below them, the canopy of the jungle raced by as she moved closer and closer. In an emergency combat situation, they could land and then rig the Apache to explode. Nothing would fall into the hands of an enemy. Akiva hated to lose a twenty-million-dollar gunship, but under the circumstances, there was no other choice open to them.

Joe spread the map across his knees, the penlight dancing across it as the gunship shook and shuddered. He could hear the port engine whining, and that meant something was wrong. "You'd better shut down the port," he warned.

"Yeah, roger. Was just going to do that. I don't want it to explode on us." And Akiva reached for the toggle switch that would shut it off. That meant they'd lose half their airspeed, and the civilian helos would catch up with them quickly.

"Find me a place to land, Calhoun. I'm getting jumpy. And we're running outta time in a helluva hurry up here...."

Joe peered intently down at the map, tracing their route with his Nomex-gloved index finger. Trying to hold the penlight steady enough with his other hand to read the fine print, he rasped, "Yeah, I'm workin' at it, gal...."

Akiva felt the Apache slow. The engine was shut down. She had to compensate immediately as they continued to limp along on one engine only. Sinking the gunship to treetop level, she licked her dry lips. Akiva could feel the helos hunting them. It was only a matter of a minute or more, and they'd jump them like buzzards on a half-dead carcass, shooting them out of the sky.

"Dammit, Joe!"

"I found one!"

Relief sheeted through Akiva. "Where? Tell me where!" Her hands were aching as she gripped the cyclic and collective. Her entire body was bathed in sweat.

Joe quickly gave her the coordinates. "It's a little meadow, near a stream," he told her quickly. "The jungle is real close."

"Good! Hold on!" Akiva swung the Apache to the north, toward their landing zone. Would they reach it in time? Would they get there before being in rocket range of the bogeys? She wasn't sure. "Get ready to egress!" she ordered Joe. Ordinarily, they would never get out of the cockpit with the rotors still spinning, but this time they'd have to.

"My harness is off," he told her. Joe stowed the optic scope into a side panel along with the binoculars. He gripped the map and, with shaking hands, quickly folded it up and jammed it inside his flight suit. They'd need a map to get back to Alpha.

In moments, Akiva had located the small patch of meadow. Without hesitation, she set the Apache down. Switching off the only engine, the rotors thumping overhead, she set the explosive device and timer that would incinerate the gunship. Luckily, the device did not rely on software.

"Okay, let's get outta here!" Akiva yelled. "We've got two minutes before detonation! Make a run for it, Joe!" And she fumbled with the handle that would open her cockpit.

Chapter 10

Joe knew he was the one in the most danger. If he completely raised the cockpit hood, it would smash into the whirling blades, or be ripped out of his hands by the powerful buffeting. The darkness was complete. Heart pounding, he saw Akiva egress successfully and leap down off the Apache. Jerking the handle, he opened the latch. Instantly, the covering was torn out of his hand. Plexiglas splintered. Metal and glass erupted, the spinning blades scattering all around him. Joe threw up his hands. Fortunately his helmet visor was down to protect his eyes as thousands of tiny projectiles exploded around him. It felt as if someone had shot two rounds from a shotgun directly at him.

Feeling the burning sensation of the glass striking his lower face and neck, he clambered quickly out of the cockpit. Ducking so that he wouldn't be cut in half by the whirling blades, Joe threw himself out of the cockpit, and aimed, headfirst, for the ground.

Striking the wet grass, he rolled over and over. Above him, he heard helicopters approaching low and fast. Hands—Akiva's hands—grabbed him. He stopped rolling.

"Get up!" she panted, jerking a look toward the sky. Now the helos had their running lights on. They were flashing red and green, approaching low and fast. Breathing harshly, Akiva helped Joe to his feet.

"Get outta here!" Joe yelled, leaping up. Then he followed her as she ran from the Apache, which sat there idling, its blades whirling slowly.

As she broke into a full run, Akiva lost her footing and fell in the thick tangle of slippery grass, her helmeted head striking a fallen log.

Joe raced toward Akiva. She lay unmoving, facedown, her arms spread out ahead of her. What the hell had happened? Gasping for breath, he knew they had less than two minutes to get away from the Apache before it blew. Bending down, he slipped his hands beneath her armpits, intending to turn her over. His shaking fingers made contact with the log. Instantly, he understood what had happened: she'd struck her head as she fell.

Glancing up, Joe saw that the jungle was less than a hundred feet away. They had to get there!

Rolling Akiva over, he pulled her into a fireman's hold across his broad shoulders. Grunting, he forced himself to his feet, moving unsteadily. Akiva was no lightweight. She was about his height and size, and probably weighed about twenty pounds less than he did. Groaning, he dug the toes of his boots into the damp grass and lunged toward the dark wall of jungle before them.

Just as Joe began to run, with Akiva flopping unconscious on his shoulders, he heard a noise that scared the living hell out of him. He'd recognize that sound anywhere: it was a rocket being fired! His brain spun. His eyes widened. Adrenaline surged through him as he took huge, leaping strides. The grass tangled dangerously around his lower legs and boots, for everything was wet and slippery.

And then the world collapsed in a thunderous explosion of heat and light. One moment Joe was running as hard as he could with Akiva, and the next, he felt himself being lifted and flung through the air like a rag doll. Just before his mind blanked out, he felt the heat of fire vomiting around him.

A cry tore from his contorted lips. Somewhere in his mind, he thought the helo was firing a rocket at the Apache. Then he realized he was wrong. They were firing at *them!* It was the last thing he remembered.

The bumpy motion of a vehicle revived Joe. He found himself lying on his side, on a rough surface of black nylon carpet. His hands and ankles were tied with thick ropes in front of him. Closing his eyes, his ears ringing badly, he thought he heard voices speaking in Spanish. There were some short barks of male laughter. He was in a vehicle…and it was bouncing along at a fairly high rate of speed over a dirt road.

He noted the metallic taste of blood in his mouth. The tightness alongside his right temple was warm—with blood leaking out of a head wound?

Akiva? Where was she? Biting back a groan, because his whole body felt bruised, he tried to turn onto his back, then stopped, looked up and blinked. It was then he realized he was in the rear of a sport utility vehicle. When he saw two men sitting above him in the seat, their backs to him, his heart pounded violently. Akiva lay unconscious against the rear door. Her hands and feet were bound as well, and the helmet she had worn was gone, revealing the bright red scarf around her head which kept the tangle of her long, black hair from covering her face.

Fear vomited through Joe. He inched toward Akiva. Reaching out, he settled his bound hands on her shoulder and shook her hard. Her face was bleached, her once glorious copper skin frighteningly pale. Not daring to speak, because he didn't want the men to hear him, Joe gripped her shoulder and gave her another sharp, short shake. Anxiously, he perused her face and head. Joe knew she had struck the log when she fell. Looking around, he realized it was daylight.

How long had he been unconscious? His memory was shorting out. And then he recalled with clarity the rocket being launched—at them. Had the Apache blown up? Worriedly, he searched Akiva's face. He saw a trickle of blood leaking from her hairline, down her left temple and onto her cheek, but that was all. Her lips were parted. Her thick black lashes were like ebony fans against her cheeks. She was achingly beautiful to him.

More fear stabbed at Joe. Behind him, he heard at least four voices, all men, talking in Spanish. Luckily, he knew the language.

Joe forced himself up on his left elbow. He inched over Akiva, his ear near her ear. "Akiva! Wake up! Wake up!" His voice was low and urgent. Turning, Joe waited to see if they'd heard him. No. The men were all talking animatedly, laughing, the air filled with the smoke of cigarettes.

Akiva groaned softly. She heard Joe's voice, very far away at first. Her head ached. The pain was drifting through her brain, which felt like a drum being pounded. Blinking slowly, she forced open her eyes. Joe was hunkered over her, his face tight with concern and anxiety.

For long moments, Akiva had no idea what had happened. Or where she was.

Joe's lips parted as Akiva slowly opened her eyes. Her once glorious gold gaze was murky; she was obviously disoriented. Giving her a wobbly grin, he leaned down, his head next to hers, and whispered, "We're captured, Akiva. Just lie there and get your bearings. We're in an SUV going somewhere on a dirt road. There're four men in the front seats and they're all speaking Spanish. Just lie still. Don't talk. Get your bearings." He lifted his head, his mouth inches from her cheek. He wanted to protect Akiva as much as he could. Joe knew his back was to his captors, and he was sufficiently stretched out so that if one of them turned around to fire a gun at them, they'd hit him, not her. Above all, he wanted Akiva to live. To survive. His heart ached with a powerful, overwhelming emotion as he watched her fight off the semiconscious state. But Joe could do nothing but feel those emotions flowing like an unchecked river of heat and hope through him. In that moment, he realized he loved Akiva. And in the next moment, he was overwhelmed by that unexpected discovery.

His mind gyrated with a million questions and too few answers. They were captured. He knew they'd be interrogated. By whom? A drug lord? Yes, most probably. And their lives would be worthless. Joe knew that. As he held her dulled eyes, his mouth stretched into the semblance of a smile. "Welcome back, gal. Somehow," he rasped, "we'll get out of this—alive. You just have to trust me like you never have before. You hear me? Trust me, Akiva. Please…" And his voice broke with the raw emotion he was helpless to control.

Mouth dry, and tasting blood, Akiva lay very still. She mentally checked her body, to see if anything was broken, or where she felt pain. With Joe hunkered near her, she felt a modicum of safety. Her heart pounded with dread. They were captured! Akiva knew what that meant. The thick hemp ropes binding her wrists together had cut off her circulation, and her fingertips were numb and looked strangely white. She slowly moved them, one at a time.

Gradually, during long minutes of bumping over the dirt road, Akiva's mind began to clear. Her head was pressed against Joe's lower arm. He kept his arm there purposely to give her a cushion to lean against so that her head wouldn't bang against the floor of the vehicle. For that, she was more than grateful. The pain in her head was like a throbbing drum, and she felt heat and pressure building to a blinding intensity behind her eyes.

"Okay?" Joe rasped near her ear.

She felt the warmth of his breath against her flesh. Absorbing his closeness, because she felt scared as never before, she nodded once.

"Anything broken?"

She shook her head slowly from side to side. Every time she moved it, dizziness washed over her. Leaning back against his proffered arm, she looked up into his stormy-looking gray eyes. She mouthed the word *concussion.*

Joe nodded. His lips became a grim line. "You slipped and hit your head on a log when we were running away from the gunship," he confided in a low tone.

Akiva closed her eyes and then opened them. Joe's face was dark and unshaven. It made his cheeks look hollow and his face narrower than usual. His hair was mussed, one black lock hanging over his bunched brow. Akiva had never seen the look that was in his eyes now, and it fed her hope when she knew, logically, there was

none. Now she was getting a hint of a man she'd never
seen: Joe Calhoun the warrior. Somewhere in her spinning head, Akiva realized she'd never fully trusted that
Joe was truly a combat warrior. Oh, he flew a gunship,
but he didn't have that kind of aggressive personality
most Apache pilots showed off like a blazing sun. He
was always quiet, steady and calm. Now, as she gazed
up at him and held his darkening gaze, she realized with
relief that Joe was a man who was up to handling this
kind of situation. That made her feel safe despite their
incredibly dangerous situation.

"W-where—" Her voice cracked. Her mouth was dry.
Akiva was so thirsty she wanted to scream out for water.

Joe shook his head. He lifted his chin and looked
around. The rear window was caked with yellow dust,
and he could see a cloud billowing up behind the vehicle
as it moved along. On either side of the thin, narrow dirt
road, he saw fields of corn. Farther away, he saw jungle
bordering the fields. Frowning, he leaned down again,
close to Akiva's ear. Strands of her hair tickled his mouth
as he whispered, "We're in an agricultural area. I see
cornfields. I don't know where we are, but there're farmers out in the fields. The jungle is a long way off. This
looks like an area I remember on the map. About twenty-
five miles inland was a cleared strip of land that was flat
and could be used for farming."

Akiva sighed. It helped if she kept her eyes open.
When she closed them, dizziness swept over her until she
felt like she was in a tornado, spinning continuously.
Joe's voice, low and tense, soothed some of her anxiety.
Akiva didn't look closely at what might happen. She was
a woman. And if their enemies were ruthless drug soldiers capable of anything, she'd be at risk in more ways
than Joe. Swallowing against her dry throat, Akiva tried

to force her fear, her wildly galloping mind, to calm. Being with him soothed her somewhat.

"A-are you okay?" she managed to whisper. Akiva saw his eyes glimmer. A slight, one-cornered smile pulled at his thinned mouth.

"I'm fine, gal. Just bumps and bruises."

"A-and the Apache?"

Joe saw the fear in Akiva's eyes. There was no way she wanted that gunship to survive the blast and fall into enemy hands. Both the hardware and software aboard the Apache were found nowhere else in the world, and they knew drug dealers and foreign governments alike would pay millions to get their hands on it.

He shook his head. "I dunno. They shot a rocket at us. I was carryin' you away from the gunship when they fired. I thought they were aiming at the Apache." He gave her a rueful look. "I was wrong. They were shootin' at us."

Akiva moved her head closer and nuzzled her cheek against his chest. She felt sick to her stomach now. Joe's closeness made her symptoms go away, if only for a moment.

Surprised at Akiva's behavior, Joe lay there, stunned. He saw her lips part and go soft. And he saw the naked fear in her face. Knowing that she was thinking about the things that could happen now that they were prisoners, his heart ached with anxiety. He feared for Akiva, because she was a woman and the enemy was male, and he knew all too well what they might do to her. Bitterness coated his mouth. He leaned down and pressed a series of small, comforting kisses against her exposed neck, where her thick black hair had parted. A fierce love welled up in him. Sensing her fear, her uncertainty, Joe rubbed his cheek against hers gently.

"It's gonna be all right, gal. Somehow...we're gonna get out of this—alive. You hear me? Alive. Both of us. I won't let them hurt you. I'll die first. Just try and take it easy. Let's take this one minute at a time. We'll both be lookin' for a way to escape...so just hang in there. I'm with you all the way...."

Joe's words were like balm to the violent fear that was engulfing Akiva now. Cheek resting against his forearm, her face pressed against his damp uniform, she tried to stop a sob coming up in her throat. Hot tears pricked the backs of her tightly closed eyes. She felt Joe's mouth, strong and sure, caressing her nape. Each kiss he feathered along her neck, then against her temple, and finally, her cheek, was like a healing unguent to the fear that was eating her alive.

In those stolen, precious moments out of time, Akiva hungrily absorbed Joe's steadiness and believed the words he spoke roughly against her ear. Somehow, she told herself, she was going to have to get a handle on her fear and turn it into strength, as he had already done. Though she was surprised at her reactions, Akiva tried not to be too hard on herself. She was in shock, and shock did funny things to one's emotions.

As she lay there, being bumped and thrown from side to side in the speeding SUV, with Joe buttressing her and trying to keep her protected, Akiva felt the darkness claim her once again. She had no strength at the moment, and it was Joe's body, his spirit, that was feeding her and keeping her safe. As Akiva spiraled down into darkness once more, she saw a set of gold jaguar eyes with black pupils staring back at her.

The discomfort of her position, the jolting of the vehicle, all dissolved as Akiva stared, riveted, at the eyes, which stared back like brilliant suns. As she felt the spinning sensation deepen, her only anchor with any kind of reality was the black jaguar's face, which slowly congealed around those sun-gold eyes burning with raw power and energy.

Finally, the spinning stopped, and Akiva found herself standing on a grassy plain near a small, burbling creek. She was beneath the spreading arms of a massive old, white-barked sycamore tree, one that she recalled from the Red Rock Reservation. Oh, how many times had she gone to that Arizona sycamore, which was probably two hundred years old, and sat with her back against it, dreaming of a happy life instead of the one she had?

And it was during those times as a young girl as she closed her eyes and daydreamed, that she would see out of the swirling mists of rainbow-colored fog, a black jaguar striding lithely and silently toward her. Akiva remembered being scared out of her wits the first time she'd seen the jungle predator. Her eyes had flown open. She'd leaped to her feet and raced back to her grandmother's house, her heart slamming into her rib cage like a frightened rabbit's.

Now Akiva stood there and watched her spirit guide, the black jaguar, approach her, his tail twitching from side to side. She felt his incredible power, until it suffused her and fed her. The heat and light moved from her booted feet, up through her uniform-clad legs and into the center of her body. As the golden energy surged through her like a tidal wave, she felt it fill her aching head. In moments, she felt it begin to heal her, so that the dizziness dissolved. Standing with her legs slightly apart, Akiva knew this was a healing and that her spirit guide was helping her. Grateful, she opened her eyes once the huge wave of energy left her. She saw the black jaguar sitting there. To her surprise, there was an Apache warrior woman standing next to him.

Gasping, Akiva immediately understood it was her great-great-grandmother, Na-u-kuzzi. Her thick black hair hung almost to her waist and she had the third braid of an Apache warrior. Around her head was the red scarf proclaiming her the mighty warrior she was. She wore a long-sleeved white tunic over loose-fitting white pants pushed into leather boots that fitted snugly just below her knees. The tips of her boots were shaped in an upward spiral that reminded Akiva of Aladdin's shoes. The wise Apaches had purposely made their boots this way because with the curved leather tip they could quickly and effectively pick up and fling a rattlesnake or scorpion aside before it bit them.

In Na-u-kuzzi's left hand was her battle ax. Akiva saw the bowie knife hanging at her left side. The look on Na-u-kuzzi's face was one of quiet strength and pride. Akiva had never seen her before, for there were no pictures of her. She only knew, based on descriptions her grandmother had related to her as a child, that this was her ancestor. Now, standing in Na-u-kuzzi's powerful energy, Akiva was astounded and mesmerized by her not only as a woman, but as a warrior.

"Granddaughter, I have come to you for a reason," Na-u-kuzzi said.

Akiva realized the older woman's lips were not moving, that she was hearing her words inside her head telepathically. "Yes?"

"You will now take your final test to become a true warrior of The People." She reached out and slid her hand across the sleek black head of the jaguar that sat at her side, his eyes upon Akiva. "Use your fear to strengthen you. Trust the man who walks at your side, for he, too, has jaguar medicine. Only if you fight together, work together, will you have the possibility of surviving this test. Do you hear me, Granddaughter?''

Akiva nodded. ''Y-yes…I hear you. I'm afraid….''

''Of course you are. A true warrior is always afraid.'' Her ancestor laughed huskily. Raising her right hand with a flourish, she added, ''What separates a warrior from a coward is that you take the fear and transmute it into action to save your life instead of letting it paralyze you like a jaguar paralyzes its prey before leaping upon it.'' Her eyes sparkled with amusement. ''Call upon me by name. Call upon my spirit guide here, who is now with you, to infuse you with skill, strength and intelligence.''

Akiva nodded. Just being in Na-u-kuzzi's presence gave her an incredible burst of confidence and self-assuredness. ''I will, Great-great-grandmother. I promise….''

''Go then, my child. We are with you at all times, no matter how dark your world becomes. Call upon us. That is all you need to do. Remember who you are. Remember that my blood runs through your veins. That you have the heart of a warrior, as the man at your side does. Allow the love you've hidden to blossom from your heart to his. If you do this, you may survive…for your biggest test as a warrior will not be whether or not you can fight, but whether or not you can trust your fellow warrior and fight your enemies together.'' Her voice grew deep with warning. ''This is an opportunity, Akiva, for you to heal your wounds. Learn to trust…really *trust*….''

Chapter 11

Akiva tried to stop her teeth from chattering, but it was impossible. The hemp rope had been taken off their ankles and they'd been marched at gunpoint to a dank cell beneath what looked like a massive, yellow-stucco bullring. Arms wrapped around herself, Akiva stood in the center of the small rectangular cell, which had a small, barred window that allowed gray light to filter in.

His face set and determined, Joe tested the door again and again. It was made of thick, dark wood on massive iron hinges.

Dizziness washed over Akiva. She saw down in the fresh golden straw that had been spread across the hard-packed dirt floor of their cell, her back to the wall, her arms around herself, her knees drawn tightly against her body. Her head ached without respite because of the concussion.

"So what do we know?" she asked Joe. "That we're on a hornet's nest. That was Luis Rios, the son of Javier

Rios.'' Akiva frowned. "We were briefed on them. Now here we are…''

They'd agreed to speak only English, though they both knew Spanish. After all, it was only a matter of time before their captors discovered they were American. The young leader, a man named Luis Rios, had their helmets. And inside the helmets, plainly marked, were the words *U.S. Army*. No, it wouldn't take much guesswork for him to figure out that they were a covert spook operation. Licking her dry lips, Akiva watched Joe, and her heart speeded up with an incredible avalanche of emotion. When the captors had pushed them out of the rear of the vehicle earlier, Joe had demanded food, water and medical attention for her. That had earned him the butt of a rifle in the middle of his back, a blow that had knocked him to his knees. Akiva had stood there, horrified by the vicious act. She'd seen the pleasure in Luis's handsome face. Obviously, he enjoyed seeing Joe in pain. If she hadn't been so dizzy, in so much pain herself, she'd have attacked him, but Akiva knew her concussion was slowing her down, to the point where she had trouble staying on her feet. She would never have been able to kick out with one foot and clip Luis's jaw like she wanted to do.

Ignoring the throbbing ache between his shoulder blades where the drug soldier had nailed him with the butt of his rifle earlier, Joe turned. In the grayish light of the damp, cold cell, he saw Akiva's pale, worried expression. He was worried, too: she needed medical attention. The look on her face—one of devastation and loss of hope—drew him over to her. Kneeling down on one knee, he placed his hands gently on her upper arms and stroked caressingly.

"I don't know what to do," he confided in a strained tone. "How are *you* doing? You look like your head's

killing you. Is it?'' He worried about the concussion.
Somewhere in his spinning senses, Joe knew enough
about medical conditions to know that a concussion could
be dangerous, could cause bleeding in the brain. If that
happened, a clot could form, and sooner or later kill the
person. His fingers gripped her shoulders. Akiva's hair
was in disarray. Earlier, the guards had taken her war ax
and bowie knife, as well as both of their watches and
their side arms.

"Yeah...this headache's a killer all right.'' She managed to lift one corner of her mouth as she gazed up into
his dark, shadowed features. Joe looked different to her.
Why? Was it because she was privy to his warrior side,
had seen his protectiveness toward her? Or was his beard
making his face look more chiseled and sharp? "What
I'd give for two aspirin right now,'' she joked wryly.
Closing her eyes as Joe's hands ranged gently across her
shoulders, then framed her face, Akiva wanted to sob.
Struggling, she swallowed hard against the lump forming
in her throat.

"Oh, Joe...I screwed up. I've lost a twenty-million-
dollar gunship, put us in this position....'' Akiva felt his
callused hands graze her cheeks tenderly. She opened her
eyes, but tears blinded her.

"Shh, gal, you didn't do any of this.'' Joe leaned down
and saw the glitter of tears making tracks down either
side of her taut, pale face. "You're gonna tell me you
planned for that lightnin' bolt to hit us?'' he teased, and
gave her a smile he didn't feel. Akiva was completely
vulnerable to him for the first time. Relief surged through
Joe as he realized why she was able to open up to him
now. It was mostly because she was hurting from the
injury to her head, and wrestling with the feeling that she
hadn't performed up to par. But there was something

else, and Joe saw it clearly: she was trusting him. With his thumbs, he brushed away the tears flooding from her anguished-looking eyes. His gaze moved down to her mouth, which was contorted with pain.

To hell with it. They were in a life and death situation. For all Joe knew, the drug dealers could come back and spray them with gunfire, killing them right then and there. Following his heart, which screamed out for him to kiss Akiva, he leaned down.

"I'm gonna kiss you, gal," he whispered, barely an inch from her mouth. "I've been wantin' to do this for a long, long time, and unless you say no…"

Sniffing unsteadily, Akiva whispered his name, her voice cracking. She reached up and slid her fingers around Joe's strong, thick neck. In the next instant, his mouth was settling tenderly against her trembling one.

Akiva couldn't stop shaking. She was so cold. So afraid. Mentally she tried to wrestle with her fears, but her body wasn't responding like she wanted it to. Maybe it was because of her injury, or shock from the combat. She just wasn't sure. Now, as Joe's warm, strong mouth moved gently across her lips in a slow, delicious exploration, Akiva drank in his heat and power, absorbing it into her shaking soul. He moved closer, his hands drifting from her face, down her slender neck, covering her shoulders and pulling her more surely against him.

Never had Akiva been kissed like this. His mouth was strong and cherishing. She lost herself in the splendor and heat created as they clung to one another. How could she have been so wrong about Joe? Right now, as his large, square hands caressed her shoulders and drew her against him, Akiva wanted more of him. Fear was over-ridden by something so incredibly beautiful and heart-stopping that Akiva surrendered to it…and to Joe. Right

now, he was strong where she was weak. As he grazed
her lips softly, worshipfully, Akiva realized in some dim
recess of her mind and aching heart that it was all right
for her to feel this way; that sometimes a man was
stronger in a moment than a woman. And vice versa. All
along, Akiva had thought that she had to be strong all
the time, that no man could match her strength or her
power. She was wrong. Moaning Joe's name against his
searching mouth, Akiva deepened their kiss. His breath
was chaotic and moist, flowing against her cheek.

Tunneling his fingers through her thick hair, he moved
it aside like a curtain and eased back from her mouth.
He trailed lingering kisses from her cheek down her jaw
and neck as Akiva moaned.

Hands moving spasmodically against his shoulders,
Akiva felt the icy coldness of fear dissolving beneath his
tender ministrations. Her heart expanded and opened in
a way she'd never known before. Euphoria flooded Akiva, left her breathless, left her staring up into Joe's
stormy gray eyes, which burned with desire for her. In
those precious seconds, Akiva realized that what she felt
for Joe was love. Never in her life had she felt this way
about a man before, and it left her frightened in new and
different ways. Yet as she clung to Joe's tender, burning
gaze, and he gently stroked her hair, Akiva knew somehow that she was safe with him. Protected. And most of
all, loved. Yes, he loved her. Blinking through her tears,
Akiva opened her mouth, but words failed her.

"Shh, gal, I know," Joe whispered unsteadily as he
framed her face once more and gave her a tender smile.
"We both feel it. And it's for real. It's ours...."

"I—I'm afraid, Joe...." There, the words were out.
She blinked rapidly again and wiped away the last of her
tears.

"So am I, gal." He eased back, his hands resting on her slumped shoulders. "Militarily, we're not in a good position." His heart cried out with the unfairness of it all. Yet as Joe searched her anguished face, her soft, well-kissed mouth, he knew that Akiva would probably never have opened up to him this way under any other circumstances. Moving his fingers along the rip in her uniform near her left shoulder, he gazed at her tear-matted lashes and pained-filled eyes.

"We have one another," he told her in a low voice. Joe didn't want to risk anyone overhearing them. For all he knew, a guard was posted outside the door and could be eavesdropping. "And we trust one another."

Trust. There was that word. Joe released her. He sat down next to her, his back against the wall, their arms and legs touching.

"Come here," he rasped, and he opened his arms and drew Akiva into them. Joe situated her so that she lay on her left side against his body, facing him. He took her full weight, as he wanted to warm her up. At first he thought she might hesitate at such intimacy, but she surprised him by nestling in his arms without a fight. Joe began to understand how vulnerable Akiva really was. As she rested her head against his shoulder, her arm sliding up across his chest and around his neck, she sighed brokenly.

"It's gonna be all right, gal. Wait and see," he whispered against her ear, which was covered with the thick black silk of her hair. "You bein' in my arms is a dream come true for me. I want you to know that." He smiled softly and closed his eyes, absorbing her softness. Akiva was a strong woman, a warrior without equal, and yet, in this moment, as their lives hung precariously by a thread, she trusted him. Trusted him! His heart soared like an eagle taking wing.

"I don't think so, Joe—"

"Shh, gal...just lie here with me. Lemme hold you. Lemme keep you warm and safe." He pressed a kiss against her hair. Little by little, Akiva was relaxing against him. He felt the roundness of her breasts against his chest, felt their rise and fall as she breathed. The warm moisture of her breath feathered across his neck. As he ran one hand slowly up and down the long indentation of her spine, he felt like a starving stray dog that had found not only shelter, but food as well. Akiva's nearness was food for his aching, pounding heart and spirit.

As he sat there with her in his arms, needing her as much as he needed to breathe, Joe wondered when it had all happened. When had he fallen in love with Akiva? Oh, he'd always been dazzled by her as a combat pilot— that reckless smile of hers, that gleam in her eye telling him she was a supreme hunter. But how long had he ached to discover this wonderful, soft, feminine side of her?

There were times when Joe sat alone at Alpha and wondered if Akiva would ever unveil her feminine side to him. When she'd told him of her childhood, he'd wanted to cry—for her, for what had been done to her. Joe understood that Akiva had had to be tough and defensive or she would not have survived. And more than anything, she was the consummate survivor. Only survivors paid one hell of a price for the hardscrabble life that had been thrust upon them as innocents. That natural innocence was something Joe had recognized in Akiva as he got to know her. She'd been a vulnerable little girl who had been thrown into a toxic, dysfunctional environment. It was no wonder she shielded herself from possible hurt. He didn't blame her at all.

As he lay there, the day dying, the grayness deepening until it was dark in the cell, Joe held Akiva as she slept in his arms. After a while, his backside became numb because of lack of circulation, but he didn't care. She was in his arms and his heart was soaring with a happiness he'd never experienced in his life.

Sitting there in the darkness, Joe heard the snort of what he thought were cattle and horses nearby. Sometimes he heard voices in Spanish, but the words were muted and he couldn't make out what the men said.

As he sat in the cell, holding the woman he loved more than life, Joe felt a kind of peace, despite their dire circumstances. In this moment that he'd never dreamed would happen, Akiva was all that mattered.

As she fell deeper into an exhausted sleep, he felt her body relax against the harder planes of his own. Her breathing slowed and deepened. Her arm slid off his shoulder and she tucked her hand against her breast, fingers softly curled. Before sleep finally claimed him, Joe wondered if Akiva had ever had a night, as a child, where she felt safe. Safe, embraced and well loved. Protected from the violence that had hounded her young life. Probably not. As exhaustion finally claimed him in the damp, chilly darkness of the cell, Joe knew that for at least this one night, Akiva slept knowing she was not only protected, but safe…and loved.

The rattling of the door pulled both of them from sleep. Joe jerked upward, instantly on guard. Akiva rolled away from him, sitting up and tensing. Both trained their gazes on the door.

Two guards dressed in camouflage fatigues and bearing military rifles stepped into the cell and stood on either side of the door.

Akiva glanced at Joe, who was slowly getting to his feet, his arms held tensely at his sides, his eyes narrowed. She saw a silver-haired man, dressed casually in a white shirt and tan slacks, a red neckerchief around his throat, enter their cell. It was Javier Rios himself. His dark brown eyes sparkled with humor. His face was narrow and he wore a silver goatee. As Akiva looked down at what he held in his hands, she gasped and leaped to her feet, her hair flying about her shoulders, her fists curling at her sides. He had her war ax and bowie knife!

One of the guards lowered his rifle barrel and pointed it at her. "Move again and you're dead," he snarled in Spanish.

Joe snapped a look at Akiva. All her attention was on the weapons the older man held in his hands. He saw her anger and her desire to have them back. Knowing how much they meant to her, Joe held his hand out to stop Akiva from moving forward. The dark looks on the guards' faces told him they'd shoot first and ask questions later.

"Ah," the visitor said, "so you are the owner of these archeological delights. Allow me to introduce myself." He bowed slightly to them. "I am Javier Rios." He looked with undisguised interest at Akiva. "Permit me to ask you some questions, *señorita,* for these weapons are very, very interesting to me. My son, Luis, took these off you out near the coast, after you were discovered by him."

Javier smiled slightly, a surge of excitement tunneling through him. This woman who stood before him dressed in black, a red scarf about her head, was a giant! He'd had no idea she was six feet tall. Luis had not said much about her, except that she was a woman. And Luis liked women for only one thing—keeping his bed warm. He'd neglected to mention that she was a warrior, no question about it.

Eagerness thrummed through Javier as he lifted the weapons for her to see more clearly. "Please, be at ease. I come to talk to you, *señorita,* about these magnificent, very old weapons they found on you." His voice lowered with excitement. "Tell me if I am correct or not, eh? I have pored over many, many archeological texts from my library, all day yesterday and long into the night. I have made many calls to museums in the U.S., even the Smithsonian, to verify what I think I hold in my hands. These are precious...." And his voice cracked.

Gathering himself, and trying to contain the thrill he felt, he looked up into Akiva's darkening face and narrowed eyes. Indeed, this woman was a true warrior! Even more excitement flowed through him. Moving his lips, he tried to steady his voice, but he always got emotionally overwhelmed when he held such treasures as these, with their history, in his hands.

"*Señorita,* I believe you are Chiricahua Apache." His eyes sparkled and he gestured with his chin. "You wear the third braid of the warrior. You have gone through arduous and dangerous trials to earn the right to wear that braid with honor. Further, you wear the red scarf of an Apache warrior. The Apaches had many women warriors in their bands. And these..." His voice trembled. "These...children of yours—why, they are priceless! I am holding a part of history...." He lifted his head and gazed at Akiva's wide eyes. His smile grew.

"According to my books, to my calls to people who are experts on Native American archeological treasures, this is a war ax that dates back roughly to 1860." He held the knife up, its leather scabbard stained from age and handling. "And this is a bowie knife! I simply cannot believe it! It is the real thing. Why, the blade has many nicks on it. The leather dates back to 1860, too, but the knife is much earlier, perhaps 1840...."

Gulping, Akiva eyed her weapons. How badly she wanted them back. The old man was positively salivating over them. He held them with such care that she was stunned.

"Tell me this is so?"

"Only when you give us water, food and medical help," Joe snarled. He cut a look to Akiva, who wanted desperately to reach out and claim her great-great-grandmother's weapons, he could tell.

"Ahh...yes, the male warrior at the side of this magnificent female." Javier's gaze settled on Joe. "I would guess, *señor,* that perhaps you, too, are part Native American? Perhaps not, eh? There were no weapons, other than a U.S. Army pistol, found on your person, so you may be Anglo after all."

"We demand to be treated according to the Geneva Convention of War," Joe said in a deep voice. When he lifted his hand, both guards went on alert. He let his arm drop back to his side.

"Yes, well..." Javier looked Akiva up and down with respect and obvious admiration. "I think we can do that, *señor.*" He smiled a little. "And then, *señorita,* will you kindly confirm what I hold in my hands?"

Akiva gulped. She knew they weren't in a military situation. Drug lords didn't follow Geneva accords any more than they followed the laws of the land. "You get us food, water and a medical doctor," she echoed huskily. "Then, maybe, I'll tell you more."

"Good enough," Javier said. He smiled at them and

again bowed slightly before stepping out into the poorly lit hall. The guards followed on his heels. One of them slammed the door shut and locked it.

Akiva felt shaky in the aftermath. She traded a silent look that spoke volumes with Joe as they waited several minutes before moving or speaking. If there was a guard outside the door, Akiva didn't want him to overhear them.

"Javier Rios," Joe finally said in a low voice. He went over to the door and tested it. It was locked. Turning, he saw Akiva sit down. She rubbed her face and pushed her hair back behind her shoulders.

"Yes," she whispered. She saw Joe looking down at her, that same tender flame burning in his eyes. The set of his mouth told her that he was ready to give his life for her, if necessary. Feeling eviscerated by Rios having her weapons, Akiva choked out, "Who is that man? How could he know so much about me?"

Shaking his head, Joe knelt down beside her, his arm going around her shoulders as he rasped, "I don't know. He's a historian, remember? From the briefing?"

"Oh, that's right," Akiva replied. "That would explain Javier's intense interest in my weapons. And it might also explain why we are being held here. From what I could see when they brought us in, there is an actual bullring built above these cells."

"Yeah, looks that way, as far as I could tell." Joe sat down next to her. His stomach was clenched with fear. With hunger. They'd had no water for nearly twenty-four hours, and he was dying for a cup right now. Running his fingers across Akiva's taut shoulders, the silk of her hair soothing to him, he whispered, "I hope like hell they give us the stuff we've asked for. You've got to be hungry and thirsty."

Nodding, Akiva looked up and almost drowned in his gray eyes. "I am, but to tell you the truth, Joe, having you here...holding me...has more than made up for everything else."

He met and held her golden eyes. This morning, in the gray light drifting in from the dirty window, he saw that she was looking more like her old self. Her skin was once again copper colored, her eyes much clearer. "Getting a good night's sleep helped, gal." His mouth hitched upward.

"No," Akiva whispered unsteadily, "it's because of you, Joe...it's you." She reached out, scared, and yet needing to touch him. Her hand settled over his. "You held me. You made me feel safe for the first time in my life. It's a miracle." Her voice quavered with unshed tears. "You're a miracle to me, to my heart. When you held me last night, my head was throbbing. I was in so much pain. Yet when you caressed my head, I felt the pain going away with each stroke of your hand. I felt it." Akiva gave him a puzzled look. "I don't know how you did it, but as I fell asleep, I was pain free. I felt so happy when you held me. Happier than I've ever been, and I don't know why. I've never trusted anyone like I trust you...."

Her words were like sunlight striking the rich, fertile earth of his heart. Akiva's voice was husky and off-key. He heard and felt her pain, her surprise, her yearning for him. Picking up her hand, he clasped it gently within his. She was so strong, and yet she was allowing him complete access to her as a woman. He struggled to speak, his emotions nearly overwhelming him.

"And I trust you, gal, with my life, my heart, my soul.... I always have and I always will." He lifted her long, slender fingers and saw small white scars that she'd probably gotten in childhood. Lifting her hand to his lips, he kissed the back of it tenderly. "What we have, Akiva, is good. It's solid." He turned and pulled her into his arms. She came without resistance, slipping her arms around him and holding him tightly. That gave Joe the courage to speak of what lay in his heart.

"I dunno how we're gonna get out of this trouble we're in, gal, but we will. I just feel it in my gut." Pressing a kiss to her hair, he whispered unsteadily, "I care so deeply for you, Akiva. I'd give my life for you in a heartbeat. I want what we have. We've earned this, gal. We've earned one another. I know we're in a god-awful mess, but I want to pursue what we have...once we get out of here...."

Akiva nuzzled Joe's hard jaw. His arms held her tightly, crushing the air out of her lungs. She felt his anxiety, his fear and his fierce love for her. All those chaotic emotions tumbled through her as she clung to him. "I do, too, Joe...." she rasped. Tears jammed into her tightly shut eyes. Fighting them back, Akiva opened her mouth, her lower lip trembling as she spoke in a haunted tone. "Your goodness, your kindness, Joe, comes from your heart and soul. I know that." Her hands tightened against his back as she held him tightly. "I—I trust you with my life...." She managed a short, nervous laugh. "I'm so afraid to say this, but life can be pretty short sometimes, and I want you to know something. I—my heart...you have my heart. I don't know when it happened...or how...I just know that I want more of what you share with me. You're unlike any man I've ever known or experienced...."

He nodded against her thick hair. "I hear you, gal," he whispered unsteadily. "When you have trust, you can build on it. And right now, that's what we've earned with

one another. You're priceless to me. You hear that, Akiva? I respect you. I admire you. I want you in my life,
always. In every way possible.'' Joe frowned and held
her tightly. His voice roughened. ''And we've got to get
out of here. We've got to escape, because I want a life
with you.''

Chapter 12

"Now that you are fed, watered and medically taken care of," Javier said in an amused tone to his two guests, who were seated in front of the massive mahogany desk in his den, "I offer you a conciliatory olive branch of sorts." He pointed to the two weapons on his desk. "These belong to you, Warrant Officer Redtail? Yes?"

Akiva's head was still aching as she stared at the neatly dressed Javier Rios. Dr. Paulo Hernandez had put six stitches in a gash there less than half an hour ago. Joe sat next to her in a carved mahogany chair with a straight back and ornate arms. Two hours after Rios's initial visit to their cell, they'd been roughly taken out of their dungeon beneath what seemed to be, indeed, a bullring, and hustled toward the main house in the huge *estancia* complex. There they were put into separate rooms, told to strip out of their clothes, given a hot shower and fresh civilian clothes. Only the clothes weren't exactly modern looking to Akiva. Her attire consisted of a rough red

woolen tunic that fell to just above her knees. A pair of
white pants went with it, tied at the waist with a rope to
keep them from falling down. Instead of being given her
flight boots, she was told to put on a pair of high leather
boots that tied just below her knees. A rough leather belt
with beaten, thin brass disks around it pulled the tunic in
at her waist. The guards had taken away her red scarf,
which she wanted to tie around her head. That made her
angry. She had just washed and towel dried her hair, but
Akiva took the time to plait her third braid of a warrior
before a guard shoved the point of his rifle into her ribs
and told her to get up and leave the room. But then the
guard had had second thoughts and had given her back
her red scarf. She felt better wearing it in front of Rios.

She and Joe had been hustled out to another room—
what looked like a kitchen in the basement of the main
house—by guards. There, frightened looking women in
black dresses with starched white aprons fed them. They
sat side by side at the crimson-tiled table in the center of
the hot, airless kitchen, where at least five cooks were
working furiously nonstop, and ate voraciously of the
salty beef-and-vegetable stew placed before them.

Afterward, they'd been escorted at gunpoint by their
two scowling guards up to the second floor. The spacious
den they entered looked more like a museum to Akiva.
She traded a look with Joe, who had shaved as well as
washed. He, too, was dressed in a red tunic and pants.

Already, they'd given Rios the standard military response to his questions: name, rank and serial number.
That was what was required under the laws of the Geneva
Convention. Javier's eyes sparkled and he seemed
amused by their response to him.

"Well?" he said again, propping his long, square fingers together, his elbows resting on the thickly padded

arms of his chair. "Do I get something other than what you've told me already? Aren't you interested in the olive branch?"

Biting her lower lip, Akiva assessed the older man. In the back of the room, his sulking son, Luis, stood, arms across his chest. He'd argued heatedly with his father earlier. From what she had gathered, Luis wanted to simply put a gun to their temples and kill them. Heart thudding heavily, Akiva weighed the son's desire against what the father wanted. She knew, without a doubt, that the older man held their lives in his hands. Because of Joe's admission of his feelings for her, and her realization of how desperately she wanted to survive this unfolding nightmare to have a life with him, Akiva decided to talk.

"Okay," she said darkly, "what's the olive branch?"

"Ahh, you are as intelligent as you look. A modern-day gladiatrix. Did you know that the Romans took prisoners, upstart warriors who fought against the greatest soldiers in the world, and brought them to Rome to fight in the Circus Maximus?" Javier leaned forward, his voice becoming animated. "And that there were women warriors, particularly among the Britons, who were gladiators? They fought just as valiantly and heroically as any male. Yes, they were a lost piece to my historical reenactments...until now."

Confused, Akiva sat there. She saw Joe's expression go sour. What was Rios babbling about? Looking around, Akiva realized that all the weapons hanging along the scrubbed white walls of the long, rectangular room looked Roman or of that era. She was no expert, but she did recognize the short swords, the long, rectangular leather shield with brass embossing on it, the brass helmet with the red horsehair plume as a crest, and other pieces of armor a Roman soldier would wear.

"What olive branch?" Joe growled. He sat up. Instantly, the guard behind him stiffened, the muzzle of the rifle aimed at Joe's head.

Giving him a distraught look, Akiva raised her hand. She was afraid the guard, a big six-foot, heavily muscled Latino with a shaved head, would shoot Joe.

Chuckling indulgently, Javier raised his hand and flipped it toward the guard. "Chico, please…they are unarmed. They are not stupid enough to try and make an escape. They know better." His dark brown eyes settled back on Akiva. "My dear, I await with held breath for you to tell me of these wondrous weapons you carry."

"And if I do?"

With a one-shouldered shrug, Javier smiled, "Then I offer you the olive branch."

Moistening her lips, Akiva glanced at Joe. His brows were drawn down, and the look in his eyes shouted silently to her to be careful what she said. Nodding slightly, Akiva turned her attention back to the drug lord, who seemed, on the surface, like a doting old grandfather type. But she didn't fool herself; he was the one who had built this illegal empire. Choosing her words carefully, Akiva told him of the proud history and provenance of the weapons. With each piece of information, Javier became more riveted. Finally, he was leaning forward, his elbows on the desk, his eyes wide, like an excited child. In the back of her mind, she wondered if he was on drugs, demented or just plain loco. Akiva couldn't decide which as she finished explaining the historical significance of the weapons.

"Ahh, this is even better than I'd hoped." He patted the war ax and bowie knife. The thick, dark leather scabbard of the latter had many nicks and scrapes across its surface.

"Now, the olive branch," Joe muttered. "What are you offering us?"

Grinning slyly, Javier picked up the war ax. The head of it was encased in thick leather to protect it. The wooden handle, made of cottonwood, was stained to an umber color from being handled so much over the years.

"You are Native American, too? Yes?" Javier asked Joe.

Mouth tightening, Joe said nothing. He wasn't about to get chatty and friendly with the drug lord. The less Javier Rios knew about him, the less power and leverage the man held over him. Joe worried most about his family. He knew a powerful drug lord could easily locate his family and have them murdered. To protect himself and Akiva, Joe might have to give his name and rank, but he sure as hell wasn't going to give Javier any more ammo to harm those he loved.

Right now, he was desperately worried for Akiva. Rios was infatuated with her; it was as if he saw her as some exotic, rare bug to be studied intently beneath a microscope. It sickened Joe, and it made him anxious. He felt Javier was dangling them like helpless puppets, and their lives were forfeit. Joe was finding it hard to keep calm as he waited for a chance to escape.

"I see." Javier sighed, obviously disappointed. "You are not going to be friendly and open, as is your partner here." His mouth twitched. "Chico, put your rifle to Chief Warrant Officer Redtail's head, please?"

Joe nearly came out of the chair. Instantly, a thick, powerful hand gripped his shoulder and thrust him back. The other guard, at least six foot five inches tall, with shining obsidian eyes, grinned down at him. He had two front teeth missing, and there was a long scar from his cheekbone to his jaw on the left side of his pockmarked face.

"*Señor,*" Javier said smoothly, "if you do not answer me, I'm afraid we are going to lose your partner, here. I will have Chico take her out into our courtyard below, stand her against the wall and shoot her." He leaned forward, opened the top of his humidor and pulled out a thick Cuban cigar. "The choice is yours...."

Gulping unsteadily, Joe rasped, "Back off, dammit. I'll tell you."

Chico grinned lethally and looked to his master.

Javier barely nodded.

Chico removed the rifle point from Akiva's temple and took a step back behind her chair once more.

"Well, Chief Warrant Officer Calhoun?" Picking up the sterling silver snippers from the right side of his desk, Rios looked over the cigar in his fingers at Joe. "Are you Native American, too?"

"I'm part Comanche," Joe spat, his anger barely restrained. He gripped the arms of the chair, breathing hard. The look of terror in Akiva's eyes when the rifle had been jabbed against her left temple almost made him lose his perspective. Under no circumstances could he let Rios know he loved Akiva. No, the older man would hold it over his head for more information.

"And your accent? Hmm," he murmured, snipping off the end of the cigar. "Southern, possibly?"

"Texas," Joe said flatly.

"Ah...of course. The Comanches were a Southwest people who came down out of the Plains and did a lot of raiding in Arizona, New Mexico and Texas." Picking up his lighter, he smiled at Joe. "So, what is this all about? Luis and I have been trying to put this together. You fly a U.S. Army gunship called the Apache. She is

Apache. You are part Comanche. What is this? The Pentagon's latest ploy? To put Indians in the cockpit on a black ops mission to try and turn around my cocaine shipments to the U.S.? I'm *very* intrigued with this new plan of theirs.''

Akiva sat very still. She and Joe still didn't know if their Apache had blown up or not. The rockets fired by Luis had rendered them unconscious before the gunship had had a chance to detonate. She tucked her lower lip between her teeth to keep herself from asking the burning question. Javier was playing them against one another. Feeling the sweat trickle down her rib cage as she sat there tensely Akiva recognized the meeting for what it was: an interrogation to find out more about them.

''We have better night vision.''

Joe glared at Akiva. Damn her! She'd purposely pulled Javier's attention back to her. His mouth thinned. In that moment, he wanted to reach out and stop her from saying more. He watched as she sat up and leaned toward the old man, who was now lighting the cigar.

Puffing contentedly, Javier studied Akiva through the white, purling smoke. Putting the lighter aside, he pulled on the cigar before answering. ''I see…well, yes, that does make sense….''

''What is the olive branch?'' Akiva demanded. ''You said if I told you the history of my weapons, you would offer us one.''

Grinning again, Javier leaned back in the chair, puffed several more times and then said, ''Ordinarily, we dispense with moles and those who would make war against us rather quickly. But over the years I've devised a different way to achieve our goals—and punish my enemies.''

Pointing to the war ax, he lifted his finger and gestured

toward Akiva. "Tomorrow, you will be given your ax back." Glancing over at Joe, he pointed to the knife on the desk. "And you will be given the bowie."

Frowning, Akiva stared at him. "What are you talking about?"

Javier looked down the length of the room toward his son, who was now smiling. Glancing at the two pilots, he said, "I am going to make you a deal that you cannot refuse. And here are my terms, which must be met. For the next three weeks, I'll be hosting a global gladiator tournament. My bullring, here at the edge of San Cristobel, becomes a combination of the Roman Colosseum and Circus Maximus. I'm sure you didn't know this, but I have set up a series of gladiator schools in Italy, the U.S., Canada, France, Germany, Peru and Mexico. People pay mucho bucks to pursue their fantasy of being a gladiator in combat."

Akiva frowned, her mind spinning. "To fight?"

"But of course," Javier chuckled. "Only, down here where I am lord of all I survey, I do not have to worry about civility or legalities. Those who take my courses come to combat one another in the sands of my bullring. And—" he smiled lethally "—I offer them blood sport. When they are done pretending to be gladiators, I offer them modern-day gladiators as the ultimate reward and entertainment."

A chill worked its way up Akiva's spine. She heard Joe move tensely beside her. Keeping her gaze on Javier, she asked in a low tone, "And how does this involve us? Is this your olive branch?"

Puffing, the smoke curling lazily about his head, Javier showed his large, perfect teeth as he smiled. "I train world-class gladiators here. You might say they are men who have refused to help me with cocaine. I give them a choice—they can become slaves who train and learn gladiatorial combat or they can die instantly, with a bullet in their brain by Chico. I'll offer you the same choice that I offer them, which is very Roman. You will fight in combat three times. If you happen to win each bout, then you will be awarded your freedom, just as the gladiators who survived fifty fights in the arena were given their freedom by the emperor of Rome."

Joe nearly choked on his rage. "You can't make us do this."

"Really?"

Akiva shot Joe a quick look. His face was set and a dull red. He was about to leap out of the chair again, his hands gripping the arms, his knuckles whitening.

"Wait!" Akiva begged him. She sat up and jerked a look at Javier, who studied them intently from beneath his gray brows. "You're saying if we go into combat, fight your gladiators or whoever they are...and if we win, you'll set us free?" Her heart was pounding. Wanting to believe Javier, but knowing better, Akiva found herself scrambling mentally for a plan. If they were loose in the bullring, there might be a way to escape at some point.

"Yes, my dear, you're correct."

"This is illegal!" Joe snarled. "You have no right to put her into such a situation. She's a woman."

"She's a warrior first," Javier said jovially. "And what's illegal about it? You're both warriors. You live to die. And that was the maxim of the gladiator—they lived and died to serve the emperor of Rome. This is no different, really. You live to die serving your country, the U.S.A. At least this way you have a chance. The other way—a bullet to the head—is no chance at all. Come, come, Warrant Officer Calhoun...you look like a sporting man. Are you going to sit there and tell me you want this beautiful woman warrior's brains splattered all over my wall? Frankly, I'm salivating over the idea of seeing both of you, as a team, coming up against my Roman soldiers in the ring. People are traveling from around the world to celebrate all things Roman for the next three weeks. They come in costume. We have parties. We have ceremonies to the old gods and goddesses…. It is as if a time machine has taken us back to the glory of Rome, in a most enjoyable way."

Akiva sat back, trying to sort through all the information. "People?"

"Yes, those who love Rome. Archeologists, both professional and amateur. Museum curators. And the thousands who are already here, camping outside my *estancia* in tents, waiting for the festivities to start tomorrow." Smiling happily, Javier said, "Your capture couldn't have come at a better time. Now they will see real warriors in action—you. I will bill you as captured Celts, Briton warriors. You are dressed in their garb already, even if you don't realize it." He chuckled and waved his hand toward them.

Akiva looked down at the rough woolen clothing she wore, feeling stunned.

"No one but us will know the truth—that you are captured U.S. Army pilots. The thousands who will jam the seats of my magnificent bullring, all in Roman costume, will simply think you are part of the show. It will do you no good to try and shout for help, for Circus Maximus brings out the howling, primitive emotions all humans have. They are going to be looking for blood sport. So don't think that you can cry out for help, for it won't do you any good. I will have guards behind the many gates in and out of the bullring, keeping an eye on you at all times."

"And if we refuse to fight?" Joe rasped, glaring at him.

Shrugging, Javier said, "Luis will be standing right behind my gilded throne, in his praetorian uniform, a pistol in his hand. If I give him the order to shoot you, he will. On the spot. Rest assured, Warrant Officer Calhoun, you'll fight for your life out there or you will be shot where you stand. It is your choice." Sitting up in his chair, his voice becoming enthusiastic again, Javier regarded Akiva. "My dear woman, you will be the hit of our event. Oh, we've had women who have trained to be gladiators, but never like this. No, you will become the star of our blood sport program. In all the years that I have been putting on this yearly event, it has always been men against men." He smiled savagely. "Now they will come up against a real woman warrior—a woman who has the blood of Apache warriors in her veins. They will get to see what it must have been like back in Rome when one of those Celtic women appeared in the arena.... Yes, this is going to be most exciting. I can hardly wait!"

Gulping, Akiva stared over at Joe. Then she looked back at Javier. "And we get the war ax and the bowie knife and that's it?"

"But of course," Javier exclaimed. "When captured enemy warriors were marched back from all points of the Roman empire, they were thrown into the arena with what they were accustomed to fighting with." His smile grew. "And I think, for your debut in the arena, you will come up against a band of Gaulish warriors, from Germania. I have five Mexican farmers who have refused to work in my cocaine factories. They have been training for six months in the art of the short sword and shield, the trident and net. Five against the two of you. That is good odds, eh?"

* * *

"I don't believe this," Joe said as he paced the length of their cold, damp cell. Night was falling. Akiva stood by the window, a pensive look on her face, her arms against her chest. "That old geezer is crazier than a loon."

"Maybe…" she murmured. She could barely see Joe, but could hear him walking back and forth in the straw that littered the hard dirt floor.

Turning to her, he said, "What are you thinking?"

"How we can turn this to our advantage and escape," Akiva said.

Sighing in frustration, Joe went over to her. He reached out and enclosed her hand in his. "He said there were a lot of doors into the bullring. Maybe we can make a run for one?"

"He mentioned that he'll have guards posted at every one," Akiva said, worried. "And every one of them will have weapons trained on us."

Joe gripped her hand. How he ached to have her fingers move across him, love him, as he wanted to love her. But now was not the time. "It sounds like Rios's blood sport features poor Mexican farmers who didn't want to be a part of his drug trade."

"Yeah," Akiva said sourly. She frowned. "I won't kill them, Joe. They're just as much pawns in this as we are. They're fighting at gunpoint, like us. They're not our enemy."

Nodding, he rasped, "We're not killing anyone. I just want to survive this with you." Worriedly, he looked down at her. The darkness was complete now; he couldn't really see her at all. But he felt the warmth of her body against his. "I'm scared. I'm scared for you. I don't want you hurt, gal…."

Snorting softly, Akiva said, "I've been thinking the same about you, Joe."

"Five to two. Bad odds."

"Yeah, but whose will to live will be the strongest? Ours. I'm not going to get hacked to death with whatever weapons they're carrying."

"All we have is your war ax and a knife."

She cut him a glance, even though she couldn't see him or his expression. "Do you know how to fight with a knife?"

"I took bayonet and rifle training in the army. Does that count?"

Chuckling at his dark humor, Akiva said, "No."

"You were taught?"

"Of course. Part of Apache warrior training."

"Ah, yes. Well, tell me all you know, because tomorrow I'm gonna have to use that knowledge to keep from bein' sliced and diced up like a beet."

Akiva couldn't help laughing softly. This was typical of Apache pilots—when things got really tense and life-threatening, their black humor surfaced. She heard Joe chuckling with her.

"My grandmother, if she were here, would be jumping up and down for joy," Akiva admitted, still smiling. "She'd tell us that the odds are even—that one good Apache warrior could take out ten white men in a heartbeat."

Raising his brows, Joe muttered, "Well, the odds are in our favor then, right?"

Mouth pursed, Akiva said, "Right." Tugging at his hand, she said, "Let's sit down. At least the old man gave us wool cloaks to go with the Celtic costumes we have to wear. If we sleep together, the cloaks around us, maybe we won't be so cold tonight."

Joe sat down in the thick, soft straw. The fragrance of it wafted upward and encircled them. They'd already laid their cloaks out. Tonight they would lie beside one another, their arms around each other, to stave off the chill and dampness. As he lay down next to Akiva Joe tried to keep desire for her out of his mind. When she'd settled next to him, facing him, he pulled one long, heavy cloak over them. He felt her head nestle in the crook of his shoulder and her hand slide across his torso. Adjusting the cloak across his shoulders, he eased it across Akiva's exposed back.

"There," he rasped against her hair. He felt the entire length of her body against his, the press of her breasts against his chest. She moved her long legs between his and they tangled comfortably beneath the cloak. Sliding his arm around her waist, he brought her fully against him.

"I'm warm already," Akiva murmured. Tiredness began to lap at her. Joe's masculine fragrance drifted into her nostrils. Closing her eyes, she smiled. "I feel like we're in a *heyoka* world, not the real world," she admitted to him in a whisper. Absorbing the sensation of Joe's strong hand stroking her back protectively, she sighed.

"Heyoka?"

"Yeah, that's a Lakota word for backward. It means chaos. Everything's turned upside down, the opposite of what you'd expect."

Akiva felt good and strong against him. Joe forced himself not to feel the burning ache in his lower body. Akiva was in his arms tonight because she trusted him, and he wasn't about to take advantage of that trust in a selfish desire to make love to her. No, right now he sensed she wanted, needed, his protection.

A feeling of deep satisfaction wove through him. It was one of the few things he could give Akiva right now—his warmth, a little solace. Because tomorrow they could die....

Chapter 13

The noise of a huge crowd rumbled through the bullring, above the cell where Akiva and Joe were being held. Akiva was sitting on the straw, tightly lacing up her knee-high leather boots, when the lock jangled and the door was pushed open. Joe was at the window and turned, his face grim. It was Luis Rios.

"Get up," Luis snarled.

Akiva looked at him and gawked. The son of the powerful drug lord was dressed in a splendid Roman uniform, replete with gold helmet topped with large ostrich plumes of bright red. Glancing over at Joe, she scrambled to her feet, her pulse skyrocketing. She had no idea what time it was, only that since dawn had filtered into their damp, cool cell, hundreds, maybe thousands of voices had begun to drift down to them.

Behind Luis were the two bald-headed guards. They, too, were in Roman uniform, except not quite as gaudy looking, and they wore AK-47s on their shoulders. So much for remaining true to history, Akiva thought sourly.

Luis adjusted the red woolen cloak that was pinned to the epaulets of his uniform. His gold metal breastplate was emblazoned with the wolf of Rome suckling the founders of the city. He wore a short sword in a leather scabbard at his side, and a dagger on the other. His eyes narrowed on them. "You're up next."

Akiva moved to Joe's side. Just his proximity made some of her fear ebb. "Where are our weapons?" she demanded hoarsely.

Grinning, Luis said, "They'll be placed out in the center of the arena. You'll be marched at gunpoint to the entrance. A guard will open the door and you will walk out to the center and pick them up." His voice lowered in warning. "If at any time you think of throwing that war ax or knife at my father or anyone in his entourage, think again." Hitching a thumb over his shoulder, he said, "These two will have a bead drawn on you at all times. Any *hint* of you throwing any weapon toward my father, and these AK-47s, which have silencers on them, will kill you. Got it?"

Joe nodded. "Yeah, we got it." His heart was pounding heavily in his chest. All morning long they'd been tense, irritable and jumpy. Who wouldn't be? This wasn't what Joe wanted at all. He wanted to tell Akiva how he felt about her, about the dreams he held for them, for their future.... But looking at the costumed enemy in front of him, and hearing the roar of the crowd, Joe felt a finality that he couldn't shake. This was real.

"The Gauls will come out. You will all turn and salute my father. Just follow along with what they say and do."

"And then?" Akiva demanded darkly.

Shrugging, Luis grinned. "You fight—to the death.

Winner walks out of the arena to fight another day.'' His eyes glittered. ''And it won't be you, I'm sure. The Gauls are all trained Latino farmers who have worked with the weapons and other gladiators for six months now. They're good at what they do. Further, they know if they kill you, they get to live to fight another day, too.''

''And I suppose,'' Akiva said acidly, ''that means they get the lucky-three contract, too? If they survive three times in the ring, they go home?''

Luis bowed slightly to her. ''Yes, of course.''

''Somehow, I don't trust you or your father to be good at your word.''

A roar from the crowd rolled down the dimly lit corridor.

''I don't care what you think.'' Luis moved out of the cell and into the hallway. ''For your information, all the other events are not to the death. My father has this rule that if one gladiator gets wounded, pulls a muscle or is in some way incapacitated, the fighting stops. You, however, have been billed to the death. There is no stopping the fight after it begins. If you refuse to fight, you'll be shot. You either do the job right or you're dead—your choice. If the crowd sees some of you killed, we will announce that it was actors pretending. They will believe it. Now, get out there. Now!''

Joe moved out first. He wanted to put his fist into Luis's smirking face, but didn't dare. Akiva followed at his heels.

The corridor was dimly lit, wide and damp. A breeze blew through it. Up ahead, Joe saw a wooden gate, at least five feet tall. A guard in Roman costume stood at it, an AK-47 in hand. The ignorant crowd beyond, all lovers of Roman reenactments, would never know the truth, Joe realized. Wiping his mouth with the back of his hand, he tried to steady his emotions. His worry for Akiva was paramount. In the air, she had no equal; that was a fact. But on the ground? In a deadly fight like this?

Up ahead, shouting of the crowds dropped and a hush fell over the arena. The guard jerked his arm toward them.

"You're next!" he shouted, and he pulled open one of the two doors.

Sunlight struck Joe as he stepped into the arena, blinding him. Instantly, he put up his hand to shade his squinting eyes. He saw a chariot drawn by two black horses being driven out another gate across from them. Several other people, reenactors, he supposed, straggled after the chariot, shields and spears in hand. As he looked around, his mouth fell open. The bullring was huge, with at least six levels to it. There were probably three thousand people in Roman costumes in the stands!

Akiva moved to his side, her stride matching his. She looked back. As the guards closed the gate, she saw the AK-47s leveled at them. All her senses became acute as she began to feel adrenaline starting to pulse through her bloodstream.

"This is incredible," Joe rasped as he spotted their weapons lying in the center of the arena. The golden sand was deep and their footing was uncertain because of it.

Akiva looked around. "Yeah. Who would've thought? Look at the old man. He looks like Caesar himself up there."

Joe saw a white canopy over a dais on the first level of the bullring. Beneath it was Javier Rios. Dressed exactly like a Roman emperor, he was wearing a crisp white toga with a purple hem, with a wreath of olive branches around his head. A group of mean-looking guards in Roman costume surrounded his gold chair. There were women there, too—beautiful ones dressed in colorful gowns.

Looking around, Akiva said, "There're four entrance-exit points. Guards at each."

Joe nodded and slowed. He reached down, and picked up the war ax and handed it to Akiva. Taking the knife, he saw that the scabbard was missing. It was a huge knife, the blade long, nicked and made of steel. The handle had leather wrapped around it, making it easier to hold. Leather long ago darkened by sweat.

Amazed by all the cheering and screaming, Akiva turned slowly. People were shouting and calling to them. Some women waved scarves and others threw flowers toward them. Akiva's heart was pounding hard in her body. She turned and faced Joe, who had a look of awe in his eyes as he, too, surveyed the crowd.

"Listen, whatever happens, I'm *not* killing these guys. They're just farmers who have the fear of God put in them," Akiva reaffirmed. "I'm a warrior. I don't fight farmers."

Nodding, Joe said, "Gal, if they come at you, you're gonna have to defend yourself. And they're under the gun, too. If they don't kill us, they're going back to their farms in wooden coffins."

Nostrils flaring, Akiva looked around. "Here they come…"

Suddenly, a dozen horns blasted across the arena, and the crowd quieted instantly. Akiva saw five men coming toward them from another gate. She didn't know much about Roman history, but she vaguely recalled that Gaul, which was modern-day France, had some of the wildest, most determined warriors and had nearly thrown off the yoke of Rome. As she eyed the men struggling across the sand, Akiva's pulse bounded.

"Farmers, hell," she muttered, stepping close to Joe. "Look at those guys. They're all built like bulls!" They moved like trained fighters to Akiva, not unsure farmers.

Joe nodded. He knew what Latino farmers looked like: they were usually short, as well as lean and hard from all the physical work they did daily. But these men, all at least six feet tall, with rippling muscles, were not farmers. "They've lied to us," he growled angrily. "They purposely misled us."

Snorting, Akiva moved restlessly, her hand tightening on the handle of the war ax. "So what's new? Why should we believe *anything* Rios tells us? The bastard…"

Joe watched the men march toward them in a broken line, his mouth flattening. They wore bullet-shaped helmets on their heads, carried round shields made of wood, with brass crosses on each. Three had swords, and the other two had a rope net in one hand, a wicked looking trident in the other.

"I think Rios lied to lull us into thinking these five good ole boys were going to be easy to fight."

Taking a deep breath, Akiva studied them intently. "Well, I've changed my mind. Those dudes are out to take us down."

"Yeah…" And Joe moved between her and the five, who were now forming a line and facing the so-called Roman emperor.

Akiva glared up at Rios, who was a good three hundred feet away. She itched to throw the war ax at the old man and split his skull open. And she could do it. The risk wouldn't be worth it, however, because they'd be shot and killed. But did they have a chance otherwise? Glancing down the line that had formed, Akiva saw the Gauls looking at them with lethal regard. Glaring back, she saw them raise their right hands, fist closed, in a salute to Rios.

"We who are about to die salute you," the five boomed out in deep voices to their emperor.

Joe refused to raise his hand. He saw that Akiva, who stood nearby, didn't, either. Her chin jutted out in utter rebellion. Good for her.

His mind whirled. How could they take on five well-trained men, who were probably Rios's guards in disguise? They ranged in height from six to six foot five inches. And they were all built like powerhouses, their muscles heavy and well formed. That meant they worked out with heavy weights at a gym with great regularity. The clothes they wore were similar to his and Akiva's, except their leggings were crisscrossed with strips of white cotton material from their ankles to their thighs and they carried protective shields. Joe's anger began to simmer and push away some of his fear. They didn't stand a chance against these men.

Javier stood up and raised his hand. The crowd quieted.

"Friends, Romans, countrymen," he began, his voice echoing around the bullring. "Lend me your ears!"

A wild cheer went up, rippling through the reenactors.

"We have a woman gladiator! She is a Celt!"

Another roar went up and echoed wildly around the ring.

Javier smiled triumphantly. "Today, she and her companion go up against five Gauls, the best of Germania. It is a fight to the death! You will now see a *real* Circus Maximus or Colosseum event. When one of them falls, give a thumbs-up or thumbs-down. It is up to you as to who lives and dies in the sands this day! Let the fight begin!'' And he threw a red rose outward. It landed on the gold sands just inside the arena.

Akiva glanced at Joe. "Did I tell you I was kick-box champion at Fort Rucker when I was going through flight training?''

He shook his head and watched as the five lowered their arms. "No…you didn't. Did I tell you I'm a black belt in karate?''

She grinned tightly as she backed away, her eyes on the Gauls. "No…you didn't." Gripping the war ax hard in her right hand, she said, "Did I tell you that Apaches fight dirty?''

Joe's mouth twitched. "No, but I'm all ears…."

"Watch me…." And Akiva suddenly leaned down, scooped up a handful of sand and lunged forward. A war cry tore from her contorted lips. She launched herself at the biggest, closest Gaul, who had a sword in his right hand and a shield in his left. Within feet of him, she threw the sand into his face.

The Gaul shouted and lifted his sword hand to his eyes, unable to see.

In one smooth, unbroken motion, at great speed, Akiva leaped off the ground, both booted feet aimed directly at the Gaul, who was peddling backward, off balance.

Her boots smashed into the man's upper chest and neck.

Satisfaction burned through Akiva as she heard the man choke. She knew without a doubt she'd damaged his windpipe with the violent, well-aimed kick. Rolling to the side, she heard shouts of anger all around her.

The fight had begun.

Joe didn't waste a second as he saw Akiva attack the biggest Gaul. Following her lead, he scooped up sand and hurled it into the eyes of the second Gaul, who was shrieking and running at him, his sword raised high. Instantly, the man shouted and lost his balance on the slippery surface. With sand in his eyes, he couldn't see Joe coming.

Breathing hard, Joe jammed the heel of his boot into the man's chest. Instantly, there was a snapping, crunching sound. Joe had just broken the man's sternum, and probably some of his ribs. The Gaul groaned. The sword dropped from his hand. Joe grabbed it. Now he had a sword and a knife.

Turning, he saw another Gaul charging him, his trident extended. Out of the corner of his eye, he saw the other two going after Akiva, who was running away from them.

The Gaul threw the net at Joe. It snaked out.

Joe leaped aside, the net barely missing him. He saw the anger in the man's dark eyes. Without a net, the man had only his trident. Perspiration ran down Joe's face. His breath came in rasps. He heard the swelling roar of the crowd, but ignored it. Moving in a circle, he jerked to the right, then the left, as the Gaul jabbed outward with the forked spear.

Joe slashed downward with the short sword, each time the trident was thrust at him. The tines of the lethal weapon barely missed him. Abruptly, he jumped sideways and swung the sword forward. The blade bit savagely into the wooden handle, and with a loud *crack* the trident snapped in two.

Joe smiled lethally. The Gaul's eyes widened enormously—he knew he was in trouble. Backing off, he looked frantically around for a way to protect himself from Joe.

Joe dropped the short sword and lunged forward, delivering a series of karate strokes to the head and neck of the Gaul. The enemy went down like a felled bull, unconscious.

Jerking around, Joe looked for Akiva. There! She was running as fast as she could from the two Gauls, who pursued her at high speed.

Digging his feet into the sand, Joe sprinted toward the closest one. They were so intent on getting to Akiva that they didn't see him. *Too bad.* In a way, Joe thought, this was just like flying combat in an Apache gunship; he was coming up behind the Gaul, who had no idea he was there. Joe was the six position, the man's most vulnerable point. Joe heard the crowd screaming. It was a blood-curdling sound.

Akiva tore forward, heading for the yellow stucco wall of the bullring. She could hear the Gaul gaining on her. He was bigger and longer legged than she. That was fine. Heading directly toward the wall as she was, she knew the Gaul would think she was trapping herself. Nothing could be further from the truth. Satisfaction soared through Akiva as she heard him breathing like a bull behind her. He was so close! Gripping the ax, she measured the distance left.

Now!

With a grunt, Akiva leaped upward. Feet first, she flew straight for the wall, her knees flexed. Behind her, she heard the Gaul gasp. As soon as she felt the solid impact of her boots meeting the wall, she doubled up, tucking her body tightly.

Joe had just felled the fourth Gaul and looked up to see something that made him gasp with surprise. As he stood over the unconscious man, he saw Akiva leap upward, her hair flying behind her. She hit the wall with her boots and then did a back flip high in the air. As she flipped, Akiva went up and over the head of the startled Gaul, landing heavily but solidly on her feet behind him.

The Gaul slammed into the wall. Grunting in pain, his head bloodied, he turned and lifted his shield and sword. Too late! The look of pure savagery and triumph on Akiva's face was very real. Her Apache war cry carried around the arena, where the people were jumping up and down, shouting with enthusiasm.

Joe stood breathing hard, hunkered over the Gaul as he watched Akiva finish off the last of their enemy. The instant she'd landed on her feet, she'd leaped up again, her boots aimed directly at the Gaul's head. In seconds, her powerful assault had smashed him back into the wall. The Gaul groaned. He sagged and slid to the ground, dropping his weapons.

Akiva turned, breathing hard. Wiping her mouth with the sleeve of her tunic, she saw Joe standing near the center, a wide grin on his face. Turning, she made sure all five Gauls were disabled and no longer a threat to them. When she saw that they lay unconscious, scattered around the arena, she walked slowly toward Joe, the shouts and cries of the crowd raining down upon her. She saw the triumph and pride in his eyes. Grinning tightly, Akiva looked toward the gate they'd come out. Luis was there, gesturing for them to come out. Javier was standing with his thumb up, indicating that all should live. The people's shouts confirmed it.

"You okay?" Akiva shouted over the roar.

Joe nodded. "Yeah. You?"

"Fine." She looked around. "Not bad for two Apache pilots, eh?"

Laughing deeply, Joe put his arm around Akiva's shoulders. The crowd's roar increased. Pulling her to him, he embraced her hard, once, and let her go. Sweat was running down her face. Her expression was taut and he saw the warrior in her now as never before.

"We'd better lay these weapons down or Luis will nail us," he told her.

Nodding, Akiva set the war ax at her feet. As she turned toward the gate, the roaring crowd kept cheering, waving scarves and throwing flowers into the arena. Joe walked at her side, his hand on her upper arm.

Her heart was pounding and the adrenaline was making her shaky. "We won...." she said, relief in her tone.

"Round one," Joe agreed. They approached the gate and it opened. Luis was standing just inside, a gold plated .45 pistol in his hand, aimed at them.

"Very good," he said smoothly. "Not exactly Roman tactics, but you did good. Now get back to your cell."

"I like how the winners are treated," Akiva said, eating wolfishly from the bowl of stew she'd been given. Sitting with Joe in a clean room at the main *estancia,* where they'd been moved from their cell once darkness had fallen, Akiva, who was starving, was glad for the meal. Javier Rios had also allowed them to take hot showers and don clean clothes. And although the clothes were the same warrior costume she'd worn earlier, Akiva luxuriated in the unexpected gift Javier Rios had bestowed upon them. They sat at a polished mahogany table. There was a tropical fruit salad available, along with fragrant black Colombian coffee and yeast rolls in a basket. To Akiva, it was a feast.

Joe ate like a starved wolf, also. He knew that food was fuel, and that they'd need it. Tomorrow, Luis had informed them as he'd brought them to the *estancia,* they would fight again. Round two.

Looking up at Akiva, who sat opposite him, her hair recently washed, Joe marveled at how beautiful she was. As he buttered a hot roll, he said, "I was impressed with your kick-boxing. You never told me you were a champion.''

"You never asked."

Chuckling, he bit into the roll with a groan of satisfaction. "At least he's feeding us right."

"Yeah, no kidding." Akiva reached for another roll, tore it open and slathered it with butter. The room was small and well appointed. It was a drawing room of sorts, with French windows that looked out over the plaza below, where there was a huge, splashing fountain. She knew the room was probably bugged. Maybe it even had a camera or two hidden in it. Akiva wasn't about to talk to Joe about anything of importance. Knowing Javier Rios, he was probably watching them. The man was a voyeuristic lunatic.

They had just finished their meal when Javier entered with his two bald guards. He was still in his emperor's clothing, the circle of olive leaves crowning his head.

"Ahh, you have become the talk of the Circus Maximus," he said genially in greeting. Holding the white toga folds on his left arm, he raised his right hand with a flourish. "This is your reward. Tonight, you will sleep in a special room reserved for gladiators who have won."

Akiva scowled, but said nothing. She kept eating wolfishly, for she didn't trust Javier to continue to provide food for them. He could just as well starve them tomorrow.

"You said if we won three times in a row, you'd let us go," Joe reminded him.

"As emperor of Rome, my word is law," he assured them jovially. He gave Akiva a warm look. "And you, my dear, surpass even my greatest expectations."

Joe nudged her leg with his toes beneath the table. He saw anger in Akiva's eyes as she lifted her head, spoon in hand. Knowing her as he did, Joe figured she was going to deliver a nasty comment. Right now, they couldn't afford to antagonize Javier. Maybe this room where Javier would be putting them was one they could escape from. As Joe's toe grazed her leg, she looked up at him. He gave her a silent look of caution.

"I just want you to stick to your promise," she told Javier.

Chuckling, he neatly rearranged the folds of his toga that hung over his arm. "Oh, not to worry, my dear, I will. Well, I must go. We're having a Dionysus party tonight, filled with wine, women, song and who knows what else? Romans were so decadent. That's what I love about them. They worked hard, but they played hard, too." His eyes glimmered. "Enjoy yourselves tonight. Get a good night's sleep. At noon tomorrow, you will take on my charioteers...."

Frowning, Akiva waited until the entourage left and the door was closed and locked behind them. Taking another roll, she tore it open. "Charioteers?"

"Chariots drawn by horses," Joe said unhappily. He stopped eating, his appetite gone. "How will the two of us combat that?"

Snorting softly, Akiva gave him a narrow-eyed glance. "You said you rode when you were a kid?"

"Yeah. And was a member at the stables at Fort Rucker. I rode every day, when I got the chance." He smiled a little. "Until I came here—" He stopped abruptly, realizing that the room was probably bugged. Clearing his throat, he said, "Yeah, I can throw my leg over a horse and stay on, if that's what you're asking."

"Good. Tomorrow is more to my liking. Horses are something that can't always be controlled." And she smiled a jaguar smile.

Chapter 14

"Are you ready?" Joe asked Akiva in a low tone. They had been allowed to stay in the main *estancia* for a while after they'd eaten, much to their surprise. Then Chico, the guard, had led them to a basement room with bars on the only window. There were two beds, a toilet and two fresh costumes for them to wear the coming day.

Akiva sat on the edge of her bed as she finished lacing up her leather boots. Her hair was loose and free about her shoulders; the third braid hung from the center part, near her brow and she had faithfully tied her scarf about her head. Joe came and sat down next to her, his solid presence reassuring to her. She gave him what she hoped was a smile. Searching his gray eyes, she reached out and slid her hand into his.

"No. I'm scared."

"Makes two of us," he muttered, looking down at her long, strong fingers as they laced through his. With his other hand, he covered them in a caress. Though they were unable to find evidence last night, both felt they were being continually photographed by a hidden camera and recorded by a microphone. For that reason, they spoke in whispers.

"Listen," Joe said, his lips near her ear, "did you see that road leading out of the villa when they walked us from the bullring to the main hacienda?"

Nodding, Akiva said, "Yeah, I saw it. Right now, it's cluttered with cars of fans coming into the place. There are hundreds of tents on either side. Looks like a huge tent party."

"Right." Joe compressed his lips and then said, "We're near San Cristobel. Luis said as much. How close, I don't know. We haven't been let out to see much of anything."

"Are you thinking what I'm thinking? That if we can somehow escape the ring today, we can make it to that little town?"

"You got it, gal." He slid her a warm look. How beautiful Akiva looked, her dark hair flowing like black lava across her proud shoulders and cascading down around her breasts. The woolen tunic she wore today was black. He wondered if that was an omen. His body responded strongly as she met his gaze with her golden eyes. Automatically, her lips parted, and he wanted to kiss her breathless. Would he ever be able to?

"There's an airport at San Cristobel," Joe rasped softly near her ear. "That's where Luis keeps his helicopter fleet."

Nodding, Akiva turned, her lips brushing his cheek. Inhaling his male fragrance, she added, "We're on the same wavelength. If we can make it to the airport, we can steal one of his birds and get the hell out of Dodge."

Grinning, Joe nodded. "You got it, gal." He patted her hand and then released it.

"The question is how?"

Shrugging, he said, "I dunno. We're gonna have to wait for the opportunity."

Rolling her eyes, Akiva rasped, "Rios is putting us up against chariots."

Joe met and held her angry stare. "Just come out firing like you did yesterday, and we've got a chance." His smile was wolfish. "Kick-box champion. That's one helluva title."

"Yeah? Well, you weren't too shabby in the clutch yesterday, either." She tapped his large knuckles, which were thick and tough from his karate training. A black belt in the discipline wasn't easy to obtain, she knew.

"We're gonna need our wits about us today. We'll have to look for *any* break we can create. Rios's goons are gonna have their sights on us, for sure."

Rubbing her brow, Akiva agreed. There was a clock on the stand between the twin beds where they'd slept. It was almost noon. Scowling, she said, "Listen, if only one of us makes it, that's okay, too. If we make a break for it, Joe, and only one of us can get out, then do it."

Eyes glittering, Joe whispered harshly, "No way, gal. It's both of us or I'm sticking around." His mouth tightened as he held her stormy stare. "I'm not leavin' you behind. I'll die here first." And he would.

Shaken by the rough emotion in his tone, Akiva had no time to respond. The door was flung open. Chico stood there, the AK-47 pointed at them.

"Get up! It's show time."

Joe nailed her with a lethal look. As he rose from her side, he said harshly in a low voice, "It's together or nothing..." and he moved toward the door. Chico placed a pair of handcuffs on him, which became hidden by the tunic sleeves when Joe lowered his arms. To the reen-actors lining the hillsides of the *estancia,* it would look like they were just going for a walk. The AK-47 was well hidden, hung on a shoulder strap beneath the red woolen cloak Chico wore over his centurion's uniform.

Akiva stood next to Joe and held out her hands to be cuffed. She saw two other Roman soldiers standing be-hind Chico, both just as big and goonish as he was. There was no way she and Joe could try and make an escape; they'd be gunned down in the hall before they ever reached the exit.

"Let's go," Chico growled, pushing her and then Joe ahead of him. "You got three thousand people salivating for your return performance. You're famous out there." And he chuckled darkly.

The roar of the crowd was deafening as Akiva and Joe walked slowly out to the center of the arena once again. Colorful scarves were raised and waved like flags. More flowers were tossed toward them. Neither responded as they walked grimly toward their meager weapons, which lay on the sand before them.

Akiva saw Javier Rios looking like a Roman emperor in his glorious gold chair, the praetorian guards surround-ing him, grim and at attention, a bevy of young beauties dressed in revealing gowns nearby. She checked the exits in the arena; all four had Roman guards at them.

Joe scooped up their weapons and handed her the ax. His heart began a slow pounding as the horns sounded and echoed across the arena.

Akiva saw one massive gate, then a second, then a third open. Out of each came a red-and-gold chariot drawn by two horses. There was a driver in each, along with another Roman soldier who carried a spear or bow and arrow.

Turning, Akiva saw Joe's face. His expression was hard and assessing.

The chariots streamed into the arena, the drivers using whips to encourage the horses to gallop around the circumference. The crowd went wild, their enthusiastic screams deafening.

Akiva watched the chariots. Backing up against Joe's back, she shouted, "They aren't gonna be able to hit a damn thing riding in those chariots. Their aim will be off."

"Yeah," he shouted. "They're leaving one gate open. See it?"

Akiva turned. The west gate was standing open. The guard was about ten feet inside, holding the huge door open. "Yeah. I wonder why?"

Before Joe could speculate, he saw four mounted soldiers come galloping through the gate into the arena.

"Damn!"

Akiva nodded. She gripped the war ax. Sending a prayer to her great-great-grandmother, she pleaded for help, for strength as she watched the cadre of Roman cavalry, riding in pairs, speed past the slower moving chariots. Each rider had a heavy, rectangular leather shield, three feet long and two feet wide, to contend with. Each had a short sword, but it was sheathed. Akiva noted that trying to control the excited horses, which were decked out in bright red-and-gold blankets and saddles, was a major job. The riders had to use their right hands to control their fractious, jumpy mounts, which obviously weren't use to the high level of noise or the arena itself.

"The gate's stayin' open," Joe called as he slowly began to turn, the knife held low and close to his body.

Heart pounding, he watched the cavalry speed wildly around the arena. The crowd cheered long and lustily.

"Yeah!" Akiva shouted. Sweat wound down her rib cage. All her attention was focused on the lead Roman, riding a big, rangy black gelding about sixteen hands tall. The horse was raw-boned, fractious and wild-eyed, and the rider was having a hell of a time keeping him at a canter instead of an out-of-control gallop.

"If we can only get to that gate…" Joe shouted. The crowd went into a frenzy as the first chariot peeled off and came directly at them.

"Yes!" Akiva watched the team of white horses send up a spray of sand as the driver wrenched them toward the center, where they stood. "Joe?"

"Yeah?" He watched a second chariot peel off and follow the first toward them. It was like watching slow-moving aircraft lumbering toward them.

"Follow my lead. We need something to ride!" Akiva dug the toes of her boots into the sand and lunged toward the first chariot.

The crowd roared. The sound became rolling thunder.

Akiva headed at an angle toward the nearest white horse. She saw the driver's angry gaze pinned on her as she sprinted forward. The soldier with the spear was being bounced around so badly that he couldn't hope for an accurate strike.

Long hair flying behind her like an ebony banner, Akiva took a huge breath into her lungs. The horses were galloping wildly toward her. Fifteen feet. Ten…five…

Her Apache war cry split the air, drowned out by the lustily cheering crowds. The horses, however, heard the high-pitched scream. The nearest white gelding shied to the right, bumping into its teammate and throwing both horses off stride. The chariot lifted up on one wheel. The Roman with the spear tumbled out.

Reaching out, Akiva saw that neither horse had on blinders, so it was easy to make them shy when something jumped at them. Her fingers caught the leather of the nearest rein. In one smooth motion, she leaped upward.

Joe watched Akiva successfully leap upon the back of the white horse as he ran toward the second chariot. The crowd went wild. Now it was his turn. He wasn't at all sure he could do the same thing; he had never trained to mount a running horse, but he was going to try.

Akiva's legs wrapped around the horse's sweaty barrel. She heard the driver behind her curse. With her war ax, she twisted around and hacked at the traces. Leather flew in all directions as the blade bit deeply into it. If she could cut this horse away, then she had a mount.

The crowd was screaming and shouting.

The whip, wielded by the driver, came down again and again on her head and shoulders as she rode the charging, bucking horse. Her ax bit again and again into the leather. Gasping, Akiva saw the trace finally break. Twisting back around, she grabbed both reins to the horse's mouth and jerked him to the left, into two Roman cavalrymen coming straight for her.

The horse grunted as she dug her heels deeply into his sides. Behind her, she heard the charioteer shout. Glancing briefly over her shoulder, she saw the chariot flip, the driver thrown out. The other horse ran wildly, dragging the upside down chariot across the arena like a plow.

There was no time to celebrate. Akiva ran her wild-eyed mount directly into the two charging cavalry soldiers. Both were bearing down on her with abandon, their heavy, cumbersome shields throwing them off balance.

Smiling to herself, Akiva leaned low on the horse's neck, the white mane stinging her perspiring face. Her eyes narrowed as she guided the horse directly at them. This was ''sky chicken'' all over again—played on the ground and not in a helicopter. Bracing herself, she prepared to slam into the careening, charging Romans.

At the last second, the soldier on the bay horse peeled off to the left. Akiva hissed, and as the man on the rangy black gelding whipped by her, she lifted her booted foot and snapped it outward. The heel of her boot connected with the soldier's hip, and he yelped. In seconds, he'd tumbled off the horse. His shield flipped up into the air, turning over and over before it plunged into the sand, as he struck the ground face first, knocked out.

Good!

Akiva turned her horse around and jerked it to a halt. Joe? Where was Joe? Breathing hard, she rapidly scanned the arena. To her surprise, Joe was still on the ground. Two of the chariots were closing in on him. Akiva saw the other two Romans on their mounts turning to charge her.

''Hiyyaa!'' she shrieked at her jumpy, dancing mount.

The white gelding shot forward. Akiva raced across the arena toward Joe. Who would reach him first? She hunkered low on the animal's neck, urging every ounce of strength out of his pumping hindquarters.

Joe turned as he heard Akiva's voice. His eyes widened. She swung her horse at almost a ninety-degree angle around him, right in front of the oncoming chariot. As the horse turned and brushed past, she shot out her hand. In an instant, Joe realized what she was doing. Thrusting out his own hand, he gripped her fingers and held on. With a jerk, she pulled him up, up, and in a

moment he was throwing his leg across her mount, settling behind her.

"Hold on!" Akiva shouted. Joe put his arms around
her waist while she jammed her boots into the white gelding's flanks. The chariot was almost on top of them. A
spear was thrown. It landed within inches of the fleeing
white steed, which was now laboring mightily with two
people on its back.

Joe clamped his legs around the heavily breathing animal. Jerking his head to the right and left, he saw the
cavalry bearing down on them. Akiva was riding the
horse for all it was worth. The roar and clamor echoed
around the arena, making it impossible to talk. He saw
her heading for the riderless black horse that was trotting
near the wall.

"Behind!" he screamed at her. A Roman on a palomino was closing the distance between them. The soldier
had dispensed with his shield and was guiding the horse
with his left hand. In his right was a short sword—up-
raised.

Akiva jerked a look to the right. She saw the palomino
approaching. "Hold on!"

Joe grunted and clung to Akiva. He felt the horse ca-
reen to the right—right in front of the charging palomino.
Collision! Everything happened in split seconds. The
white horse turned, clipping the shoulder of the charging
palomino. The soldier's sword was coming down at them.
Joe thrust his long, wicked looking bowie knife upward
to stop it. Metal bit into metal. And then the palomino
went down, the Roman soldier thrown over its head,
screaming as he smashed into the wall.

"Whoa!" Akiva shrilled at the horse. The white horse
practically skidded on its rear as she hauled back on the
reins.

"Joe! Grab the palomino!"

He slid off and ran for the horse, which was standing there, dazed. Luckily for him, there was a saddle on it, unlike Akiva's steed. Grabbing the reins, he was quickly mounted.

The crowd's roar was now wild. He turned the horse around. Akiva had trotted over to the rangy black and literally leaped off the white horse, flush onto the stronger mount. Her face was savage looking, her eyes slitted with lethal ferocity. Grinning, Joe knew they had a chance to survive.

"Go after that chariot!" Akiva shouted, raising her war ax.

Joe saw the plan. He watched as the last Roman soldier, on a brown-and-white pinto, kept his distance from them. The man probably didn't want to end up like his comrades. Digging his heels into his mount, Joe followed Akiva as she sped across the sands of the arena toward the chariot, which was heading for the open gate. Her hair flew behind her as she forced the black to a wild ground-eating gallop in pursuit of it.

The other chariot was at the far end of the arena, along with the last cavalry soldier. Joe whipped his mount across the withers with the leather reins. Hunkering down, he closed the gap on Akiva.

The charioteer's eyes were huge as they bore down on him, and the man screamed at his partner to shoot at them. But the other man was fumbling badly with his bow and arrow. The sands of the arena had been dug up, creating deep ruts. Hitting bump after bump, the chariot was being tossed around like a bobbin on the surface of the ocean.

Akiva raced her horse up alongside the chariot. She was breathing hard, and sweat drenched her straining body, but she didn't hesitate for an instant. Giving a throaty war cry, she saw the driver's eyes bulge with terror. He held up his hand to try and avoid the oncoming ax as it slashed downward. As he released the reins, the horses, seeing the open gate, headed directly for it. The chariot lurched violently as the horses made the unexpected turn, throwing out both passengers.

Akiva followed the careening chariot now speeding down the wide tunnel. Jerking a look over her shoulder, she saw Joe riding in hot pursuit, no more than twenty feet behind her. She saw the gleam of triumph on his sweaty, hard features. In his hand, he held the bowie knife ready—just in case. Her war ax was now situated in her waist belt.

The chariot swayed drunkenly from side to side, scattering the few people in the tunnel. The horses were panicked. Every time the hub of a wheel struck the wall, sparks flew.

Akiva saw the opening at the other end. She restrained her charging horse and kept him just behind the chariot. There were no Roman guards there, only surprised fans. They, too, scattered like a flock of startled birds as the wild-eyed, runaway horses thundered at them.

Joe pulled alongside Akiva. She pointed to the opening. "Our freedom!"

"Let's get the hell outta here!" he shouted, his smile tight with triumph.

As the chariot and horses came charging out of the tunnel, Akiva saw the road—the only road that led in and out of Javier Rios's estate. Laying the leather to the black gelding's sweaty withers, she flattened herself on his back.

"Stay down!" she shouted to Joe, "and follow me!"

They galloped on, sending people flying in all directions. As Joe galloped past them, bringing up the rear, he twisted his head back toward the bullring. People thought this was an act, apparently. They were cheering and waving them on. He saw no guards…not yet.

They galloped down the dirt road, weaving around arriving cars, trucks and recreational vehicles. On either side was a huge tent city, spread out on the gentle green slopes around the bullring. Joe kept his attention on Akiva, who was pushing the huge black horse relentlessly. The animal was covered with sweat, flecks of foam flying from his neck and flanks. She was riding him hard, and he saw her objective. Down at the base of the hill, the road forked in a T.

Remembering the map, he whipped his horse alongside hers once more as they raced through the oncoming traffic. Drivers kept screeching to a halt when they saw them, gawking out their windows. Some waved. Others smiled. They all thought this was part of the reenactment excitement.

"Go to the left!" Joe shouted at her. He jabbed his hand in that direction. "San Cristobel is that way!"

Nodding, Akiva remained in perfect rhythm with her black gelding. The horse was powerful—a Thoroughbred with long, sturdy legs. Though he was wild-eyed, with foam streaming out his open mouth as Akiva sawed on the snaffle bit, he followed her directions flawlessly as she guided him down the last green hill and to the left.

There was a lot of traffic on the dirt road. Akiva wanted to reserve the horse's energy as much as she could, understanding that Rios would be after them shortly. The snarled traffic would hinder Rios's men from getting to them, however. No enemy could catch up with them in this kind of traffic—not in a car. So unless he had a helo at the *estancia,* they were going to get away, Akiva realized with soaring confidence.

Triumph swept through her as Joe pushed his mount abreast her own. They rode hard and close, their legs sometimes brushing. The country around them was flat and agricultural. Up ahead, Akiva could see the small town, which lay in a shallow valley.

"See it?" Joe shouted, jabbing his hand to the right.

"Yes! The airport!"

He grinned. It was a brief, tight grin.

Akiva rode the horse like she was part of the animal. Joe could see how all her warrior training as a child was paying off. The black was a big, stubborn animal, but he gave up all thought of battle under Akiva's knowledge-able hand. She pushed the animal to his limits, and his long stride ate up miles of the rutted road, the dust rising in clouds behind them.

Joe watched in awe as Akiva bent forward over the animal's neck. Her hair was flying across her shoulders, her body hunched and rhythmic as she squeezed every ounce of power from the black horse, and he couldn't help but marvel at her many natural abilities.

He had no idea how much time had elapsed as they galloped their winded mounts down the hill and into the bowl-shaped valley of San Cristobel. The sun was no longer above them. It might be around 1300, Joe thought, as he followed Akiva along the roadside. Cars would slow down or stop as they approached. That was good, because Joe didn't want to get hit. His legs were tiring, and he wasn't riding well. At least he could still hang on.

As they swept off the main road and over a green, grassy hillside toward the tiny airport, Joe could see four helicopters there. He was sure they belonged to the Rioses. Were there guards posted? Scanning the area, he saw only a farmer in a wide-brimmed straw hat near one of the two airport buildings.

Worried, Joe pulled alongside Akiva. "We gotta watch for guards!"

Nodding, she shouted, "You go around the buildings. I'll ride up to that first helo."

"Right."

Akiva dug her heels into her horse's heaving flanks as they galloped down the hill. Once on the hard dirt surface of the airport grounds, she slapped the reins against his wet sides and headed directly for a Bell helicopter. Though she scanned the area, she saw no guards. To her left, she saw Joe circling the buildings to make sure they were safe.

"Whoa!" she shouted, and pulled hard on the reins. The black skidded to a halt within three feet of the helicopter. Akiva leaped off. She slapped the animal on the rump, and, startled, the gelding trotted away.

Akiva ran forward, praying that the keys to the helo were there. As she jerked open the door, she saw them.

"Yes!" she shouted. Quickly, she untied the tether on the blades and threw the nylon rope to the ground. Climbing in, she settled herself in the seat. Instantly, the blades began to turn as she fired up the engines on the ship. Lifting her head, she saw Joe ride around a corner of one building. There was relief on his face. The horse leaped sideways as it saw the helicopter and Joe tumbled off. He quickly got to his feet and sprinted toward her.

Jerking the door open, he leaped in. He was covered with dust.

"Fuel?" he demanded, slamming it shut.

"Full tank. We're in business," Akiva growled triumphantly. She took the cyclic and collective in her hands. Giving him a tight grin, she said, "We're outta here, Calhoun. Hold on. We're makin' a run for the border!'' using the slang to indicate to him that they needed to get the hell out of there as fast as they could and head back to their covert base.

Chapter 15

"I think we should maintain radio silence," Joe told her over the helicopter intercom. They were twenty miles south of San Cristobel, and he was worriedly looking back toward the town to see if any other helicopters were taking off after them. So far, so good; there was no indication that Luis Rios and his henchmen were getting ready to chase them down.

Wiping his mouth, sweat still running off his face, Joe glanced over at Akiva. Her profile was set and serious, her mouth curved downward as she guided the helicopter swiftly at treetop level.

"No, we need to stay silent," she agreed.

Joe took a shaky breath and tightened the straps of his seat harness. "Heck of a day in the arena, wouldn't you say?" He cut her a quick glance. He saw Akiva's expression thaw momentarily.

"Yeah. It reminded me of my trials to get my third braid."

"Javier Rios is crazy."

"Maybe," Akiva muttered. "He's got the perfect setup there. He's seen as a philanthropist, he's got a global reenactors thing going on…. People don't have a clue what he really is underneath—a drug trafficker." She kept glancing at the instruments. The helicopter was shaking around her, and it felt good. Comforting. Being back in the air was where Akiva belonged. Still, her heart was pounding in her chest and fear was making her adrenaline run high. They weren't safe yet, not by a long shot.

"Isn't that the truth?" Joe drawled. He kept twisting around and checking the sky out behind them. Luis would get airborne as soon as he could make his way to the airport. Judging from the snarled traffic, Joe knew it would take a while.

"I'm heading back to Alpha," Akiva told him.

"Yes. But we don't know who'll be there. It's possible that Major Stevenson yanked the plug on the black ops when we didn't show up. I'm sure the women there contacted the main base to let them know we never came home."

"Yeah, and with Sat Intel," Akiva murmured, "they'd see what was left of that twenty-million-dollar Apache I blew up."

Reaching out, Joe pulled the heavy curtain of hair away from Akiva's drawn face. Instantly, her lips parted. An incredible love for her welled up through his chest, momentarily chasing away the fear tunneling through him. "If we make it home, I'm askin' Major Stevenson for some leave. You and I deserve some time alone… together."

Just the brush of his fingers along her hair sent prickles of pleasure across her cheek and neck. Akiva gave him a quick glance. She saw the smoky look in Joe's gray eyes. "You know what? You're the bravest person I've ever met. I was so glad you were with me…. We were a team. And we got out of there because of what we did—together."

Joe rested his hand on her shoulder, atop the ebony blanket of her thick, soft hair. "We're alive because we threw whatever prejudices we had aside, gal. And you trusted me. That's what really got us out of that fire. Trust."

Holding his warm gaze, Akiva managed a shaky smile. Every mile between them and Luis made her relax just a little more. "Trust? Yeah, a big hurdle for me. But you helped me overcome it, Joe. And yes, I'd sure like some time off. I'd like to spend it with you, somewhere quiet and peaceful…."

When they were within two miles of Alpha, Joe made a call to the base. He'd chosen a civilian channel that was least likely to be picked up or used. If Luis Rios's men were in the air, he and Akiva hadn't seen them. Joe acutely missed the Apache's wonderful radar equipment, which could spot aircraft thirty miles away.

As Akiva flew straight for the hole in the jungle, he called again.

"This is Alpha. Over," came a female voice over the line.

Joe smiled at Akiva. "Hey! That's Major Stevenson's voice! She must have flown in!"

Akiva grinned broadly. She brought the helo into a hover and then began to descend. "Our luck's changing!"

Joe radioed back and filled Major Stevenson in on their unexpected arrival. He didn't want to risk getting picked up over the airwaves by Rios. Sitting in the helo, Akiva smoothly guided the bird down under the canopy. Once there, she headed toward the dirt strip. On their final approach, Joe saw two black, unmarked Apache helicopters sitting just outside the hangar. His heart rose with joy. Gripping Akiva's shoulder, he rasped unsteadily, "We're home. Everything's gonna be okay now…"

A huge wave of emotion, mostly relief, broke through Akiva's intense focus as she sat the helicopter down two rotor lengths away from the familiar Apache. She nodded. "Yeah…home—" Her voice broke. Choking back a lump forming in her throat, she shut off the engine and waited.

Out the Plexiglas window, she saw both majors, Maya and Dane. Akiva knew she'd left the base in the hands of her X.O., Dallas Klein, so that she could be here. Wild Woman was there, too, the red streaks in her blond hair standing out like flames. So was Cam and Ana. Grinning, Akiva also saw Sergeant Paredes, the Angel of Death, beside them. She was waving her hand with joy. Akiva lifted hers in return.

"They look so good to me," she whispered, taking off the headset and putting it between the two seats. "I didn't realize how much I missed them until just now…."

Joe laughed. "Yeah, they're a sight for sore eyes, that's for sure. Come on, let's go meet them and fill them in on our wild ride."

Akiva hurriedly opened the door and got out once the rotors stopped spinning. In the late afternoon light, she saw all her friends, dressed in their black, body-fitting uniforms, move toward them in unison. The relief was evident on their smiling faces. As Joe dropped to the ground beside her, Akiva laughed. It was a laugh of sheer, unadulterated relief—of joy—that they were alive.

Wild Woman gave a screech and ran forward, her arms wide open. The smaller woman—she was only five foot four—threw herself at Akiva, wrapping her arms around her neck.

Laughing, Akiva caught Wild Woman and staggered back.

"Hey! You're alive!" Wild Woman whooped. She embraced Akiva, placed a big kiss on her cheek and then released her. She then went to Joe, threw her arms around him and did the same thing. Joe nearly toppled over as she spontaneously assaulted him with affection. Laughing, he hugged her and accepted her welcome-back kiss on his cheek.

Akiva came to attention and saluted Majors Stevenson and York. They returned her salutes, their faces filled with concern as well as happiness and undisguised welcome.

Joe released Wild Woman with a laugh, straightened up and saluted the officers in turn.

"At ease," Maya told them. Then she stepped forward and threw her arms around Akiva. "You had us worried," she muttered.

The simple fact of Maya's arms wrapping around her made Akiva sob involuntarily. Hugging Maya, she whispered, "Thanks for coming…. We were worried, too. We weren't sure we were going to make it back…."

Maya finally stepped away, tears in her eyes. "Thanks for showing up. We've been worried sick." Turning to Joe, she embraced him, too. "Joe? You okay?" she asked, releasing him.

A little shaken by Maya's uncharacteristic embrace, he grinned foolishly. "Yes, ma'am, I'm fine now that we've got the BJS here."

Dane York came forward, shook Akiva's hand and

welcomed her back. He did the same with Joe. "We're glad to see you two show up. Welcome home," he murmured, his voice filled with undisguised emotion.

Angel Paredes was next, grinning from ear to ear as she approached. She gave both Akiva and Joe welcome-home hugs. Looking at them critically, she said, "Well, I can see a few Band-Aids are in order here. Why don't you two come with me to your mess building? I've got my paramedic bag in there. And we got chow. Hot chow, ready to serve. You two look like starvin' jaguars to me."

"Sounds good!" Joe said, rubbing his hands together and grinning. "I'm starvin' for some good ole squadron chow."

Akiva kept looking skyward nervously.

Maya grew serious, understanding her concern. "We've got a third Apache on alert, just in case you're worried about Rios following you and strafing us where we stand."

Akiva nodded, relief dissolving some of her tension as she walked at Maya's side toward the building. "Good, because once that bastard gets airborne, he's got three civilian helos armed with rockets that will be looking for us."

"Because of the info on Rios's helos you fed into our computers," Dane told her with grim satisfaction as he walked between Joe and her, "we're expecting them. And if they show up, they're as good as dead."

Joe gawked at Major York, whose face held a look of grim satisfaction. "Sir? You mean…"

Maya gave him a predatory smile. "We've got permission to take 'em out, Joe. From the Pentagon itself. They didn't like the idea of having an Apache knocked out of the air. It's war now."

"Whew!" he whispered. "If Javier loses his only son, he'll be pissed off and in a get-even mode."

"That's okay," Maya said. She reached the door of the mess hall and opened it for them. Gesturing for everyone to enter, she followed them in.

Akiva sat down at the table. The fragrant odor of spaghetti cooking made her mouth water. The enlisted women who had served at Alpha came over to them, and Akiva shook their hands. They were all crying. Maybe it wasn't a soldierly thing to do, but Akiva understood their tears. She wanted to cry herself, out of a sense of relief, more than anything.

"We never lost hope for you, ma'am," Iris Bradford sniffed, taking a tissue and wiping her nose and reddened eyes.

Akiva nodded. "I'm glad." Angel was already pushing up the rough wool sleeve of her Roman tunic. Akiva's knuckles were red and oozing blood. Paredes quickly cleaned them up with a few expert swipes of an antiseptic damp cloth.

The other two enlisted women sat down at the table opposite them. Spec Robin Ferris said, "When we lost radio contact with you, we called in the alarm to BJS." She smiled triumphantly. "They came right away."

"Yes, ma'am," Spec Susan Dean chimed in, "they were here in a heartbeat. We've been working a search grid trying to find you. After the Sat Intel showed the Apache destroyed, we hoped that you might have survived."

Maya stood near the table. It was clear that Akiva's stint as a C.O. had been successful. Her people doted upon her. Maya saw the eagerness in their young faces and heard the joy in their voices at the fact that Akiva was back, safe and sound. Maya felt good about her choice of leader for Alpha.

Joe looked up at Maya as Angel tended his many wounds and abrasions. "Major, did you realize we'd been kidnapped by Luis Rios?"

"We realized something happened," she admitted, her brows knitting. "We found the remains of the Apache, but no bodies with it. That's when we knew you'd escaped or were captured. We didn't know what had occurred."

"And then," Dane added, coming to his wife's side, "we found where someone had fired a rocket about two hundred feet away from the downed bird. There was a hole in the earth."

"Yeah," Joe said wryly, "I was carrying Akiva away from the Apache. She had been running with me and tripped over a root and hit her head on a log. It knocked her unconscious. I picked her up and started sprintin' for the jungle, but Rios got there and fired a rocket at us."

"It was the last thing Joe remembered," Akiva told them, and she filled them in on the rest of their extraordinary capture and escape.

Paredes had just finished her medical duties and closed her paramedic bag when Iris Bradford got up and called to her buddies to help her dish up the evening meal for everyone.

Maya shook her head and gave her husband a look of disbelief after hearing their story of capture and escape. "This is incredible. A modern-day Roman arena? Gladiator reenactors?"

Joe gave Akiva a look of respect. "Yes, ma'am, it was. I mean, I don't know if you're aware of this, but we got thousands of people in the U.S. who are Civil War reenactors. It's big business. And I guess in Mexico, Roman reenactors are 'in.' The biggest joke, though, was that the thousands of people comin' to the shindig didn't have a *clue* that we weren't there because we wanted to be." His voice deepened. "And I've gotta tell you all, Akiva here is an *incredible* gladiator. She gave the term woman warrior a whole new meaning out there in that arena. She bested the boys at their own games."

Eyes sparkling with pride, he saw Akiva lower her lashes, her cheeks turning a bright red at his enthusiastic and heartfelt praise. "She truly is a warrior in the finest sense of the word. If it hadn't been for her athletic ability—for her grabbin' that horse as it pulled that chariot—we wouldn't be sittin' here now." Joe looked up at Maya's dark features. "Ma'am, I strongly recommend that Akiva be put in for a medal of some kind. What she did was extraordinary. We owe our escape to her. There's no doubt about it."

"Ohh, Joe..." Akiva protested, embarrassed.

Maya smiled at her. "Ease off the throttles, Akiva. I'm *sure* both of you will be receiving commendations and medals."

"The episode serves to warn us about future secret installations that are not within BJS reach," Dane interjected in a worried voice. He scowled and settled his hands on his hips as he watched the three Alpha crew bring out steaming plates of spaghetti with huge meatballs.

"No kidding," Akiva said, her voice turning emotional. She thanked Iris, who brought over plates for her and Joe. "Let's eat, shall we? I'm starving to death!"

Turning around in the seat, Joe chuckled indulgently as he picked up his fork. "At least this time around, it doesn't feel like we're eating the Last Supper."

There were chuckles all around as everyone took

places at the tables and began to eat. Maya and Dane sat with Akiva and Joe, while the other pilots and personnel spread out at the other two tables. In moments, everyone was devoting all their attention to eating.

"This smells so good," Joe whispered. "Real American food…" And he dug into the spaghetti with unabashed relish.

Akiva chuckled and sprinkled some salt over hers. "This is the best gift I've had in a long time," she murmured. Still, worry threaded through her as she picked at the food. She looked across the table at Maya, who was eating with gusto.

"I'm sorry we had to blow up the Apache," she murmured. "I didn't want to…."

"You got struck by lightning," Maya offered gently. "You didn't have a choice, under the circumstances."

"Being a leader has made me respect tenfold what you do," Akiva told her in a low tone. She saw Maya lift her head, her emerald eyes widening with silent laughter.

"You'll get used to it, Akiva. Don't worry."

Staring at her, the fork halfway to her mouth, she said, "Get used to it? Don't we get to go home? Back to the base? I'd like to be just a pilot again."

Dane gave her a steady look. "Your operation here at Alpha has been very successful, Chief. According to the Pentagon and everyone concerned, Alpha is still on an operational footing."

Gulping, Akiva shot a look at Joe, who was frowning. "So, we're back in the frying pan here?" she asked. Right now she didn't feel as gung ho as she had before. She felt emotionally shredded, and she knew she was in shock over the last week, with the crash and loss of the Apache, and having their lives on the line day in and day out.

Maya cut up her spaghetti with her knife and fork. "Slow down, Akiva. I know you're fried right now. Major York and I have been talking, and here's what we're going to do." She laid down the knife, placed her hands on the table and looked at Akiva. "First, we're going to use that civilian helo you brought in. I'll have Wild Woman fly you to the nearest town in Mexico that has access to civilian airlines. You'll dress in civilian clothes, of course. She'll drop you off, you'll buy tickets and get to Cuzco, Peru, as soon as you can. From there, we'll pick you up and fly you back to the base." She picked some spaghetti up with her fork and popped it into her mouth.

"At the base, what I'll need ASAP are your reports. Akiva, because you're the C.O. of Alpha, I really need you to seriously evaluate what went right and wrong here. Joe, I'll need your input on how to fix what is weak about our black ops mission."

Joe nodded. "Yes, ma'am, I can do that."

Maya stole a look at her husband, who was seated at her elbow. "We felt that, because of the shock of your crash and subsequent capture, you both deserve about seven days R and R. We've got two suites at the Liberator Hotel in Cuzco lined up and waiting for you. The rooms even have hot tubs, and I'll bet you would like to soak away some of those bruises I see on your arms."

Brightening, Joe glanced over at Akiva, who had a surprised look on her face.

"R and R. Hoo doggies, now that's somethin' I can handle just fine."

Akiva smiled slightly at Joe. She saw the desire for her burning in his eyes. Yes, they needed—and deserved—that kind of time with one another. She cut one of the huge meatballs with her fork. "Thanks, Maya. We can use some downtime. I'm still in shock. I'm not feeling much emotionally—yet.''

Nodding, Maya murmured, ''I know. I can see it in your eyes.''

Dane smiled congenially and finished off his plate of spaghetti. ''In the meantime, we're putting Cam in command of Alpha until your return.''

Akiva stared at Maya. ''You want me back—here?'' She sat up, her heart beating a little harder in her chest.

Maya lifted her head, her emerald eyes filled with amusement. ''Why not? You were doing a good job.''

''But…I lost an Apache….'' Akiva knew that usually, if a helicopter was lost, the pilot's reputation suffered unless it was due to a mechanical problem. Getting struck by lightning wasn't exactly her fault, she knew, but it had cost her an expensive machine.

Waving her fork, Maya murmured, ''We've been here since you went missing. I've had a chance to go through your paperwork and see the way you set up and were running Alpha.'' She gave both of them a warm look. ''We saw nothing wrong with what you had laid out and were doing. Both Major York and I believe you two are best outfitted for this black ops.''

''I don't know whether to be happy or sad about that,'' Akiva griped in a low voice.

Joe chortled. ''Just say thank you, gal.'' And then he stopped, instantly aware of his mistake. Calling her the endearment in front of their commanding officers was a huge faux pas. Eyes widening, he shot a look at Maya. There was a slight hint of a smile on her lips as she continued to eat her meal. Dane glanced at his wife, at Akiva and then back at Joe, as if the feelings between Akiva and Joe had just become apparent to him. Watching Major York's face fill with surprise, Joe said nothing.

Mentally castigating himself for the slipup, he saw Akiva flush. She didn't look at him. Joe didn't blame her. Sitting there, he wondered if he'd screwed up but good. Although they were both of the same rank, romance wasn't exactly what the army had in mind between officers, and it was discouraged. Would Maya and Dane understand? Hands damp on his legs beneath the table, Joe felt angry at himself for not thinking first before he shot off his mouth. It was so easy to call Akiva "gal"...for she owned his heart, body and soul. Worriedly, Joe pushed his empty plate away and slowly put the flatware on top of it.

"I take it that we should have reserved only one suite, and not two, at the Liberator Hotel?" Maya asked wryly, her lips lifting and curving.

Akiva stared down at her plate. Yet as she heard not only the amusement in Maya's tone, but her acceptance that there was something serious between her and Joe, Akiva could hardly believe her ears. Although BJS was run by Maya, it was still a U.S. Army installation.

Lifting her chin, Akiva stared at Maya, who was grinning like a jaguar who had found her quarry. The merriment, the approval in Maya's eyes were obvious. Akiva felt an incredible warmth and acceptance from her C.O.

Heartened, she murmured, "Yes, one suite would be fine."

Chapter 16

"At ease," Maya murmured to Joe and Akiva as they entered her office at Black Jaguar Base. She gestured to two chairs in front of her desk. "Have a seat." Frowning, she looked at the two neatly typed reports she held in her hands.

Joe, who had been using an office down the hall, gave Akiva a wink. She smiled slightly as she sat down. He could hardly wait to get out of here and go to Cuzco. The idea of having Akiva all to himself was elating. Although she was once again dressed in her black uniform with the war ax and bowie knife once again tucked away beneath her belt, her hair tied back in a ponytail that fell to the middle of her back, he could see desire burning in her eyes—desire for him. It set his heart skittering with a happiness he'd never felt before.

Turning his attention to Maya, who was also in her black uniform, her hair cascading across her shoulders, he saw her brows draw downward as she flipped through their reports. Was something wrong? Joe sensed that Maya was juggling a lot of things; but then, as C.O., she was in a constant state of organized chaos. He waited, but not very patiently.

"Okay..." Maya murmured, looking up after they'd made themselves comfortable. She smiled a short, perfunctory smile. "Your reports are impeccable. Full of useful information for us and for the boys at the Pentagon to disseminate. I know it has taken nearly a day since your return to file these, and I want you to know how grateful I am. I know you'd rather be other places, and that's what I want to talk to you about."

Joe's heart fell. Wasn't Maya going to let them go to Cuzco? He had an uneasy feeling as he watched her tidy up the reports, put them to one side and fold her hands in front of her on the green metal desk. Trying to gird himself for disappointing news, he sat very still and waited.

"Akiva, you're Native American and aware that you each have a jaguar spirit guide?"

Taken aback, Akiva sat in silence, momentarily stunned by Maya's question. Ordinarily, they only talked military business, not about something like this. She saw the seriousness of Maya's emerald gaze. Opening her hands, she murmured, "Yes, ma'am..."

And then it dawned on Akiva that she'd never told anyone about it, except Joe. She glanced over at him. He had a nonplussed expression on his face. Feeling her gaze, he looked at her.

"I didn't say anything," he said, as if reading her mind.

Maya smiled thinly. "No, Akiva, Joe didn't talk to me."

"Oh...I see...." Well, she didn't, really, so she sat

quietly and waited, because she could see Maya had more to say.

"Joe, I know through my own mystic sources that you come from Comanche bloodlines. There has been a female jaguar spirit guide that has come down through your lineage to you, whether you're aware of it or not."

"...Okay, ma'am...." Unsure of where his C.O. was going with this unexpected conversation, Joe again traded looks with Akiva. She appeared just as confused as he was.

Maya stood up and rubbed her hands down the sides of her thighs. "You have heard, I'm sure, that I'm a member of a jaguar clan here in South America?"

Both nodded.

"It's like a black ops," Maya said wryly. She moved around the desk and quietly closed the door to her office so they could have absolute privacy. Walking slowly back to her seat, she sat down.

Akiva noted the door being shut. Maya rarely closed her office door; it was one of her hallmarks as a leader that her door was always open, so that anyone, officer or enlisted, could walk in and talk to her. Maya's openness as a C.O., her strong ties to her people at the BJS squadron, were legendary in the army. No C.O. did what she did. And for Maya to shut that door signaled something very serious to Akiva. Her heart pounded briefly with dread. Automatically, she clasped her hands in her lap, her gaze riveted on Maya, who sat looking somewhat amused as she picked up a pencil and tapped it against her desktop for a moment.

"Okay." Maya sighed, and giving them a quick smile to dispel the worry she saw etched in their faces, she continued, "What I'm going to say to you is absolutely confidential. Consider it a Q-clearance kind of thing, all right?''

Both nodded their heads.

Maya saw some relief in their expressions. They understood that Q-clearance represented the highest level of secrecy within the government. It was given on a need-to-know basis only.

''Originally, I intended to send you to Cuzco for your R and R. Well, that's changed,'' she murmured. ''I'm going to ask you to go somewhere else. Actually, it's even better, but you don't know that, and you're going to have to trust me on this.''

Frowning, Akiva stared bluntly at Maya. It wasn't like her C.O. to beat around the bush like this. Biting back questions, Akiva squelched her impatience. She saw Maya drop the pencil and fold her hands.

''I'm sending you to a place called the Village of the Clouds. It's a community up along the Peru-Brazil border—very hidden, very secret. Only special people go there…by invitation only. And your invitation is that you each have a jaguar spirit guide with you, whether you know it or not.'' Maya shot a look at Joe, whose brows were rising. She could see a lot of questions coming.

''This is a village that sits at the foot of the Andes, between the jungle and the mountains. It's a very unique agricultural village with a small community of…well, a certain type of people.'' Clearing her throat, she said, ''I got orders last night for you to go there, instead of going to Cuzco for your well deserved rest. Both of you are still in shock over what happened to you. This village is a place people go who are sick, or who are in training with the Jaguar Clan.''

Joe cocked his head. ''Which category do we fall into?''

Grinning, Maya said, "Both."

"This place...I've heard of it," Akiva murmured. "It's a spiritual training center."

"Correct. You may be more familiar with Spirit Lake, which the Eastern Cherokee have in North Carolina." With a shrug, Maya told them, "Among the myths and legends of the Native Americans of North America, or Turtle Island, there is a sacred and secret place people can go for healing and help. The legend is that if people bathe in the waters of Spirit Lake, they will be healed."

"Yes," Akiva murmured, "I've heard of it."

"The Eastern Cherokee nation was the largest on the East Coast," Maya murmured. "Suffice to say, this lake does exist, but it doesn't unveil itself except to those who have earned the right to find it, and be healed by its special waters."

Joe scratched his head. "Ma'am? Is this village where you're sending us like that?"

"You got it, Joe." Maya smiled warmly. "Again, you have to trust me on this. The Village of the Clouds is one of the most peaceful, healing and beautiful places on the face of Mother Earth. You go there by invitation only." She glanced at Akiva. "Since Akiva is more steeped in her people's spiritual traditions, she understands better what I'm talking about. Joe, you've been away from your people's traditions, but this is an opportunity, if you choose, to reconnect with them. And if you don't, that's fine, too. No one is going to force you to do something you don't want to do. Just use your time there to soak up the peace and love that's so much a part of the place."

Akiva stood up. "I think I see what's happening." She looked down at Joe, who had a confused look on his face. "This mission at Alpha was a test, wasn't it, Maya?"

She nodded gravely.

Joe frowned. "A test?"

Akiva laughed sharply. "Yes. My people believe that you are tested through life and death situations. If you pass, a new door—a better one, with more opportunities—is opened, granted to you because you not only passed the test, but lived to tell about it." Darkly, Akiva glanced over at Maya. "This is a reward for surviving the mission, isn't it?"

"Yes," Maya murmured, "it is."

"Why didn't someone tell us earlier about this test?" Joe demanded.

"Joe," Akiva said, "the path we walk, because of our blood, is a spiritual one in the long run. From time to time we all get tested. You don't know going in that it's a test. Only afterward, if you survive it, do you figure it out."

"Okay," Joe muttered, "does this get us a brass ring?"

Maya chuckled. "You could say that."

Excitement began to thrum through Akiva. "Joe, I think we just got the gold key to the city. Am I right, ma'am?" She couldn't keep the sudden excitement out of her voice.

Pleased, Maya nodded. "That's a roger. Okay, there's a helo warming up on the mining side to take us to Agua Caliente. We need to take the bus up the mountain to the temples of Machu Picchu. That is where one of two entrances to the Village of the Clouds is located." She stood up. "Are you ready for your next adventure?"

Grinning broadly, Akiva whispered, "Oh yes, ma'am!" She turned to Joe, joy bursting through her. He stood, an unsure look on his face. Reaching out, she gripped his hand and squeezed it momentarily. "Come on, Joe. Just

trust me. This is going to be a mind-blowing and wonderful experience.''

"Will it help me understand my Comanche heritage?"

"Yes," Maya said. "You're hungry to know about
your Native American background and there you will
start training to connect back to it."

Joe grinned. "That's a wish come true."

"Open your eyes," Akiva told Joe softly.

Joe felt dizzy as he opened his eyes. Akiva was standing next to him, her hand gripping his. There was fog
moving around them, thinning and thickening, as if whim
to some breeze that he did not feel. Seconds earlier, they
had been standing at the center of a place called the Temple of Balance. Maya had instructed them to stand in a
particular spot, close their eyes, take a deep breath and
relax. Joe had done that. When he'd closed his eyes, Akiva took his hand in a warm grip. He'd heard a popping
sound, like a champagne bottle being opened, and felt a
quick sense of movement, then nothing.

Looking through the cool, drifting fog, he saw the excitement on Akiva's face. Lifting her hand, he kissed the
back of it. "Okay, where we goin', gal? You seem to
know a lot more about this than I do."

"Keep trusting me," Akiva whispered, and she tugged
on his hand and started walking through the fog. "At one
time, Maya told me about this village and how to get
here. I always wanted to come but never thought I'd be
given the invitation."

They hadn't walked far when the fog began to rapidly
thin. Joe saw that they were in the jungle, standing at the
bottom of a small wooden bridge that arced across a
small, burbling stream of clear water. Beyond it, the jungle disappeared and he saw a village of thatched huts.

People walking about—men, women and children—were dressed in pastel clothing, mostly long-sleeved cotton tops and pants that hung comfortably. Everyone wore sandals. A number of iron pots hanging from tripods over fires were being tended on the hard-packed ground at the center of the village. Joe could smell mouthwatering scents of food drifting through the air.

Excitedly, Akiva said, "Let's go!" and she leaped onto the bridge. Joe followed, grinning. He liked seeing Akiva in this childlike mood. They were now in civilian clothes, for they never left the base in their black uniforms. Akiva had on a pair of dark green nylon hiking pants, her hiking boots and a long-sleeved, pink cotton shirt. She wore her hair loose and free.

As they leaped off the bridge and onto a path that would lead them into the village, Joe saw an incredible sight to his left. In the distance, across a huge, flowered field, he saw the bluish slopes of the Andes. High above them the granite crags glistened with snow. Between the mountain and the village, a wall of white clouds billowed, rolling and shifting continually. He was sure they were due to the steamy heat of the jungle meeting the colder, drier air descending off the mighty Andes. It was a beautiful and awe-inspiring sight.

"Welcome," a male voice boomed.

Joe, who had been looking at the clouds, hadn't been watching where Akiva was leading him. He stopped abruptly. On the path in front of them was a very tall, regal looking old man with a beard. He wore a pair of dark blue pants, sandals on his feet and a pale blue cotton top that fell to midthigh.

"I'm Grandfather Adaire," he said with a welcoming smile. "And you're Akiva and Joe." He held out his thin hand toward them. "Welcome to our humble village. We're glad you could come."

As Joe slid his large, square hand into Adaire's, he felt a jolt of warmth move instantly up his arm and into his body. It was like getting a slight shock of electricity, but one that was pleasant. Adaire had long, silver hair that hung below his square, proud shoulders, and his aged skin looked paper thin, with deep lines and wrinkles. His eyes gleamed with warmth, however. Joe liked him immediately and enthusiastically pumped his hand.

"Hello, sir."

Chuckling, Adaire said, "Around here, we just go by first names. You may call me Adaire, or Grandfather, or Grandfather Adaire—whatever is comfortable for you."

Joe grinned.

As Adaire turned his attention to Akiva, her eyes widened with surprise—especially when Adaire stepped forward, opened his arms and wrapped them around her.

"Welcome home, Daughter," he rumbled.

Tears instantly flooded Akiva's eyes as she embraced the older man. The intense heat of his hands, as he slid them gently around her shoulders, permeated her like a bolt of unexpected lightning. Ordinarily, Akiva wanted no man to touch her...except for Joe, whom she loved and trusted with her life and her heart. But Grandfather Adaire melted all her usual barriers, and her heart burst open. Heat, soothing and healing, moved into her body. All Akiva could do was gasp softly, cling to his tall, bony frame and close her eyes.

Joe watched Akiva's face soften miraculously as Adaire eased back from their embrace. He was smiling down at her with such love that Joe swore he saw a gold color around the man's head and shoulders. Even more touching were the tears streaming down Akiva's cheeks as she gazed at the old man. Wanting to somehow help her, Joe stepped up and slid his hand into hers. She turned, her eyes wet with tears. He gave her a tender look that told her he loved her. Akiva squeezed his hand in response and his heart soared.

"We want to welcome you to our village," Adaire told them with a slight smile. "Your hut is ready for you. If you'll follow me, we'll get you acclimated to your new home away from home."

Joe walked with Akiva, hand in hand. The path, hard packed by many who had walked it, was bordered on one side by jungle. He saw several red and yellow bromeliads in the limbs of the trees, as well as green and silver moss growing there.

As they walked around the central plaza, where many were helping with the cooking chores, Joe was amazed. He saw every color of skin on earth represented by the people who lived in the village. They lifted their hands and called to them in greeting as they passed by. The strange thing was their lips didn't move. And then it struck Joe that he was hearing their sincere greetings in his head and heart simultaneously. That was when he realized mental telepathy was being used, rather than spoken words. Shaken, he saw Akiva wipe the last of her tears from her cheeks.

At the end of the village was a small hut. The burbling stream wound behind it. Adaire led them inside, for there was no door. He turned and stood in the foyer.

"You will find everything you need here, children. You may wear the clothes you have on, or you may want to shed them for ours." He gestured to two sets of neatly folded clothes on a hand-hewn table. There was a bowl of fruit on it, as well. "Look around, explore and enjoy yourselves. Tonight, you'll have dinner at our hut. I'll have someone come and get you at that time. If you need anything, you may ask those who are living here. They will be eager to help, or to answer your questions." Adaire smiled gently. "There is a path just outside your hut. It leads to a beautiful waterfall—very secluded and healing. If you feel like it, you might go there once you're settled in here."

"Thank you, Grandfather," Akiva said, her voice low and emotional. "This is…overwhelming…."

With a deep laugh, Adaire nodded and folded his hands inside the sleeves of his tunic. "I know it is, children. But you have time here to heal, and to open your hearts to one another. You have *earned* this privilege."

Joe watched Adaire leave. Turning, he gripped Akiva's hands. "This place… It's somethin' else, gal…." He looked around in awe.

"Yes, it is," Akiva sniffed. She self-consciously wiped the tears from her eyes. "What I couldn't say until now is that for as long as I can remember, I've seen Grandfather Adaire in my dreams, Joe. I remember, when I was so small and my father would beat me, and I'd cry myself asleep in my room afterward, I came to this place…and Grandfather would be here to greet me. He'd hold me and I always felt better afterward." Akiva's voice lowered. "He was the only male I ever trusted—" she smiled brokenly "—until you came along…." She reached out and slid her hand up Joe's arm.

Shaken by her admission, Joe rasped, "I don't pretend to understand all this. It reminds me of magic…." And he brought Akiva into his arms. She looked like she needed to be held, and he was just the man to do it. As her arms slid around his waist, Joe buried his face in her soft, clean hair and inhaled her special scent into his flaring nostrils.

"It is magic," she whispered unsteadily, nuzzling his neck with her cheek. When Joe held her, Akiva felt safe. Completely and utterly safe and loved in his strong, caring arms. She felt his lips press against her hair and she sighed brokenly and surrendered to him. "You're magic...." she whispered.

Rocking Akiva gently in his arms, Joe closed his eyes and simply held her. "My daddy always said truth was stranger than fiction, and I guess this village falls into that category," he chuckled against her ear. "But I don't care how strange it is, Akiva. All I want—all I need—is you, gal, and everything else, strange, magical or otherwise, will fall into place for me...for us...."

Nodding, her throat tightening with more tears, Akiva absorbed Joe's strength and quietness like a thirsty sponge. Finally, she said in a broken whisper, "Joe, Grandfather Adaire gave me a healing. When he held me back there, something beautiful...something wonderful happened." Closing her eyes, she murmured, "I felt so much of my anger and rage, my sense of injustice, dissolve. As he held me, he was filling me with this incredibly beautiful gold light. I saw it flowing out of his hands—I felt it! It was like warm, liquid sunlight, filling me and flushing out the darkness. My fears, my negativity, my rage toward men—I felt it oozing out of my feet, back into Mother Earth, who took it all away from me."

"You feel so soft and good to me," Joe murmured, kissing her hair once more. He felt her arms tighten around him. More than anything, he wanted to love Akiva. To fill her with his heart, his soul by touching her, kissing her and making her one with him.

"Why don't we change clothes," he rasped near her

ear, "and go find that waterfall? I don't know about you, but right now, all I want, Akiva, is you...the beauty of this place...the healing that's going on. I want to love you, gal...want to share my heart, my soul with you...."

Chapter 17

"**I**'m afraid," Akiva whispered. She sat facing Joe on the grassy bank of the pool beneath the waterfall. She had come and knelt between his thighs, resting her hands on his knees. They had decided to blend with the villagers and were wearing the soft cotton clothing that had been left for them.

Joe heard the waterfall in the background, the scream of monkeys and macaws in the jungle that surrounded this place of unearthly beauty. Although the music around him lifted his spirits, his heart beat hard in his chest as he searched Akiva's unsure eyes. Her hands were cool and damp as he grasped them with his own. The breeze was slight, and lifted some strands of her black hair, which shone with reddish highlights in a ray of noontime sunlight.

"Of what? Me?" he asked in a low tone. He watched as Akiva sat back on her heels. She had taken her shoes off earlier and wriggled her toes luxuriously in the short green grass that edged the bank of the large, shallow pool.

Bending her head, Akiva closed her eyes and concentrated on Joe's warm, strong hands enclosing hers. How much she needed his quiet strength right now! When she finally answered, the words came out low and halting. "...Yes and no... I'm mostly afraid of myself..."

Sliding his hands up her bare arms, he whispered, "Look at me, Akiva." When she lifted her head and opened those glorious golden eyes fraught with shadows, Joe felt hot tears behind his own. He fought them off, because right now, Akiva was completely vulnerable. It was a massive gift, one that touched his heart in a way he'd never felt before. Seeing her lower lip tremble as she gazed at him, he moved his hand caressingly across her proud shoulders. "Whatever it is," he told her in a rasp, "we'll handle it—together. We're a good team, you and I. We proved it in the arena. We trusted one another there with our lives. How can we not trust one another now?" He managed a slight, nervous smile, afraid of saying or doing the wrong thing right now. Afraid that he'd bumble and make an error that would cause her to retreat.

The feel of his strong hands on her shoulders, moving gently down her arms to where her hands were rigidly clasped in her lap, soothed Akiva. She gave a jerky nod in response to his searching question. Joe's gray eyes were wide, and she heard the incredible gentleness in his husky tone, felt him trying to engage and support her, even though he wasn't really aware of what she was afraid of—yet. Unable to hold his lambent gaze, though it made her heart lift with hope, she bowed her head and forced out the words gathering like a lump in her throat.

"Joe...I've never trusted men...white or red...not ever...."

"No wonder. Your father beat you. And then your stepfather.... You had no reason to trust men, Akiva. Anyone with an ounce of brains could understand where you're comin' from on this." He closed his hands around hers. They were so cold!

Seeing the suffering on her face now made Joe want to cry. Akiva was allowing him the privilege of seeing her without any defenses in place, allowing him access to her hurting heart and wounded soul. The love he felt for her was so deep and wide that it stunned even him as he responded emotionally to her needs. Akiva invited him to share a depth of love that Joe had never felt before, or was even aware could exist. But it did, here and now, with her....

"Well," she quavered uncertainly, "I guess you're right. I guess I've been blindly stumbling around all my life without understanding myself."

"Men wounded you and men weren't high on your list of people to trust."

Nodding, Akiva stole a glance at him through her damp lashes. Joe's face was strong and tender looking. His eyes burned with a fire that enveloped her, made her feel strong enough to go on. Joe deserved her honesty. He, more than anyone, did. He'd earned it the hard way: he'd fought in life-and-death circumstances at her side. He'd shown her that he had earned her trust in a way only a warrior could know and honor.

"I have been so angry all my life...angry at men. I hated them for a long time. When I got to Fort Rucker for Apache training, and Major York was breaking us down—or trying to, because we were women and he wanted to see us fail—I just saw red." She blinked and lifted her head, looking over at the waterfall. It was so clean and clear, and she felt so raw inside right now. As the mist from the falling water collected above the pool, a shaft of sunlight struck the myriad droplets and created a rainbow. A rainbow meant much to Akiva. To the Apache nation, it was a sign of grace, of blessing, from the Great Spirit. The shimmering bands of color gave her hope that she could share with Joe what was eating her up alive inside.

"Lucky for me, I had kick-boxing as a positive activity to take the edge off my rage and hatred of men. The way York was pushing us, trying to get us to fail, well, I was ready to lash back. Fortunately, Maya saw the steam building in me and she got me into kick-boxing as an outlet. I took my fear, anger and sense of injustice about what was occurring to all of us there, out on my poor opponents." She managed a clipped smile and pulled her hand from his. Pushing several strands of hair from her face, she placed her fingers across Joe's hand. "I beat the living daylights out of the men who challenged me in the kick-box ring. I *wanted* to hurt them."

Nodding, Joe said quietly, "What Major York did was wrong. He's admitted that now, and he's made amends. So much so that he's given his heart, his life, to Maya. But it didn't help any of you women going through flight school then. I'm glad you went into kick-boxing."

With a ragged sigh, Akiva looked up at him. "It was all a mask, Joe. I was really afraid of men, of what they could do to me if I trusted them. I just couldn't—" Her voice broke. "Oh, I had a few guys, off and on through my life, who wanted a relationship with me, but I froze. I wouldn't let them into my life. I couldn't—I just… couldn't…."

"And with good reason," Joe whispered. He saw the

tears beading on her thick, black lashes. Her lips were parted, and he felt her suffering so acutely that he felt overwhelmed by it, by the sheer torture of what she had carried all her life within her. "I don't know how you managed to reach out to me, gal...." He lifted his hand and grazed her cheek.

Closing her eyes, Akiva absorbed the wonderful pressure of his fingertips upon her flesh. "Every time...every time you touch me, Joe, I feel my heart opening up more and more to you. I feel like you're the sunlight to my dark, dark soul, which has been left freezing in the winter of my wounded heart."

Cocking his head, he studied her closely. Her lower lip was wet with tears that fell silently down her face. "Maybe because we share Indian blood?" he suggested softly. It was hell to sit here with her and not pull her into his arms, for he knew that was what Akiva needed right now. Not raw sex, but love. He wanted to show her his love by holding her, giving her a sense of protection from the world around her. More and more, Joe was realizing the many colors and depths and shades and tones of love. Before, he'd been pretty much like any other guy—he'd equated it with sex. But he was finding out, in the past months with Akiva, that love was like the rainbow shimmering over the pool beside them. It was colorful bands and striations of rich and fragile emotions all combined. And he knew from loving Akiva that he had the emotional capacity to respond to every one of them.

The realization filled him with a stunning awareness. Just as she had the courage to open up to him, share her vulnerability, her fears, her secrets and darkness, he recognized that he had a similar capacity to absorb them all. It left Joe stunned, left him feeling humbled by love itself, for it was so profound and deep that he knew he'd only scratched the surface of it before with other women. Akiva was opening up a whole new, wondrous world to him emotionally.

Akiva sat there wrestling with her fears and the rocketing emotions that were battering her inside. "Yes... your being Indian helps...because we're aware that we're part of spirit, too, Joe. I know you haven't been steeped in our traditions, but I've seen you, time after time at Alpha, use your heart, your intuition with our team...with me...and it helped me begin to open up and trust you. I realized after our confrontation that my real problem was distrust of men, no matter what color their skin was. I know you didn't realize it at the time. You may not now, but you have such goodness and strength within you. For me, it was easy to turn to you. You are like sunlight and I couldn't help but open up to you."

"I think," Joe told her in a husky tone, "that all people are fragile, delicate flowers deep inside. That sometimes we get stomped on by life and nearly destroyed, gal." He reached out and stroked his fingers caressingly along the side of her face, tucking a few strands of hair behind her ear. "I know I don't have the training in Native American traditions you had, and I can see how they've helped you, how they've sustained you in the dark night of your soul. I came from a pretty happy family. My problems were I saw myself comin' from the wrong side of the tracks, and worried that no one would see my abilities, my talents. That they'd put me in a box and never let me prove my worth." He shared a sad smile with her. "I didn't want people to think I was a dumb box of rocks, just because my daddy was poor and a truck driver."

She managed a partial smile and moved her fingers gently across his dark, hairy hand. "I understand, Joe. I really do. I guess I never saw myself as being a poor, underprivileged Indian kid from the res."

"You were too busy surviving your father and step-father," Joe rasped, his brow dipping. He saw her try to smile. As she lifted her head, the path of her tears gleamed against her copper skin. How beautiful she looked in that moment! "Listen, I'm here for you, Akiva. In any way I can," he murmured. "The gift of yourself, your trust, is all I want or will ever need." He gestured to the rainbow shimmering above the pool. "You're my rainbow. Did you know that? You make me feel like a rainbow inside. Every time I see you, my heart races. And when you smile—" he touched the corners of her mouth with his thumbs "—I feel like bursting out in song."

Just the touch sent a shiver of yearning through to the core of her heart and body. Catching his hands in hers, Akiva tilted her head and gazed into his dove-gray eyes. Joe was so open, so accessible, that it gave her the courage to speak of her worst fears and secrets. "I love the idea of being your rainbow...but I never felt that way inside myself. Joe, I need to tell you the rest of what burdens me."

"I'm listenin'," he whispered rawly. "We'll handle it—together."

Taking a deep breath, Akiva said in a broken tone, "I was so afraid of men, I never slept with one. I didn't want to. I didn't want to put myself under their control. I couldn't trust my feelings with them, and if I couldn't do that, I wasn't going to sleep with one."

Gulping, Joe absorbed her halting words laced with so much tortured pain. "And that's your big secret?" he asked, meeting her tear-damp eyes. "That you're a virgin?"

Wryly, she said, "Yeah, at twenty-four…"

"There's no shame in that. How can there be? With what happened to you, Akiva, I don't blame you." Joe opened his hands and placed them over hers, adding, "I don't even see how you can open yourself up to me. I'm sitting here stunned by how much I love you, want you, and I'm riding on a wave of happiness just having you here…."

Frowning, Akiva gazed into his eyes. "You mean…it doesn't bother you that I'm not…well, experienced?"

Shrugging, Joe whispered, "A woman's body is sacred, Akiva. It's too bad more boys who masquerade as men don't honor that, or get it." Slipping his fingers through hers, he added in a low voice, "No, it doesn't bother me at all. It scares me a little, because I don't profess to be the world's greatest expert on makin' love. I've got some experience, yes…but I worry I'll hurt you, or do something to make you retreat from me. I worry that I'll blunder, or cause you pain—and that's the *last* thing I want to do, gal. You're so precious to me, as special as that rainbow out there over the water. I worry about *me,* not you." And the corners of his mouth lifted with sad irony.

"Joe, you would never hurt me. Not ever." Akiva's voice grew raspy with tears. "You never realized it, but the three months at Alpha were some of the best and happiest I've ever experienced. I really looked forward to seeing you every morning…sharing coffee with you at the mess. Having those stolen moments when we were completely alone…" Sniffing, Akiva raised her hands and tried to wipe away her tears. "I was worried that I wouldn't be good enough…that I couldn't please you. Or I wouldn't know how to do it…''

Laughing gently, he opened his arms. ''Come here, gal,'' he murmured huskily.

Akiva moved into his arms. She snuggled against him and rested her head on his shoulder as he held her tightly. A ragged sigh tore from her lips.

''*This* is what I need, Joe. You…''

His heart ached with such love for Akiva, for her brutal honesty and her simplicity, that Joe could do nothing but hold and rock her for a long, long time. They sat there on the bank, the roar of the waterfall behind them and the rainbow glinting in an arc of pale pink, gold, green and lavender colors. All Joe wanted was to share his spirit, his heart with Akiva as he sat there with her in his arms.

In some ways, she was still a hurt little, eight-year-old-girl who had sobbed out her heart in her room after her father had beaten her. Joe couldn't understand how any parent could do that to a child. It was beyond him. Now he was getting a raw taste of what it had done to this magnificent woman whose heart was that of a jaguar, who never quit, who had fought back and survived even when the odds were against her. As he slowly rocked Akiva in his arms, to an ancient rhythm known only to the beating heart of Mother Earth, many awarenesses avalanched upon Joe.

In that time out of time, as the earth seemed to hold her breath, the sun stopped moving and the rainbow— the symbol of their love for one another—became stronger and more colorful, Joe felt his fears of hurting Akiva dissolve. In their wake was the driving, raw need to connect with her heart and share what he felt with her.

As Joe eased Akiva to the ground, the grass soft and

fragrant, like a living blanket beneath them, he smiled
tenderly into her face. He saw the gold in her eyes, saw
that the darkness was gone. Her lips parted as he eased
her onto her back. Her hair cascaded like silk around her,
becoming a dark halo about her head as he leaned down
to find her mouth.

The moment Joe's mouth brushed hers, Akiva felt
some of her fear dissolve. As his tongue tenderly laved
her lower lip, she felt more at ease. She concentrated on
the sensations, the tingling, the delicious heat moving like
a flowing stream from her lips, toward the center of her
body, to her swiftly beating heart. As his mouth cherished
hers, she became lost in the splendor of golden stars beginning to explode deep within her lower body. It was
then that Akiva felt, for the first time, the stirrings of her
as a woman who needed her man. Sliding her arms across
Joe's broad shoulders, she leaned up and boldly returned
his kiss.

Akiva felt Joe's smile across her mouth. His hand
moved to her cheek and pushed the curtain of her hair
aside. Fingers grazing Akiva's neck and moving slowly
down the soft cotton of her shirt, he cupped her small
breast. The sensations that sparked as he moved his
thumb languidly across the tightening peak of her breast
caught her by surprise. It was a delicious feeling, and she
moaned and pressed closer, wanting more of the pleasure
that he was creating within her.

Heartened by her moan of rapture, Joe lost a little more
of his anxiety. Akiva's mouth was soft and bold beneath
his. Her breath was becoming chaotic, and she was twisting and turning, obviously enjoying what he was doing
to pleasure her. The elation in his heart grew and he
became bolder because of his need to show her how
much he loved her.

In minutes, Akiva was divested of her top and slacks. She lay on the grass, warmed by the afternoon sunlight, and watched through half-closed eyes as Joe undressed. He was powerfully built, his shoulders broad, his chest deep and darkly haired. Her gaze drifted to his lower body, and she felt her heart quicken. But it wasn't out of fear, it was out of anticipation and a driving need to couple with him, to make them complete and whole.

As he settled beside her, his length against hers, she turned toward him and smiled softly. Easing her fingers upward across his hair-roughened cheek, she whispered, "Why was I so afraid?" and she smiled softly into his stormy eyes.

"I love you, Akiva," Joe rasped against her smiling mouth. "Love never hurts. It can only heal...." And he leaned down and brushed the peak of her hardened nipple with his tongue. Instantly, she responded. Her hands gripped his shoulders, and she gasped in surprise. Taking the nipple into his mouth, Joe suckled her gently. With one arm he brought her strong, writhing body against his. She was moaning with incredible pleasure as he followed his heart's voice and turned off the fear in his head. In that moment, Joe transcended his own dread of hurting Akiva instead of giving her happiness and elation. For the first time, he gave himself free rein, letting his sense of smell, taste and touch tell him what Akiva would enjoy.

The rainbow colors deepened. The sun glowed more strongly in the sky, its rays warm upon them. The music of the water tumbling into the emerald green pool below became part of the rhythmic music and magic as Joe eased her long, curved thighs apart with his knee. As he moved over Akiva, he placed his arm beneath her head. She was smiling up at him, wonder in her eyes, sunlight dancing in their depths, plus a love so clean and clear it went straight to his pounding heart and heated body. Everything was perfect. So perfect. As he smiled down at Akiva, he brought his other hand beneath her wide hips, lifting her just enough to move into her hot slick depths. Moving slowly, he allowed her body to accommodate his entrance. Akiva's eyes widened with surprise, and then her lashes fell. As he gently continued the slow rhythm just within the gates of her moist, feminine core, Joe began to see desire replace her surprise. And when her arms slid around his shoulders, he smiled down at her.

"It feels good, doesn't it?"

Akiva nodded, but couldn't talk now. Her body was beginning to burn, and a hungry desire, like that of a starving jaguar, began to gnaw at her. She was no longer satisfied with Joe's slow entry. Primal knowing took over, and Akiva slid her long legs around his. She arched and pulled him more deeply into her singing body. The world tilted, and she closed her eyes. A soft, ragged sigh issued from her lips as she felt Joe's weight more surely upon her, a warm, safe blanket.

Like the rainbow that shimmered and undulated behind them, Joe established the rhythm Akiva wanted. The burning knot in his lower body quickly magnified, a volcano ready to explode. He heard her soft cries of pleasure, saw the sensuous look on her face. They were linked to one another—one heart beating hard, one body moving and flowing, like the restless beauty of the waterfall plummeting into the emerald waters below. All of nature was embracing them, and all of nature was inside them—connected, heated, throbbing with new, pulsing life.

When the sunlit explosion occurred deep within Akiva's wildly writhing body, it took her by utter surprise.

She gave a sharp cry. Instantly, she arched and froze in Joe's protective arms, her hands opening and closing spasmodically against his back. He seemed to understand what was happening. Cradling her face into his shoulder, he continued to move strongly within her, prolonging the savage pleasure and heat fanning out through her like raw sunlight spilling across the surface of wildly frothing water. Like a million dappling, glistening lights dancing— that was how Akiva felt as she gave Joe the ultimate gift of her body, heart and soul.

Within moments, she felt him tense. His arms became strong bands about her, crushing the breath from her lungs. He groaned like a jaguar claiming his mate. Understanding on a deep, primal level that Joe had just given the gift of himself to her, Akiva clung to him. She tasted the salt of his perspiration on his shoulder as she pressed small kiss after another across his tense flesh. As they lay locked in that timeless moment of heat, passion, love and life, Akiva had never felt so fulfilled, so satiated and at peace with herself, or the world that now hazily intruded upon them in the aftermath.

Joe groaned and rolled off her. He brought Akiva into his arms and they lay on their sides, facing one another. Her skin was slick with perspiration, and he eased the dark hair that clung to her cheek away from her face. Akiva's eyes were half-open, the glorious gold color of dancing sunlight.

"You are my rainbow woman," he told her in a roughened tone. "I love you like I've never loved anyone." Continuing to smooth her mussed hair away from her face, he saw the joy and pleasure in her expression. There was wonderment in Akiva's eyes. And the happiness that exploded through Joe was like a volcano flowing outward, spewing wave after wave of hot lava.

"I...can't talk...only feel," she whispered as she caressed Joe's face. "I love you so much...." And she did, with all the brightness and strength of her heart and soul.

Joe understood. Lying back on the grass, he pulled Akiva close to him. Her long, strong body flowed against him like water flowed against a rock. In many ways, he realized, he was a rock to Akiva—stable and steady, someone she could rely on, someone who would be there to cushion her moments of anger and hurt, but also to share her joy and laughter.

Inwardly, Joe knew that their relationship would be fraught with highs and lows as Akiva worked on healing that old wound deep within her. He'd already experienced it at Alpha: one day she would reach out to him, tentative and unsure, and the next showed him that freezing glare of anger that bubbled so close to the surface. In many ways, he'd been her whipping post, but he hadn't taken her mood shifts and swings negatively. Because he loved her, he could tolerate them, and now, understanding where they had come from, he had no problem at all absorbing her darker moments. In the end, that wound would be cleansed by his love for her, and would one day cease to exist. As he leaned down and pressed soft kisses to the top of her head, which was resting against his chest, Joe smiled to himself.

Yes, he knew he could give Akiva what she needed in order to heal. And she, without knowing it, was healing him of his past, too. Joe was realizing he had nothing to prove to anyone. Over the months of working with Akiva, he had lost the drive to impress her. His past habits had dissolved, freeing him up as never before.

He sighed euphorically. The sunlight warmed him, the breeze softly touched his damp body to dry him. The grass was springy and embracing beneath his naked flesh. And best of all, Akiva's long, sinuous form lay like a warm blanket against his. Life didn't get any better than this, and Joe absorbed it all.

Akiva smiled softly as she sat between Joe's thighs. He was leaning on an old log on the bank, overlooking the waterfall. As Joe's hands came to rest on her shoulders, she tipped her head back against his strong body and sighed. The sun had shifted, although she wasn't aware of time passing. The rainbow was still there, but faintly, because the sun's rays now slanted at a different angle. It didn't matter; the rainbow burning brightly within her body more than made up the difference.

The songs of birds, the music of the water splashing into the green depths of the pool made her heart mushroom with such joy that Akiva opened her eyes and looked up at Joe. His hair was ruffled, that one precocious lock falling over his broad, smooth forehead. He smiled down at her wordlessly, his gray eyes burning with love—for her. Lips parting, Akiva whispered, "You are my sun. The Apache people worship the sun, for it gives not only light, but life, my darling. You have brought light into the darkness of my heart and soul. Your warmth, your love, has allowed me to let go of the past and believe there is a better way to live." Akiva's fingers slipped upward over Joe's strongly corded neck to his cheek. "You've given me my life back, beloved. You gave it with your love. You had such patience with me...."

Capturing her long, artistic fingers, Joe kissed them gently, then brought her hand down to her breast and held it there. "I'll be your sun," he said in a husky tone, "if you'll be my rainbow. Fair enough?"

Laughing softly, Akiva leaned down and kissed his hand. "Fair enough."

As she lifted her head and stared out across the pool, she was suffused with a joy she'd never known before. Words were inadequate. The late afternoon mirrored that feeling in all respects, for she knew Mother Earth loved her children and would talk to them in symbolic ways. Right now, Akiva and Joe were one with her, and one with each other. The moment of integration was magical and made Akiva feel like a wondrous child, wide-eyed and as open as that fragile flower Joe had compared her to earlier.

Brushing her cheek against his hand, Akiva could only smile and feel the continuous joy that ran through her like a wild, tumultuous river. She was free. Really free, for the first time in her life. And Joe's love for her had been the key. He'd taken her edginess, her hardened rage, and transformed it patiently simply by loving her and seeing who she was beneath all that armor she wore.

"I might be a warrior," she told Joe quietly, "but I'm a woman first. And I want to share and explore that part of me with you. Always...."

Reaching down, Joe slipped his arms around Akiva. She sighed and tipped her head back to rest on his proffered shoulder. Brushing her cheek with kisses, he murmured, "You're the bravest, gutsiest woman I've ever known, gal. You have the heart of a jaguar, the soul of a rainbow. I just hope and pray I can always do right by you...."

Opening her eyes, Akiva drowned in Joe's burning gray ones. "You will, because you love me...and I will become more the rainbow for you over time, and less the warrior."

Smiling gently, Joe kissed her brow. "You'll always be a warrior for those who need you to be that, Akiva. In the quiet moments, alone, you'll share the rainbow with me. It doesn't get any better than that. Not ever..."

Epilogue

Akiva sat down with Joe in the planning room at the Black Jaguar Base. With them were Maya and Dane, Cam Anderson, Morgan Trayhern and his assistant, Mike Houston. An aide shut the door to the small but well lit room and quietly left them alone. The table was oval and made out of highly polished mahogany with a golden grain.

Maya sat at one end, Dane at the other. Akiva was glad Joe was at her side, as she noted the seriousness in everyone's faces. She and Joe had returned just a week ago from the beautiful Village of the Clouds. And now they were preparing to return to Alpha and run it. Joe cocked his head and gave her a wink. She smiled slightly.

"I'm glad everyone could make it," Maya said, opening a file folder marked Top Secret. "We're here to initiate the second thrust of a three-pronged assault on the Mexican drug trade. Thus far, our insurgence into southern Mexico, into Javier Rios's area, has been an unqualified success.'' Maya gave Akiva a warm look and then shifted her gaze to Joe.

''Akiva and Joe are doing an admirable job at Alpha. We're sending them back with two Boeing Apache Long-bows, plus the Blackhawk they presently have. They will also have a civilian helicopter that they'll use at their discretion, to fly to the spook base west of them for any supplies they might need. Things will continue as before there.''

Maya smiled a jaguar smile. ''The Pentagon is constantly eavesdropping on Rios's communications. He sends a lot of satellite transmissions, and the Pentagon is taping them all. To say he's upset about Akiva and Joe dodging his clutches and leaving his arena is putting it mildly. Good job, gang. I'm proud of you. We've got him unsettled. The helicopter you stole has never been reported to the police or anyone else. They're writing it off. His son, Luis, is buying a new one, only this time it's a Russian Kamov Black Shark.''

Akiva scowled. ''Great. We're back to square one. The Apache won't be able to pick up the radar signature on it.''

''Don't be griping too much,'' Maya teased darkly. ''We just found out on a Sat Intel that the two new drug lords moving into Peru to take over after the last one I dusted off are buying four new Kamovs to replace the ones we blew out of the sky that day.''

''Ouch,'' Joe muttered. ''Looks like everyone is gonna have their hands full.''

''Yep,'' Maya sighed, ''business as usual.''

''Druggies keep it interesting,'' Dane said in a dry, humorless voice.

''At least,'' Mike Houston put in on an upbeat note,

"you are now getting replacements here at BJS to give your original women pilots some downtime and rest."

Nodding, Maya said, "Yes, that's true. We have ten new Apache pilots, male and female, coming on temporary duty to us. But the pressure on my original pilots to train them under combat conditions provides *more* stress, not less right now, Mike. About three months after the initial training period, the pressure will start to ease. But not until then."

Morgan brightened and folded his large hands on the table, his own copy of the top secret file beneath them. "I've authorized the army to send down six of their best instructor pilots to work with you, Maya."

Her brows raised. "Oh?"

"Yes." He smiled slightly, his hair black and silver beneath the washed-out light of the fluorescent fixture above the table. "I talked the army chief of staff into seeing it my way. You need to train in a group of instructors who will know the lay of the land down here and what these Apache pilots are getting into. They're coming down here to look, gauge and then set up another program at Fort Rucker that will mimic what is being done here. I see this plan as an interim step. Right now, you're on combat footing. You don't need to be stretched even further training these pilots. You need something in between, and I think we've got a fix on it."

"Good," Maya murmured. "We need all the help we can get."

Dane leaned forward and said, "This is good news, Morgan. Thanks. Maybe, if Maya approves it, I can work with that IP team. I'm pretty good at making up charts, blueprints and templates."

"Say no more," Maya muttered with a grin, "it's all

yours, Major York. I've got enough to do, thank you very much.''

Akiva nodded. Because she'd had a taste of being a C.O., she understood as never before the strain, the demands and stresses on the major. And her admiration for Maya skyrocketed even more. Akiva only hoped that she could juggle her tasks half as well as Maya could.

She felt Joe's hand sneak beneath the table where they were sitting. His fingers moved over hers, which were resting on her thigh. Giving him a glance, she saw him smile slightly, his gray eyes warm with love for her. It was as if he was reading her mind and feeling her worry about her job as C.O. at Alpha. With him at her side, she knew she could do it.

Dane rubbed his hands together, flashing everyone a triumphant grin. ''Excellent. Thank you, Major.''

''You're welcome, Major. You're a real glutton for punishment, if you ask me. But—'' Maya sighed and looked down the table at her husband ''—better you than me. Thank you.''

Dane nodded and gave her a slight, gallant nod of his head. ''My pleasure, Major.''

Maya snorted and gave him a narrowed look that was filled with playfulness. Everyone at the table tittered. And then they grew solemn once again as she flipped to the next order of business on her agenda.

''Okay, let's move on to Chief Cam Anderson's mission.'' Maya looked down the table at Cam, whose copper-colored hair hung in heavy curls around her proud shoulders as she smiled tentatively back.

Pages were shuffled as Maya made sure she had all Cam's orders in front of her before she continued. ''Now, I've talked to the new president of Mexico, Alejandro Feliz. He basically got elected on a reform platform, promising to wipe out the connection between the major drug families in his country, clean up the police department, which is being paid off big time by the drug families, and generally scrub house. I talked to his secretary of defense, and they both said they want our help.''

''*How* do they want our help?'' Morgan demanded in a heavy voice. ''Payoffs from druggies are legendary in their country. We've tried working with them before, but it puts our people at too high a risk. You can't trust anyone. The drug families have moles in every local, regional and federal police agency.''

Shrugging, Maya said, ''That's true. But President Feliz says he's going to make a clean sweep. At first I was skeptical, but after two phone conversations with him, I'm convinced he means business. He knows he's got a dysfunctional country that's run by the shadow legacy of the drug families. And he knows the only way to clean it up is from the inside out.'' Maya shot a glance at Cam, who was dressed in her black flight uniform. ''The president asked for our help. He wants to know how to create a black ops situation with his elite air force helicopter units so that they can fly into areas where drugs such as marijuana are being grown, and drop the troops off and let them destroy the fields. This is a big deal,'' Maya told them.

Houston nodded. ''It is. Mexico has a lot of mountainous agricultural areas where marijuana is being grown alongside other legal crops. Many farmers in northern Mexico, especially along the Baja coast, are trading in their traditional crops for marijuana. It pays them a hell of a lot more than potatoes, yams or corn can.''

''That's right,'' Dane murmured. ''The economy in Mexico sucks, and people are struggling to survive. Raising and selling marijuana is an easy way to make a buck.

The U.S. border at San Diego is less than an hour away, so it's a real easy proposition for them.''

"Well,'' Maya growled, "I'm not wasting one of my key pilots by sending her after some dirt-poor farmers in Mexico. The president is gonna have to deal with that particular problem. Cam is going on temporary duty to Tijuana, Mexico, where she's going to be training an elite helicopter squadron to go in and begin to interdict drug flights that are heading north over the U.S. border. It doesn't matter if it's cocaine, marijuana or whatever. Her job is to teach these Mexican pilots interdiction routines we've learned and perfected here in Peru.''

"Do they have Apaches?'' Akiva asked.

Maya shook her head. "No, but the U.S. Army, thanks to Morgan's work, is going to 'loan' four original Apache models to the Mexican pilots. Right now, eight pilots are going to be graduating in about another week from Fort Rucker. This is a top secret operation. The drug families haven't got wind of any of this yet…but they will.''

"And my job,'' Cam said in a clear, firm voice, "is to teach these guys the ins and outs of air interdiction? How to turn these flights back into Mexican airspace?''

"Correct.'' Maya's eyes glittered. "Just like here, you won't be authorized to fire upon any civilian fixed-wing or rotor aircraft. I don't want those boys getting trigger happy. The moment one of them fires a cannon or rocket at some civilian aircraft, whether it's carrying drugs or not, all hell will break loose. You're going to teach the fine art of sky chicken and other wonderful assault tools that we've created down here at BJS over the last three years.''

Cam smiled grimly. "It will be a pleasure.''

Morgan scowled. "I've been running into a lot of prejudice against women by the Mexicans. Their country is very backward about women being equals," he warned. Looking at Cam, he added, "The eight pilots now going through Fort Rucker are being given a quick shakedown on women being equals in the cockpit, but I can't guarantee that it's going to be a picnic for you, Cam."

"No," Houston warned in a gravelly tone as he stared at Cam. "You need to know going into this that you're going to be locking horns with all of 'em. They aren't going to want to take you seriously. If you were a man, no problem. But you're a woman, and unfortunately, in their country, women stay home as housewives and mothers. They don't fly combat helicopters."

"So," Maya summed up, "Cam, you're going into a highly charged prejudicial situation and you're going to have to get firm, put up strong boundaries and make them do it your way or no way."

Cam smiled slightly. "I'd like to think I'm a steel hand in a velvet glove, Major."

"I know you are," Maya said. "That's why you got chosen for this backbreaking TAD." She slid Akiva a look. "If I sent Akiva, she'd have these guys running and screaming in eight different directions because she doesn't put up with any kind of male prejudice toward a woman."

Akiva had the good grace to flush. "That's true," she murmured, her mouth drawing upward.

Maya laughed briefly. "Akiva doesn't suffer second-class citizenship at all. Nor should any of us," she said, losing her smile. Her emerald eyes narrowed on Cam. "You have a lot of diplomacy, and even though you're strong, you can bend without breaking. Your main job is interdiction. We've got to start cutting down on the hundreds of drug flights a week, originating from all over

Mexico. We've got to stop them from crossing the U.S. border.''

Nodding, Cam said, "I feel strongly I can do this, Major. And I'm appreciative that you're letting me.''

Joe grinned across the table at Cam. "Just kick butt and take names like you do down here,'' he chuckled.

"Humph,'' Akiva groused, "if those eight didn't square away pronto, I'd hang their hides off the Apache's blades.''

"Precisely my point,'' Maya said, as she looked at Akiva and then over at Cam, who was smiling. "I need a woman pilot who doesn't want to do that first. But as a last resort…''

Everyone chuckled.

Leaning back in her chair, Maya gave Joe and Akiva a thoughtful look. "And I have a happy announcement to make—one you can spread like gossip around the squadron.'' Maya knew that any news flew around the BJS like wildfire, so it was an inside joke. "Joe?''

Akiva frowned and looked at Joe. He smiled nervously and stood up after releasing her hand beneath the table. Smoothing down his black uniform, he dug into his left pocket.

"I thought this was a good place to share something happy with ya'll,'' he told them. Digging deeper into his pocket, he found and pulled out a small gold box. His heart speeded up with anticipation. Akiva gave him a quizzical look. Grinning uncertainly down at her, he said, "This is a surprise, gal…''

"I guess so,'' Akiva murmured.

Everyone at the table chuckled indulgently again.

"There,'' Joe said with relief. He was so nervous that he was fumbling with the small box. Finally, he got it open. "This is for you, Akiva…an engagement ring.''

He placed the open box on the table in front of her. "The major helped me pick it out in Cuzco last week, after we got back. It's gold topaz, pink tourmaline, purple amethyst and green emerald put into a channel setting, so it's flush with the gold of the ring. That way, you can wear it...if you want...and it won't catch on your clothes or anything." Mouth dry, he sat down and pushed the box a little closer to the edge of the table where Akiva was sitting. Placing his hand behind her chair, his arm around her shoulders, he swallowed hard and began.

"I'm askin' you to be my wife, Akiva. When the time's right, gal, I'd like to tie the knot with you. Major Stevenson has already given us the green light to fly north, to our families, to have the wedding." Searching her eyes, he saw shock and then such warmth in them. "Well? I know this is a little surprisin' to you and all...but I thought this was the right place to ask you...with all your other family bein' here...." His heart raced as Akiva stared down in shock at the proffered set of rings.

Joe watched with trepidation and anxiety as Akiva lifted her hands and touched the set. One was a plain gold wedding band; the other, similar band was set with seven small squares of expensive gemstones.

"I chose the design because it reminded me of you, gal," he admitted in a strangled tone. Shrugging, Joe looked around at the people in the room. They were all grinning, expectation and happiness clearly written in their expressions. Heartened, he added, "I know you had a dark, stormy beginning in your life, your childhood."

Akiva looked at him. Hot tears filled her eyes as she took out the engagement ring and held it gently between her fingers.

"And I just wanted you to know how much of a rainbow you are to me," he added thickly, his voice turning emotional. "You color my life with such beauty. The way you see the world through those sunlit eyes of yours makes me feel like I'm flyin', gal." He lifted his hand and enclosed hers as she held the ring. "Would you do me the honor of being my partner? My best friend? My wife?"

Choking back tears, Akiva melted beneath his pleading tone, which was raw with feeling. No one had ever loved her as Joe did. Akiva was constantly amazed by his thoughtfulness, his sensitivity toward her and her needs. It was as if he could read her mind and her healing heart. "Y-yes, you know I will...."

Reaching over, she threw her arms around his shoulders and embraced him. Burying her face against his neck, she started to sob. Akiva couldn't help herself. Joe brought out everything good and kind within her. As his arms wrapped around her, she heard the room burst into shouts, laughter and clapping. The joy that swirled around her and Joe in that moment made Akiva feel giddy. She was overflowing with so much happiness that she didn't know what to do except feel his goodness and love overwhelm her.

Maya rose, a smile lingering on her mouth. "Congratulations, Akiva and Joe. We couldn't be happier for you. You *deserve* one another."

Sniffing, Akiva lifted her head as Joe raised her left hand and slid the engagement ring onto her finger. Even in the fluorescent lights it sparkled and scintillated as she moved her hand slightly. A rainbow...she was *his* rainbow in life. What a wonderful thing to be for another person. Leaning over, Akiva placed a quick kiss on his mouth.

"Thank you," she murmured softly, tears drifting

down her cheeks. "I'll try to be more a rainbow than a thunderstorm in your life, Joe."

"But it's the rain from the thunderstorm that creates the rainbow," Joe reminded her softly.

Everyone laughed. Akiva turned and looked at her friends. Their eyes were warm and she knew in her heart they were truly happy for her and Joe. Cam, who sat across from her, was self-consciously wiping the tears from her forest-green eyes. The way her lips were pulled into a smile made Akiva wince inwardly. She knew of Cam's own unhappy past. And more than anything, she wished happiness for her, for not much good had followed Cam through her twenty-five years of hardscrabble life.

Joe rose to his feet and pulled Akiva's chair back so that she could stand. Everyone came around the table, shook hands and congratulated them. Maya stood back, her fists resting languidly on her hips, her smile wide.

As Morgan joined Maya, she looked up at him. "Well, let's see," she said conspiratorially, "Jenny Wright is marrying Matt Davis, the mercenary who came down here with her. Ana has married Jake and they work here with us. Now, Joe and Akiva. Looks like we're on a roll, eh?"

Grinning, Morgan said, "Marriages forged in the fires of hell always grow into heaven. I know. It happened to me. I guess my people at Perseus are going to follow my lead," he agreed in a low tone, a smile playing across his mouth as he watched Akiva with Joe.

"Hmm, like our own," Maya murmured as Dane came to stand with them at the end of the table. She watched as Mike opened the door and everyone else began to file out of the room. Soon the four of them were alone.

"I'm your heaven," Dane reminded her archly, his

grin confident and cocky as he dropped his arm across her shoulder and gave her a quick embrace.

"Oh? So I'm your hell?"

"Ouch...no! I didn't mean it that way...."

Morgan chuckled. "Considering you two were arch enemies when he came down here, I'd say whatever hell you had between you is long gone, and you're both in heaven, from the looks of it." His eyes glinted knowingly as he surveyed them.

"Love takes working on a day at a time," Maya murmured.

Dane kissed his wife's hair and then whispered, "Yes, and I love every second of it with you."

"You're such a romantic, York." She jabbed him playfully in the ribs. "And so full of it."

Houston chuckled and joined them. "I think all of us have pretty good marriage partners." His eyes brightened. "Did I tell you Ann is pregnant again? We've got number two coming along in about six months."

Stunned, Morgan looked at him. "Congratulations. Does my wife know?"

"Oh, yeah," Mike chortled. "Laura was the *first* to know. Your wife may not work at Perseus, but she knows *everything*."

"That's true," Morgan said, his brows dipping, "and I'm always the last to know."

Dane gave his wife a warm look and kept his arm around her. In this room, away from prying eyes, he could show his affection for Maya. Out there on the base, he couldn't, due to military regulations. "So, you're going to be a father two times over. Congratulations, Mike." He offered his hand to the man.

Grinning proudly, Mike shook it. "Thanks, Dane."

"Is Ann happy about it?" Morgan asked.

"Oh, yeah! She wants a bunch of 'em. The more the merrier. She's been a flight surgeon so long that she really missed her mothering years, so she's makin' up for it now." He smiled softly. "And I like being a dad to these kids we're having. Nothing is more satisfying."

"Humph," Morgan groused good-naturedly, "wait until they hit their terrible twos and then the hormone strike in their teen years. That's when you want to give them away."

Laughing, Maya said, "Oh, Morgan, you love your four kids through all their ups and downs! I think you and Laura both have broad enough shoulders to ride through those little tempests in a teapot."

"True," Morgan murmured, offering his hand to Mike. "Got a name picked out yet?"

Houston shook his head. "Naw, we're workin' on that right now. Anne's got about fifty baby name books spread all over the house. She's makin' lists, and I'm sure I'll have a ton of 'em to look at when I get home."

"Somehow," Maya said wryly, "you get through it and love every moment of it with her."

Having the good grace to flush, Houston stuck his hands in the pockets of his dark blue chinos. "Guilty as charged. I like having a life partner." He threw a look over his shoulder toward the open door. "Joe and Akiva are gonna have the same kind of marriage we have. A working partnership based on mutual respect and love. It doesn't get any better than that."

Maya slid her arm around her husband's waist and gave him a look of open affection, something she had to be careful not to do among the squadron personnel. "Akiva needed someone like Joe. He's going to take good care of her. She's very wounded in some ways, but I can already see the changes he's helped her to make."

"Yeah," Houston said, impressed, "she's lost a lot of that tough armor she was wearin' like a good friend. I think you're right—Joe is going to be her safe place where she can let down, just be, and find out that some men are trustworthy, after all." He grinned, pleased with himself. "Like us. We're great role models for men."

Snorting, Maya said, "Isn't *that* the truth? Frankly, I'd like to shoot all the rest and put them out of their misery and clone you guys. Women would be a lot better off."

The room was filled with a raucous round of laughter.

Morgan shook his head. "Getting serious for a moment, Maya, how do you think Chief Anderson is going to get along on this mission?"

Leaning languidly against Dane's tall, strong frame, Maya murmured, "Cam has some problems. She's still emotionally wounded from the time we were shot down."

"Yes," Dane agreed, worried. "Cam thinks she abandoned Maya to the drug lord. She didn't. She made the correct tactical decision. Maya was unconscious and there was no way Cam could have carried her into that jungle. They'd both have been captured if she hadn't made a run for it on her own. But Cam isn't convinced of that, even now. I see it every day, in small ways around here."

"Yeah," Maya sighed. "She's developed into a mother hen, smothering her chicks. I've had a couple of talks with her about this, but it's like she's trying to make sure no one on her watch or under her wing gets hurt."

"Well," Morgan said, "that's pure folly. If she's in command, things can happen out there."

"I know, I know. But that's a cross she bears and takes with her on this mission." Maya frowned. "I just hope that she doesn't get in trouble with it. Mexican men aren't exactly thrilled about equal rights for women. They aren't going to take kindly to a woman being their boss."

"Yeah," Mike said, "I can see there's going to be hell to pay on that front. But you wouldn't have chosen Cam if she didn't have what it takes to make this a successful mission."

Maya nodded and glanced around at the men. "Sometimes you put an officer in charge who doesn't have all the job skills in place, and hope that the mission will train and teach them. This is the case with Cam. She has the abilities. It's just a question of whether or not she'll pull out these tools and use them or knee-jerk back because of this wound."

"All we can hope for," Dane told Morgan, "is that she'll grow into the mission. Cam has that potential."

"Well, with those Mexican pilots," Maya growled, "she's gonna have her hands full. I just hope one of them is a little less Neanderthal and a little more forward looking and thinking. If there's one out of the eight, then Cam has a chance. If not, then her mission objective is doomed to fail."

As Akiva and Joe walked across the roughened black lava surface within the hollow echo of the cave, they shared a smile with one another. Joe saw her lift her left hand once again, to look at her sparkling engagement ring.

"You like it, gal?"

"You know I do." Sighing, Akiva tossed her head and gave him a soft smile. "It was a beautiful surprise, Joe."

Wriggling his thick brows, he gave her an elfin grin. "I like surprising you. You deserve nice surprises. You had enough of the other kind."

Losing her smile, she gave him a warm, longing look.

"You're the nicest surprise I've ever had, Joe Calhoun. I always thought life was going to treat me rough, like it always had, but you walked into my life and turned me upside down and inside out."

"Give yourself credit," he said as they slowed to allow an electric car carrying supplies pass by them. "You took me in stride. That took a lotta courage." Around them, the cave was like a hive of busy bees, the activity nonstop. Voices echoed mutely throughout the hollow area.

Trailing her fingers through black strands of hair that had wafted across her lower face, Akiva said, "I realized my problem was distrust of men, not just Anglos, and you helped bring that awareness to me. Once I realized that, I started growing because somewhere in my soul, I knew I could trust you."

"You trusted on blind faith knowing," Joe whispered, giving her a tender smile. How he ached to touch Akiva as they continued their walk back into the cave recesses. But he couldn't. Not now, at least.

"Yes…yes, I did." Akiva walked closely enough so that her arm brushed against his momentarily. "And I'm going to keep on trusting you, Joe—with my life and my heart."

At her words, Joe reached out and gripped her long fingers and gave them a gentle squeeze.

"Forever, gal. Forever."

* * * * *

Look for Cam's story next year in the Silhouette Special Edition line, when **MORGAN'S MERCENARIES: DESTINY'S WOMEN** *continues!*

In the meantime, you won't want to miss a brand-new **MORGAN'S MERCENARIES** *miniseries beginning this summer in Silhouette Special Edition.*

Turn the page for a sneak preview....

Chapter One

Lieutenant Wes James studied the stranger as he came
to a stop before him and Lieutenant Callie Evans. The
man was tall and carried himself like an ex-military officer. Wes would recognize that bearing in anyone,
whether in uniform or not.

"Yes, sir?" Wes began. "How can I help you?"

"I'm Morgan Trayhern," he said, his voice deep and
shaken. "Are you two part of the earthquake rescue
team?"

"Yes, sir, we are," Wes said, and quickly introduced
himself and Callie.

"My wife, Laura, is somewhere in that collapsed hotel," he began, his voice breaking. Battling back tears,
he rasped, "I'd left her five minutes earlier, to go down
to the hotel bar and meet an old friend for drinks." Rubbing his dirty, unshaved face, Morgan closed his eyes for
a moment. When he opened them again, he looked directly at Callie. "When the quake hit, everything just

exploded around us. I made it out the front door before...before it collapsed.'' Morgan turned and looked at the fourteen-story heap of concrete and steel that was stacked like broken gray pancakes.

"You were lucky, Mr. Trayhern," Callie said soothingly.

Wes frowned. "Wait a minute...you're *the* Morgan Trayhern? You were in the Marine Corps?"

"Yes, that's right, Lieutenant James."

Eyes widening, Wes glanced over at Callie. "You remember him, don't you?" Morgan Trayhern was a part of Corps history, because of his role in the Vietnam War. "He's a living legend among us...." Wes felt his heart contract for the man, who had obviously been digging and hunting for his missing wife since the earthquake occurred. He pulled a canteen from his web belt. "Here, sir. You must be thirsty. Have some."

Gratefully, Morgan took the canteen and drank deeply, then returned it.

"What floor was your wife on, Mr. Trayhern?" Callie asked, her heart filled with anguish for the man she felt she knew well, after learning about him in Corps history.

"The fourteenth floor, Lieutenant Evans. Why? Does it make a difference?"

Nodding, Callie said, "Yes, sir, it often can. As these floors pancake on top of one another, most survivors are found on the upper floors, because the crushing weight lower down is so intense." She saw hope ignite in his murky gray eyes. Holding up her hand, she added, "I can't guarantee you she's alive, sir, but it's hopeful. Okay?"

"It sounds good to me, Lieutenant. I've been digging through that rubble all night, calling out for her. So far I haven't heard her...." He choked on a sob.

"Voices don't carry well through the rubble, sir, so don't take that as a good or bad sign," Callie said softly. She patted his shoulder gently. "Why don't you rest for a while here with Lieutenant James? Let me and my dog start the first grid search that Lieutenant James has prepared."

Morgan shook his head. "Rest? When my wife might be alive?" He wiped his reddened eyes. "No...I'll keep hunting till I know...for sure...one way or another. I won't leave her up there alone. I need her. I love her and I won't desert her now...."

Callie gave him a sympathetic look that she hoped spoke volumes to his torn spirit. Giving Wes a heartfelt glance, she pulled on her thick, protective gloves and said, "I'll see you after I'm done with the first grid."

"Be careful up there," Wes warned in a low tone. "The aftershocks are almost as bad as the original trembler." Suddenly Wes was afraid for her. His heart ached, knowing he could lose her just as he had lost a loved one in the past. He wanted to protect Callie. He wanted to reach out, grip her shoulder before she went off to climb the dangerous rubble, but he couldn't...not under the circumstances.

Their first priority was finding Laura Trayhern. And Wes believed they *would* find her. He only hoped it wouldn't be too late—for Morgan and Laura. Or for him and Callie....

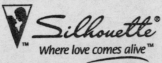

MONTANA *Born*

From the bestselling series

MONTANA MAVERICKS

Wed in Whitehorn

Two tales that capture living and loving
beneath the Big Sky.

THE MARRIAGE MAKER by Christie Ridgway

Successful businessman Ethan Redford never proposed a deal he
couldn't close—and that included marriage to Cleo Kincaid Monroe!

AND THE WINNER...WEDS! by Robin Wells

Prim and proper Frannie Hannon yearned for Austin Parker, but
her pearls and sweater sets couldn't catch his boots and jeans—or
could they?

And don't miss

MONTANA *Bred*

Featuring

JUST PRETENDING by Myrna Mackenzie

&

STORMING WHITEHORN by Christine Scott

Available in May 2002
Available only from Silhouette at your favorite retail outlet.

Silhouette
Where love comes alive

These New York Times *bestselling authors*
have created stories to capture the hearts and minds
of women everywhere.
Here are three classic tales about the power of love—
and the wonder of discovering the place
where you belong....

FINDING HOME

DUNCAN'S BRIDE
by
LINDA HOWARD

CHAIN LIGHTNING
by
ELIZABETH LOWELL

POPCORN AND KISSES
by
KASEY MICHAELS

Available only from Silhouette
at your favorite retail outlet.

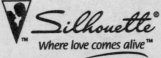

Every day is

A Mother's Day

in this heartwarming anthology
celebrating motherhood and romance!

Featuring the classic story "Nobody's Child" by Emilie Richards
He had come to a child's rescue, and now Officer Farrell Riley was
suddenly sharing parenthood with beautiful Gemma Hancock.
But would their ready-made family last forever?

Plus two brand-new romances:

"Baby on the Way" by Marie Ferrarella
Single and pregnant, Madeline Reed found the perfect husband in the
handsome cop who helped bring her infant son into the world. But did his
dutiful role in the surprise delivery make J. T. Walker a daddy?

"A Daddy for Her Daughters" by Elizabeth Bevarly
When confronted with spirited Naomi Carmichael and her brood of girls,
bachelor Sloan Sullivan realized he had a lot to learn about women!
Especially if he hoped to win this sexy single mom's heart....

Available this April from Silhouette Books!

Where love comes alive™

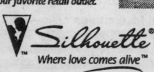
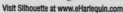